HER ONLY CRIME

A KATE REID NOVEL
BOOK 14

ROBIN MAHLE

HARP HOUSE PUBLISHING, LLC.

Published by HARP House Publishing
January 2022 (1st edition)

1

With the window rolled down on her patrol car, Police Officer Louisa Espinoza basked in the tepid breeze that brushed against her cheeks. Hard to imagine that it was December. Most places would've been blanketed with snow, but not here in Somerset, Texas.

She drove along the two-lane road through town that was bounded by a few older homes, vacant dirt lots, and the occasional discount dollar retail store. Roughly 20 miles south of San Antonio, the rural community of about 2000 had a police force of 5. Espinoza was the youngest on the force.

Her police-issue Dodge Charger turned down Payne Road and continued beyond the elementary school. Espinoza had been called out to the new housing development on the city's outskirts with a complaint of a pack of wild dogs running loose. "Why the hell Animal Control can't come out..." She groaned with exasperation.

The young officer of barely 26 was born and raised in San Antonio. Recently married, she and her husband moved to

Somerset about 2 years ago. The houses were cheap, yet it was still close enough to the metro area for her husband to make the commute. And gaining experience on a small police force would be a nice steppingstone for her.

Espinoza spotted an elderly man on the side of the road near the convenience store. He waved her down. She rolled to a stop and stepped out of her car, greeting him with a pleasant smile. "Good morning, Mr. Ortega. How are you today?"

"Well, I've been better, Officer."

She observed his appearance and noted that he looked slightly more disheveled than usual. In his 70s, he hadn't owned a car and took the buses to get around. "How can I help you this morning?" Espinoza adjusted her hat that barely contained the thick black hair tucked under it in a tight bun.

"I was just picking up some groceries and turns out, I forgot my damn wallet. Walked all the way here and didn't bother to check before I walked out the house," Ortega replied.

"You walked a mile and a half?" Espinoza asked.

"I sure did."

"Good for you, Mr. Ortega. Would you like me to give you a ride home so you can get your wallet?"

"Now that would be a very kind gesture, Officer. I would appreciate it."

"No problem at all." She started back to her cruiser. "Hop in. I'll take you home and even bring you back so you can get your food."

Mr. Ortega carefully stepped into the passenger side and closed the door. When Espinoza returned behind the wheel, he gazed around the patrol car. "I'll tell you what, I haven't been in one of these things in some time."

She turned the engine and chuckled. "Well, I hope not.

Although, I know your granddaughter and if she's anything like you..."

The old man laughed until he coughed. He pounded his chest with the side of his fist. "Damn cigarettes. Should've quit a long time ago."

Officer Espinoza turned onto 6th street. "You know those things will kill you."

"So I've been told by my doctors," he replied. "This is it right here, Officer."

She turned onto the long gravel driveway and stopped near the front of the manufactured home. "You need help getting inside?"

"No, ma'am. I got this. I'll only be a minute." He stepped out.

While Espinoza watched the old man slowly reach his front door, she assessed the area. Another prefab home was across the street and down about half a block. This part of town was mostly sparse desert and the people who lived here relied on Social Security, sometimes Disability. As she continued to look around, a glint of light captured her eye. Espinoza narrowed her gaze as the morning sun shone low. "A reflection?" she whispered.

The old man was still inside and so Espinoza stepped out of her patrol car. A reflexive check of her weapon and she carried on down the driveway toward whatever had caught her gaze.

A large black bird swooped down toward her as she neared. She ducked to avoid a direct hit. "Holy shit. Damn bird." Slightly embarrassed, Espinoza looked for anyone who might've seen her, but the area was deserted. She cleared her throat and walked on, glancing back at the old man's front door. Still no sign of him.

Ahead of her, several yards from Ortega's driveway, was a shallow channel of silty sand that traversed through the desert and only carried water during heavy rains. Near the low bank of the wash was what appeared to be a mound of recently overturned soil.

The town had suffered a dry spell and the ground was otherwise cracked from dehydration, except for right there. Espinoza reached the spot and squatted for a closer look at what had caught her eye. "What the?" Her heart jumped into her throat, and she shot up, reaching for her radio. "Dispatch, it's Espinoza. I need backup."

"What's going on, Louisa?" the dispatcher asked. "What's your location?"

"I'm at the home of Mr. Ortega down on 6th. He flagged me down and needed help, so I brought him home. I started looking around and..." She paused to gather her senses. "I found a finger."

"Sorry, say again."

"A finger with a ring on it. The sun bounced off the metal and caught my eye. Oh, Lord, you gotta get someone down here now. I'm not sure there isn't more to this."

"Captain's here. I'll tell him."

Espinoza set her sights on the unsettling discovery once again. The dainty severed finger lay on the ground, dirty and picked at by small scavengers. No way was she touching it without gloves. She turned back toward the home in the distance and spotted the old man emerge. "Damn it." She ran toward him. "Mr. Ortega?"

He gripped the stair railing and walked down the steps of his porch. "Sorry it took me so long. I forgot where I put the damn thing." The old man's gaze sharpened. "What's wrong? You all right, Officer?"

"Fine. I'm just going to need you to stay in your home for a little while. Can you do that, Mr. Ortega?"

"What on earth for?" he asked.

"I found something out there on your property, or near it. I need the captain to come and check it out, but you'll have to sit tight for a while," she replied.

He peered beyond her. "What the hell you find? Got all sorts of critters around here, you know."

"I know. This wasn't an animal."

"Wasn't?" His eyes softened and his lips slightly parted.

"Please, sir, I need you to go back inside." She reached for his shoulder.

"Yes, ma'am."

When he returned inside, Espinoza jogged back to the spot. For several moments, she stared at the finger and the nearby mound of dirt. "Please don't let the rest of you be in there."

FOR THE PAST SIX MONTHS, Dr. Yost had been there for Kate Reid. The recently promoted FBI Supervisory Special Agent hadn't really known she needed the good doctor. Had it not been for friend and co-worker Levi Walsh, Kate would've continued to ignore the warning signs. In her position, the results could've been —and nearly were—deadly.

The arduous task of revisiting a history Kate had worked so hard to forget, Dr. Yost pulled no punches. "I think we're done here, Kate. What do you think?"

"I think you might be right, Doc. I'm happier than I've been in a long time. Lighter. I'm starting to think that not everyone is out to get me." She laughed.

At 35, Kate Reid was a far cry from the young woman she had been when she joined the Bureau. Convinced she could do good there; the results hadn't gone exactly as planned. Though with her recent promotion to lead profiler for the Behavioral Analysis Unit 4 at Quantico, maybe her time had arrived. Just exactly as Nick Scarborough predicted.

"I imagine that belief stems more from your line of work rather than a personality trait," the doctor added. "But I couldn't be happier to hear that, Kate. I think you have made great progress.

And I think as long as you continue to trust yourself, listen to your gut, and not let what happened to you in the past get in the way of your future, you'll do just fine." Dr. Yost grabbed her prescription pad and started to scribble on it.

Kate looked on. "What are you doing? I thought we were good?"

She ripped off the script and handed her the slip of paper. "You are good."

Kate read it and smiled. "You got it, Doc. I will follow your instructions to the letter." She reached for her carrier bag and stood up.

"I certainly hope so. It's time you stop doubting yourself, and you're well on your way. Because once you do that..."

"No one else will doubt me," Kate replied.

"That's right." She offered her hand. "It was an absolute pleasure getting to know you, Kate Reid. Good luck in your future but remember that I'm always here."

"I appreciate that. Thank you, Dr. Yost." Kate stepped into the corridor and made her way outside to the parking lot. A measure of remorse overcame her as she climbed into her Ford Explorer, as though this had been the end of something. Not quite a friendship, but a regret that Yost would no longer be her fallback. Maybe she hadn't needed that anymore. It was kind of the whole point.

Kate pressed the call button on her steering wheel. "Call Nick on cell."

The line answered. "Hi, so how'd it go on your last day?"

"A little sad, I guess, but otherwise it was good," she replied.

"Dr. Yost was good for you. Now you have the tools you need and I'm so proud of the work you put into this," Nick replied.

"Thank you. Listen, I'm heading into the office now, but I wanted to let you know all was well."

"I'm glad to hear it. I've got a meeting to run to, babe, but you have a good day and I'll see you tonight."

"I will. You too. Love you."

"Love you too," Nick replied.

When the call ended, Kate reminded herself that they had both come a long way. Nick would always be in AA, and he came to understand that it was part of his life. He was a recovering alcoholic. But both had come out the other side relatively intact. Kate didn't want to jinx it, but she'd begun to feel normal, if there was such a thing when one hunted down killers for a living.

She arrived at the Quantico guard gate and displayed her ID.

The security guard nodded. "Have a good day, ma'am."

The Behavioral Analysis units of the FBI were located in Quantico, which was also a military installation and was where the FBI's Academy was housed. She arrived at the offices of Unit 4 and when the elevator doors parted, Agent Jonathan Surrey stood on the other side.

"Oh, good morning." Kate stepped out. "You off somewhere?"

"I was just going to get something I left in my car." He stepped into the elevator. "You look good this morning, Reid. Must've gotten a good night's rest."

Kate smiled. "Something like that."

Surrey was the newest member of the team and had essentially taken on the role formerly filled by Cameron Fisher, who was now the senior unit agent. Surrey came from the Denver field office and had an impressive career in profiling.

Divorced and in his mid-thirties, he always appeared as though he'd stepped off the pages of a men's fashion magazine. His black hair was styled on trend, long on the top with a gentle wave to it. He was fit, but not particularly muscular. But what had impressed Kate the most was his ability to leave his job at the office and maintain an arm's length from office drama. In here, there was a fair bit of that to go around, even while it had improved since Nick's lateral move to Unit 2 and Noah Quinn's departure.

Kate continued down the hall and reached her office. While she'd kept busy doing consultations for other field offices, the team hadn't had a large-scale investigation since Pittsburgh and the bomber who had committed suicide, but not before taking a handful of innocent people down with him. It was that case that brought Kate's mental state to a head and prompted Walsh's intervention.

No sooner had Kate sat down at her desk than Agent Eva Duncan arrived.

"Good morning." The Chicago native with caramel hair and an athletic build walked inside in beige dress pants and a starched white button-down. "When did you get in?"

"Just a few minutes ago. What's going on?" Kate asked.

Duncan continued inside and dropped down onto one of the guest chairs. "I moved out."

"What?" Kate drew up at attention. "I thought you two were taking a 'wait and see' approach?"

"We waited. I don't think either of us liked what we saw." Duncan chewed on her lower lip for a moment. "I love him, Kate, but he's the boss. In the current environment here at the Bureau, it's too big a risk for both of us."

"Oh, Eva, I'm so sorry. Couldn't you talk to Chief Cole and make sure he knows you two were together before Cam was promoted?"

"Honestly, Kate, I doubt it would make a difference." Duncan twitched her nose as if shrugging off rising sentiment. "We knew it could come down to this. It was only a matter of time."

"So, what do you want to do?" Kate asked.

"Find another place to live, I guess," Duncan replied. "I'd been looking for an apartment for a while and I got one not too far from here. Actually, it's in Walsh's building. He and I will be neighbors."

A tender grin appeared on Kate's lips. "Well, if you're going to have a neighbor, no doubt Levi would be one of the best."

"What's that now?" Walsh stopped in the hall outside Kate's office and peered in. "Did I hear my name?" The husky Alabama native, who was the team's Investigative Analyst, sauntered inside. "You ladies talking about me again?" He laid on the southern charm as thick as molasses.

"Eva was just telling me that you two are going to be neighbors," Kate replied.

"That's a fact." He glanced at Duncan. "She asked if I knew of any apartments for rent in my building. You know, we could carpool."

"Maybe so, but I should probably get moved in first," Duncan replied. "It'll be a couple of weeks."

"Where you staying now?" he asked.

"In a hotel. Just until the apartment is ready," she added.

"Well, I look forward to having you for a neighbor." Walsh leaned on one of the chairs and turned to Kate. "You have a few minutes to spare at some point today?"

"Sure. How about after lunch?" Kate replied.

He winked and clicked his tongue. "You got it. I'll see you both later, then."

Officer Louisa Espinoza spotted the captain's SUV approach. She'd been standing guard over the severed finger for nearly 20 minutes.

Captain Eli Brown, the 43-year-old Texas native and 15-year Somerset police force veteran, made his way over. With his thumbs tucked into his belt loops, the lean man eyed her. "Where's Mr. Ortega?"

"In his house. I asked him to stay put until I got some help." Espinoza squatted low and pointed to the find. "What do you make of this, Captain?"

He turned down his gaze. "Looks like a finger. Painted nail, though most of it's chipped off. The ring looks like maybe some costume jewelry."

"Yes, sir. It looks to be a middle finger and she's wearing a dolphin ring."

"She?" he asked.

"That's how it appears to me, Captain. It's dainty, and the ring looks feminine, the polish."

"Anyone can polish their nails, but I agree that it looks an awful lot like it could be female."

Espinoza pulled up again. "Should we dig around and see if the rest of her is here? I mean, look at the mound of dirt. It looks like a grave, doesn't it?"

"Good Lord, I hope it isn't." He peered at her. "You got a shovel?"

"Um, no sir, but I could ask Mr. Ortega."

He raised his hands. "No, don't bother the old man. I brought one when Dispatch told me what you found." Brown started back to his car. "Besides, we find more on Ortega's property, he might not be willing to help us out with much of anything."

Espinoza glanced back at the old man's house. "No way he knows anything about this, sir."

When the captain returned with a shovel, he regarded her. "I wouldn't count out the old man just yet. How about we see what we can find here, huh? Let's start digging."

Espinoza stood back while the captain carefully removed

material around the exposed body part. "Captain, have you ever had to do this before?"

He stopped and looked up at her. "Dig up a body? No, Louisa, I haven't. Although I have seen my share of dead bodies. I wouldn't recommend it."

"Should I go talk to Mr. Ortega and at least tell him what we're doing on his property?"

Brown glanced at her while he pierced the mound with the tip of the shovel. "You want to tell him we should have a warrant too? Besides, I'd be hard pressed to be certain this was Ortega's property. He has a sizable plot of land, but with this wash being so near, could be state-owned."

She cast away her gaze. "Yeah, of course, but I think Mr. Ortega would be the first to say he'd…"

"Hold up, now. What's this?" Brown squatted low and used his hands to move away the dirt.

Espinoza joined him and narrowed her gaze. "Oh no."

"Damn it to hell." Brown stood again with the aid of the shovel. "We need to get a team out here to secure the area. Now you can tell Mr. Ortega what we're doing because he might have a few things to answer for."

2

Floodlights mounted high on heavy-duty tripods shed light on the arid desert landscape. Nightfall arrived and the temperature dropped amid the painstaking task of unearthing the human remains. Captain Eli Brown contacted the San Antonio Police Department for assistance after the gruesome discovery. Officer Espinoza had found the severed finger, but as the captain peeled back the clumpy clay soil, what lay beneath prompted the call.

Now, not only was Brown's entire police force of five observing the dig, so were several of San Antonio's finest crime scene investigators.

Brown stood next to his young officer. "Louisa, why don't you go home? You've been here since this morning."

"Captain, I don't want to leave. I need to know if there are more," she replied.

"They could be at this all night."

"I don't care," Espinoza added.

"Excuse me, Captain?"

Brown turned to see a member of the CSI. "Yes?"

"You want to come take a look?" The officer started back toward the dig site. "We uncovered the remains you found, but unfortunately, that wasn't all of it."

Brown glanced with uncertainty at Espinoza, who trailed them.

The CSI officer walked inside the circle of light and crouched next to the find. "Here."

Brown aimed his gaze downward. "Dear Lord, is that an arm?"

"It does appear to be." The officer pulled up again. "We think there could be numerous body parts in this vicinity, and we're going to need to recruit additional help."

"I'll help," Espinoza cut in. "I can do this. I'll be careful."

"Appreciate that, Officer, but this is a situation that requires those trained in this type of recovery," he replied.

"What exactly are you saying?" Brown asked.

The officer held up his hands. "No offense. I'm saying we may need to get the feds down here. I can put in a call to the San Antonio FBI field office and request some assistance. Captain, it looks like we could be dealing with a mass burial site here. This is something the FBI should be involved in, at least until we know more."

"Sure, yeah, okay. If that's what we have to do," Brown replied.

When the officer retreated, Espinoza stepped forward. "You know that'll mean they won't want our opinion, or our help."

"Let's not jump the gun, Louisa. He's being overly cautious. I don't believe for a second we have some sort of killing field right here in Mr. Ortega's front yard. By the way, how's he doing?"

"All right, considering... He's shocked, like the rest of us. His daughter's with him inside the house. We should probably let her take him out of here. We've already talked to him. We searched his home. He cooperated fully. He doesn't know anything about this. I know you saw that too."

Brown placed his hands on his hips and nodded. "Yeah, I saw it. Still, I wouldn't mind keeping tabs on him. Go ahead and get his daughter to take him to her house. Make sure we know where that is."

"Will do, Captain." Espinoza retreated.

The San Antonio police lieutenant approached Brown. "Your people hanging in there?"

"So far, so good. It's a hell of a shock, for sure. Nothing much happens around here."

"Yeah, well, you should spend a day in the city. It'll make you glad you're here; I'll tell you what."

"Your CSI officer said he wants to get the feds down here. What do you think?" Brown asked.

"He's right. God knows what else we're going to find in that ground," the lieutenant replied.

"What do you think? Is this some kind of mass burial site? If so, what the hell are we talking about? Immigrants? Transients? What?"

The lieutenant shook his head. "Your guess is as good as mine. All I know right now is that they appear to be female."

The captain looked on. "Go figure."

SSA Victor Romero, a 10-year veteran of the Bureau, had been at the San Antonio field office for almost 4 years. After a few calls and a few hours, he'd arrived at the scene before dawn.

"Evening." The dark-haired, bearded Agent Romero approached the lieutenant.

"Is it still evening? He checked the time. "Nope. It's 3am, so, good morning. You must be Agent Romero."

"Yes, sir." At about 5 feet, 10 inches, Romero looked to be in his late 30s. He thrust his hands into the pockets of his overcoat. "I hear y'all have found human remains, likely from more than one victim."

"Sadly, we have. Follow me, I'll introduce you to the Somerset police captain. It was one of his officers who uncovered this." The lieutenant started toward the captain.

"Captain Brown?" the lieutenant began. "FBI Agent Romero just arrived, and I reckon you two have a lot to discuss. Agent Romero, this is Captain Brown and Officer Espinoza."

Romero offered his hand. "Espinoza. You drew the lucky straw, I see."

She revealed a closed-lip grin. "You could say that. It's good to meet you, sir."

"None of that 'sir' crap. Romero's fine. Since you're the one who started all this, why don't you show me around and start from the beginning about how you came to be here on this cold night."

Espinoza glanced at her captain.

"Go on," Brown replied.

"Okay, then, follow me." She walked toward the cordoned off area. "This morning, I was helping out one of our local citizens, Mr. Ortega. I gave him a ride home and while I was waiting to take him back out, I caught a glint of shine coming off something out here."

"A glint?" He nodded. "Okay. And so you figured you'd come and inspect."

"Yeah, I was just curious and sitting on my thumbs waiting for the old man. I mean, Mr. Ortega. Anyway, when I got closer, I saw what appeared to be a severed woman's finger." She led him to the table where the evidence was collected. "This one right here."

Romero picked up the bag and examined the contents. "Yep, that's a finger. Looks like a woman's finger. We'll go with that until we know more. And so that was when you called your captain to check it out?"

"Yes, sir. That was around 10am this morning. Been here ever since. We don't have a CSI team, so Captain called on SAPD to help us out. They found a lot more than I thought they would."

"I'd say so," Romero added.

"What's the plan then, sir, I mean, Agent Romero?" Espinoza asked.

But before he could answer, the CSI officer approached him. "You're Agent Romero?"

"The one and only," he replied.

"We could use some guidance if you wouldn't mind following me."

"You got it." Romero started ahead and glanced back. "Espinoza, you coming, or what?"

"Yes, sir." She jogged to catch up.

The CSI officer stopped at the edge of what amounted to be a considerable hole in the ground. "At the moment, we've recovered ten different body parts. But this one here, well..."

Romero didn't wait for him to finish and squatted low. "Ah, hell."

"This one is clearly mutilated and dismembered but..."

"All the pieces left in the same location." Romero stood up again. "Arms and legs positioned next to the torso. Head placed above the severed neck. And the body hasn't been here for long. Not much decomp, not that I claim to be an expert."

"Yes, sir," the CSI officer replied. "My team is still excavating, but aside from right here, they haven't come across anything else in a while. We may have opened up the extent of what's here."

Romero nodded. "Keep looking. Let's get what we have sent to the medical examiner. He'll have to start trying to ID the victims, however many we have here."

"What's your best guess, Agent Romero?" Espinoza asked.

"Hard to say, maybe three or four victims." He turned to her. "Enough to make this one hell of a serious situation. And where is Mr. Ortega right now?"

"We suggested his daughter take him to her house."

"You didn't want to question him?" Romero asked.

"We did talk to him and had a look around his place, but he's 72 years old. No way could he have done something like this," Espinoza began. "And I've known him for a couple years now. He's not capable..."

"You'd be surprised, Espinoza, at what people are capable of," Romero cut in. "Get him to your station. It's time we have a chat with Mr. Ortega."

It was the light from his cell phone that roused Nick Scarborough from sleep. He peered back at Kate to be sure she hadn't been disturbed. He sat up and reached for it before stepping out of their bedroom to answer the call. "Scarborough here."

"We need you at the office," the caller replied.

Nick cleared his throat and rubbed his eyes as he walked down the hall into the living room. Wearing only boxer shorts, he scratched at his firm chest. "What's going on? It's 4 in the morning."

"I just got word of a major cyberattack against Amtrak. Their entire system is down. No trains are moving."

Nick grew more alert and pushed his hand through his dark hair, now streaked with grey. "Okay. Yeah, I'll be there as soon as I can." He ended the call and returned to the bedroom.

"What's wrong?" Kate whispered.

He turned at the sound of her voice. "Go back to sleep. I have to go in early." He opened the closet door and pulled out a suit.

Kate sat up in bed and brushed away the rogue strands of dark hair from her face. "Something happened. What is it?"

Nick turned back to her. "Amtrak's been hacked. Their entire system is down. It's going to be chaos in about an hour when commuters learn their trains aren't running."

"Is there anything I can do?" she asked.

"I wish, but no." He started toward the bathroom. "I have to jump in the shower and get out of here. I'll call you later. Go back to sleep." He stopped at her side and kissed her cheek.

Fat chance she was going back to sleep now. Kate sat up in bed and checked her phone. No messages or calls, so she walked out into the hall and reached the kitchen. Nick was going to need coffee to-go, so she made the pot and scrolled through her phone while it brewed.

The implications of what lay ahead for him today were unknown, but this sort of thing was happening with greater frequency. Nick would have his hands full.

She heard his shoes click on the wood floor and peered up at him. "That was fast."

"No time to waste." Nick wore a fitted white Oxford shirt that accentuated his trim waist. The navy-blue suit jacket rested perfectly on his square shoulders.

Kate grabbed a travel mug and poured the coffee. "Take a cup with you. I have a feeling you're going to need it."

"Thanks. I have no idea how today is going to play out, so I don't know when I'll be home."

She pressed her hand against his chest. "I know. I get it."

He smiled and leaned in for a kiss. "I'll do my best to keep you posted, okay?"

"Okay."

"Love you." He started toward the door. "And thanks for the coffee."

When he closed the door behind him, Kate dropped two slices of bread into the toaster. "Luckily, I'm not taking the train today."

DAWN HAD BROKEN and light spilled into what passed as an interview room inside the modest Somerset Police Station. Agent Romero stood behind an empty chair and regarded the old man. "You mean to tell me you had no idea what was buried on your property?"

"I swear to you, I didn't. I'm still not sure that's my land." Mr. Ortega's voice fractured, and his face wore confusion and fear. "I don't go out much, except to get food."

Espinoza was invited to sit in on the questioning and grew uncomfortable at Romero's pressure tactics. "It's okay, Mr. Ortega. If you know anything at all, you should tell us now. The surveyors will check the boundaries of your property to be sure, but this still does involve you."

"I don't know a damn thing except I haven't slept all night and y'all are telling me I got dead bodies on my land. No, ma'am. Nothing about this is okay. Do I even get a lawyer?"

"Do you feel you need one, Mr. Ortega?" Romero asked.

"Well, the way you're looking at me, I'm starting to think so," he replied. "Louisa, I've known you since you and Pete moved here. You know I got nothing to do with this."

Espinoza glanced at the agent. "It's just that this is really bad, Mr. Ortega, and we're just looking for answers."

"Well, I ain't got none. You hear me?" His eyes reddened. "Where's my daughter?"

"She's still in the lobby," Romero replied. "I'll tell you what, Mr. Ortega, you continue to fully cooperate with our investigation, and I'll let you go on home with her in a few minutes. Will that do for you, sir?"

A trace of hope sparked in his eyes. "Yes, sir. I promise you, I got nothing to hide. I'll let you have access to whatever you need."

Romero nodded. "Then you're free to go—for now." He walked out of the room.

Espinoza spotted Captain Brown outside the door when Romero opened it. They traded glances and he nodded to her. She turned back to the old man. "Okay, Mr. Ortega, let's get you back with your daughter."

Romero followed the captain to his office. "He doesn't know anything."

Brown continued inside. "Sorry to say, but I could've told you that on the outset."

The agent sat down across from Brown's desk. "I had to see for myself his reaction. But whoever did this knows that man doesn't get out much. In fact, they likely counted on it. No neighbors close enough to care, meaning, this could be a local we're after. What we need to find out is how long those remains have been in the ground."

"They looked fairly fresh to me. Then again, I didn't see all of them," Brown replied. "So what happens now?"

"We'll wait for the M.E.'s reports. See how many victims we're talking about and get an approximate date of when they were murdered," Romero replied.

Brown lowered himself onto his chair. "Who the hell could've done something so heinous?"

Romero scratched at his full beard. "Someone who's plenty pissed off about something."

As KATE DROVE INTO WORK, news of the cyber-attack consumed every radio station. Callers who'd been affected by the shutdown voiced their thoughts, while transportation officials did their best to assure the Eastern Seaboard the situation would soon be resolved.

Nick was the senior unit agent for BAU's Unit 2. He'd taken the position after transferring out of BAU 4. The move had been called voluntary, but his options were to make the lateral move or stay and work under Cameron Fisher after his demotion. It wasn't much of a choice.

On her arrival, Kate stopped in to see her boss. "Hi."

"Morning." The 48-year-old former NYPD detective, now senior unit agent, pulled the toothpick from between his lips. "How's Scarborough handling all this? I assume he's involved."

"Oh yeah." Kate walked inside. "He got called in at about 4 this morning."

"The entire building is buzzing about this. Any idea who's behind the attack?" Fisher asked.

Kate returned a cockeyed grin. "I think we all have a pretty good idea, but we'll see how top brass lets this play out."

"So, what's on your mind, Reid?" Fisher's eyes narrowed as he peered at her. While the lines on his face were profound, they enhanced his rugged appearance. The salt and pepper hair helped, too.

"Just seeing how you're doing; whether you're going to have to step in with this situation," she continued.

"Don't see a need for that. You sure there's nothing else? You look like you want to ask me something."

Kate shrugged. "Nope. I'd better get to my desk. I was

expecting a file to come through from the Miami field office. Maybe it's arrived."

He pulled up at attention. "Oh? What do they have going on?"

"Don't know yet. I'll keep you posted, though." She turned on her heel and walked into the hall again. She'd wanted to ask how he was doing now after ending things with Duncan, but coming out with something like that wasn't appropriate, she supposed. He was still her boss, even if Duncan was one of her closest friends. She returned to her office and sat down.

"Morning." Surrey walked in. "What's going on with Scarborough? His team get pulled into this train hack?"

"Good morning, and yes, they did," Kate replied. "I have a feeling he's going to have his hands full."

"No shit." Surrey took a seat. "You get that file yet?"

"The consult request from Miami? I don't know. I just got in and I haven't checked my emails. Everyone's been pretty consumed with this breach," she replied.

"What are Scarborough's thoughts on it?" Surrey pressed on.

"He didn't say. He was out the door pretty early."

Surrey got to his feet again. "Well, I'll let you get settled in this morning. Let me know if you get that file and we can see what's going on. I wouldn't mind a quick trip to Miami if it meant getting the hell out of this D.C. winter."

Kate regarded him. "You're from Denver. It's worse there."

He turned down his mouth. "What can I say? I've never been one who appreciated the cold. See you later, Reid."

3

The remains of what was believed to have been from multiple bodies were transferred to the Bexar County Medical Examiner's Office in San Antonio. It was up to them to determine just how many victims were buried in the old man's yard in Somerset.

As morning arrived, Agent Victor Romero walked into the M.E.'s office just as it opened. "Good morning." He flashed his creds. "FBI Agent Romero. I need to see Dr. Bauer regarding the Somerset victims brought in a few hours ago."

The older woman eyed the badge. "One moment, sir. I'll let him know you're here."

"Appreciate it." Romero meandered inside the lobby for too long when the doctor finally arrived.

"Agent Romero. I'd like to say it's good to see you, but it usually never is."

Romero extended his hand. "Back at ya, Doc. I know it's early, but you got anything for me?"

"Considering the remains were only brought in a couple of

hours ago, I'd normally say you've jumped the gun, but I do actually have some news. Follow me back." Dr. Bauer entered the corridor with his white coat flapping in his wake. The 55-year-old had been the county's M.E. for nearly ten years, and he'd ceased being surprised by anything. "I have one of my finest doctors working on it as we speak."

"What'd you find?" Romero trailed him into an autopsy room.

Another doctor stood at a table where at least some of the remains were laid out. "Dr. Bauer."

"Dr. Fenmore, this is FBI Agent Romero. He's the one who sent us the Somerset victims."

"Good morning, Agent Romero. Dr. Bauer and I have been working on literally piecing together the parts and we think we know how many victims you have here."

"Do tell." Romero folded his arms.

"First of all, are you certain there is nothing more to be found?" Fenmore asked.

"I'm not certain of that at all. San Antonio PD still has a CSI team out there excavating. However, they haven't uncovered anything else since and I'm not sure they will. This could be it."

"That's good news, but also not." Fenmore walked around to the table and stood behind it. "From what we've gathered at the moment, it appears these remains are from four different women."

"Four. Okay." Romero stepped closer. "And you're sure they're all female?"

"Oh, yes. All of them," Bauer cut in. "The mutilated torso with the extremities removed is that of a single victim. Clearly tortured, as evidenced by the multiple abrasions, contusions, and lacerations on the torso. The arms were carved with a straight edge knife just deep enough to penetrate the layers of the skin. This appeared as a means only to inflict pain. From there, a more appropriate saw was used to cut through the bone."

"Doc, you've been around here for a long time. This look like the work of a cartel to you?" Romero asked. "Revenge for a rival gang, or drug deals gone bad. In other words, is this something I should get the DEA in on?"

Bauer raised his pointed chin as he appeared to contemplate the question. "At this stage, it's too early to know. But I can tell you, it well could be. You know as well as I do the tactics the cartels employ. Mostly to scare those around the victims into compliance, or what have you. However, I can't say definitively whether that's the case."

Romero nodded. "How long before you can get any of these vics ID'd?"

"Days, at best, weeks if there's a substantial backlog, I'm afraid. There isn't much to go by, with the exception of this victim here. The rest I have to piece together as best I can unless your people uncover more. You have to know that we may not be able to identify any of them, especially if they're undocumented. But again, it's too soon to know anything right now."

"Okay." Romero turned on his heel. "Just keep me posted. Thank you." He returned to his car and headed back to Somerset.

The only person of interest he had wasn't that interesting at all. And the idea the old man could've tortured and chopped up four women, whose ages were still unknown, seemed the least plausible of all the scenarios. The cartel was at the top of his list. This was what they specialized in—torture, beheadings, dismemberment. Still, why had they chosen to make a mark in Somerset? It was a small and quiet city, still part of the San Antonio metro area, but well on the outskirts. And the cartel was fond of making known their crimes by leaving the victims in plain sight, so that others knew not to cross them. Lastly, these were all women.

"Ah shit." He reached for his cell phone and made the call to someone who might have better knowledge of something like this. "Jonathan Surrey. What's up, brother? Vic Romero."

"Romero? How the hell are you, man? It's good to hear from you," Surrey replied.

"Doing all right. You know how it goes, same shit, different day. I hear you made a move to Quantico a few months back, is that right?"

"Sure did. It's been damn near a year already."

"They give you an offer you couldn't refuse?" Romero laughed.

"Not exactly, but it's going all right. What's on your mind, brother? We haven't talked in a long time."

"That's on me," Romero began. "San Antonio's been keeping me hopping these past few years. And not in a good way. So, uh, the reason I called is that since you're at BAU now and y'all are the experts in goddam horrific murders, you think I could get some advice on a new case?"

"Sure, of course. What are you working on?" Surrey continued.

Romero turned off the highway toward Somerset. "Right now, I got four dead vics. All women. Cut all to hell, dismembered."

"Jesus," Surrey replied.

"Tell me about it. Although, I'm sure you've seen worse, my friend. Thing is, first thought in my head was that it was the work of the cartels. Then I thought, they don't just go after women and bury them."

"They like to show off their work," Surrey added.

"Yes, sir. So I started thinking, well shit, if it isn't the cartels, then it could be some sick son of a bitch who hates his momma, you know?"

Surrey grunted. "Sure. What are some of the specifics off the top of your head?"

Romero filled him in on what he knew to date. "I thought, who better to call and pick a brain than the main man over at BAU."

"I'm not the main man, but yeah, sounds interesting for sure. I can take a look at what you got. You want to shoot over the files? We do consults all the time."

"Yeah, I'd appreciate that, man. Thanks. I gotta run. I'm headed into a meeting. I'll get it over to you today."

"I'll keep an eye out. Hey, it was good talking to you, Vic. I'll do what I can."

Romero ended the call and parked his car. He'd arrived at the Somerset Police Station and walked inside.

Officer Espinoza hurried toward him. "Agent Romero, I'm so glad you're here."

"What's going on? Everything okay?"

"We found another burial site. An anonymous tip came in early this morning. The person said they found a woman's shoe with blood on it not far from the new housing development on the edge of town. Same place I got a call about yesterday. Some stray dogs, I guess. Anyway, I told the captain and he arranged for SAPD's CSI to get out there."

"An anonymous tip? We need to know where that call came from, first and foremost. Secondly, how many have been uncovered?" Romero asked.

"They think two, so far. But they just got out there." Espinoza started away. "Come talk to the captain. He'll fill you in."

"Uh, hang on a sec, would you? I need to make a quick call." Romero picked up his phone as Espinoza carried on toward the captain's office. "Hey, Surrey, it's me again. Sorry to be a pain in the ass. But about that consult..."

"Yeah?" Surrey replied.

"Might need a little more help than I thought. You think you could make a trip to visit an old friend?"

Agent Surrey returned his phone to his pocket and marched ahead to Kate's office. "Reid, hey, you got a minute?"

She peered up at him. "Sure. What's going on? Did you review the Miami file?"

He walked inside and sat down. "This isn't about Miami. I just got a call from an agent in San Antonio. I knew him from way back and it looks like he's got a serious situation on his hands." Surrey leaned over with his elbow on his thighs. "Yesterday, in a city called Somerset, outside of San Antonio, four female victims were unearthed on the property of an older man. They've already concluded he had nothing to do with it."

"Why is that?" Kate asked.

"Because he's in his 70s, been in that town for decades and never had any trouble. And these victims were dismembered. In fact, they haven't uncovered any whole bodies yet. Just pieces."

She turned away. "Oh my God."

Surrey nodded. "There's more. This morning, they got a tip, two more bodies uncovered in another location not far from the first one. San Antonio police have a CSI unit on scene working to uncover more."

"Your friend at the San Antonio field office..."

"Agent Victor Romero," Surrey cut in.

"He's asking for our help?"

"Yep."

Kate leaned back in her chair and appeared to consider the information. "They're somewhat near the border. Does Romero suspect the cartels?"

"That was his first thought, yes. He's not positive. Listen, I think it'd be worth our time to head down there and see what he's got," Surrey replied.

"Okay, let's get with Fisher for his authorization. We can be there today." When Surrey stood to leave, Kate added, "You said they got a tip. Any idea who called it in?"

Surrey turned back to her. "Anonymous. But we sure as hell better try and track that down."

She pushed off her chair and joined him. "Okay, let's get with the boss and get his take." As they made their way into the hall, Kate continued. "The newly found victims, are they female too?"

"I don't think they've made that determination yet. But based on what they know now, I'd say it's an almost certainty." He glanced at her. "Wouldn't you say?"

"Probably." Kate knocked on Fisher's open door. "You have a minute to talk?"

He pushed back from his desk and eyed Kate. "Course I do. Have a seat. Tell me what you have."

Kate turned to Surrey. "The floor is yours."

He nodded. "The San Antonio field office is looking for our help. Multiple mutilated bodies buried in a suburban offshoot called Somerset. I'd like Reid and myself to head down there and see what they have."

Fisher pulled the toothpick from his mouth. "What else you two have on your plates?"

"Profile review for a case in Miami," Kate replied. "Offering our input, but they haven't requested any additional support. We can put our heads together before we get to San Antonio and give them something they can use. It's already a suspected hate crime. The profile practically writes itself."

"And we'll be sure to answer their calls. We won't leave them hanging," Surrey added. "I think Agent Romero in San Antonio could use our help. He suspects it's the work of the cartels but isn't sure."

"Given the proximity to the border, that's a fair assumption," Fisher replied.

"Except that the first four victims unearthed were all female," Kate added. "No confirmation yet on the latest find. If it was the cartel, I'm not sure of the point they were attempting to make. And we all know that's how they operate. Intimidation tactics and extreme violence to get across their point."

Surrey regarded Fisher. "What do you think? I'd like to get there as soon as possible."

"I'll authorize it. Get on the next plane out."

Agent Romero peered into the so-called burial pit while the San Antonio CSI team continued their search. "How far is this from the first location?" He turned to Officer Espinoza.

"About a mile south," she replied. "One hundred yards that way is state-owned land." She turned back. "Over there is a property previously owned by a now bankrupt retailer. They never did build anything on it."

"And who owns this piece of land? The developer?" Romero pressed on.

"It's slated to be a dedicated community park once the new homes go in," she replied. "So, there's no connection to old man Ortega. What do you make of that?"

He peered at her. "Right now? I'm starting to think whoever this killer is knows the town well. Why these sites aren't out in the middle of the desert somewhere is what really concerns me. It suggests someone wanted these victims found. And there's no way to figure out who called in this tip?"

Espinoza shook her head. "No. The call was made from a payphone."

"A payphone? You guys still have those here?"

"We do. Not everyone can afford a cell phone, Agent Romero."

"I guess not, but it doesn't help us figure out who made the call. We need some kind of lead until we get back forensics and autopsy reports and hope to hell someone left something behind."

Espinoza looked away a moment. "I might have some people I can talk to. I don't know if they'll want to talk to me..."

"Who?" Romero asked.

"We're a pretty tight-knit community. I've worked hard to make myself known to the people around here. So when I say I might be able to talk to them, they'll trust me to keep their confidence."

Romero placed his hands on his hips. "What are you saying, exactly?"

"If this is the work of the cartels..." She shrugged. "Some of the neighbors around here might have some idea whether that's true."

"And you know who these neighbors are?"

"Of course I do," Espinoza replied. "But it'll have to be me, alone. They see you coming and they'll clam up."

He held up his hands. "No, I get it. That's fine. Do whatever you can. In the meantime, I've asked some experts with the Bureau to come and take a look at what's going on. They're due here in a few hours. How about I bring them to your station late this afternoon and we'll huddle up again? Will that give you a chance to talk to some of these folks?"

She nodded. "I think so. Experts, huh? What kind of experts?"

"The kind whose job it is to track down sadistic killers who like to chop up women."

∽

KATE SHUT off the light in her office and had her phone at her ear. "We're heading to the airport now. Should be in San Antonio by around 5. It'll be getting dark soon after, but I imagine they'll continue excavating through the night."

"Who's the agent at the field office?" Nick asked on the other end of the line.

"Victor Romero. Apparently, Surrey knew him from way back. He's the one who got the call. How's everything going with the train situation?"

"My team's working on it. Hell, pretty much all of Unit 2 is working on it along with the Maryland field office, DHS, CIA. Just about all the acronyms. The specialists tell us the system should be up and running again in about 48 hours."

"No commuter trains for two days and no idea who brought them down?" Kate continued into the hall to meet Surrey at the elevators.

"Nope. It's a mess right now," Nick replied.

"What's your first thought on responsibility?" she pressed on.

"No surprise there. They've done it before and no doubt, they'll do it again. As long as private businesses for national industries continue to handle their own cyber security, I don't ever see an end to it."

"You think it's the Russians?"

"They are at the top of my list," Nick replied. "Listen, hon, I gotta go. Have a safe flight and keep me posted."

"You do the same. Love you." Kate ended the call as she spotted Surrey. "You ready to go?"

"Mind if we stop by my place so I can get a bag? I don't know how long we'll be there, but at least for tonight." He looked her up and down. "Don't you need to pack some stuff?"

"Me? I keep an overnight bag in the back of my car at all times."

The elevator doors parted, and they stepped inside when Surrey continued, "Well, aren't you the perfect Girl Scout."

Kate pressed the button to the parking garage and smiled. "What can I say? I like to be prepared for everything."

He clasped his hands at his front and gazed up at the numbers as they descended. "I'm not sure either of us will be prepared for what awaits us in San Antonio."

4

As a cop in Somerset, Louisa Espinoza understood that getting to know everyone in the community was a necessity and that included those who hadn't wanted to be known. Those who were afraid of the cops. Their backgrounds weren't all that dissimilar to her own and she used that to gain their trust.

So when she rolled up in her Dodge Charger patrol unit to the part of town where people didn't talk much to the cops, they didn't run from her. And her reputation with them would go a long way into learning who had made the anonymous call to the station and perhaps who knew more than they might have let on. Espinoza stepped out of her car and approached the government run single-level apartment homes.

While this part of Texas didn't experience bitter winter weather like many other places, it dipped into the low 60s on occasion, like today. Cold, for those who were acclimated to the desert. And as the sun lowered in the sky this afternoon, Espinoza felt particularly chilled.

Ahead of her lay a barren landscape with a few dormant shrubs, yellow grass and rock-filled planter beds. The masonry-block building was rundown. Chipped and dirty white walls, shingles on the roof that needed to be replaced and single-pane windows that didn't keep out the cold in winter or the heat in summer. If this place had been run by a private company, it would've been fined for neglect. But since it was government run, it was largely ignored.

Three women sat on lawn chairs in front of one of the units. An older woman, and two younger ones. She knew they were family. "Hi there."

"Officer Espinoza, how are you?"

She eyed the young woman, who was barely 18. "I'm doing all right, Vangie, and you?"

"Fine, I guess," she replied. Evangeline Cordova had been born here, but her mother hadn't, and she hardly spoke English. Her older sister, Lupe, short for Guadalupe, sat next to her. "We haven't seen you around in a while. Is everything okay?"

Espinoza stepped closer. "Not really."

"This about the cut-up bodies on Mr. Ortega's property?" Lupe asked.

"Do you know anything about that?" Espinoza replied.

"No. I mean, people talk, and Mr. Ortega has a big mouth for an old guy," Lupe replied.

"So you heard it from him?"

Lupe glanced at her sister. "No, but he's been talking to people. Do you know who would do such an awful thing?"

The officer sat down on an overturned milk crate. "That's what I wanted to talk to you guys about. I wanted to know if you've heard anything or seen anything." She raised her hands. "And you know I won't say who told me."

The sisters glanced at each other while their mother carried on with her game of Solitaire on the glass table in front of her.

"All's I know is that girls around here are scared," Vangie replied.

"Scared of the cartels?" Espinoza asked.

"Cartels?" Vangie shook her head. "I don't know about that."

"They could be trying to expand their territory."

"No," Lupe cut in. "This isn't the cartels. I don't know who it is, but if it was them, they'd make sure we all knew it."

Espinoza knew she was right. Everyone around here knew how those people operated. Some had lived it first-hand, and it was a major reason why they were here now. "Well, we have a lot of FBI agents coming to town soon, so I'd stick close to home, you understand? It's safer. Who knows what the hell's going on, but it's best you stay around the hood."

"Thank you. But Officer Espinoza, if it wasn't the cartels who killed them girls, then who do you think it could be?"

"I'll find out, Lupe. I promise you. I'll find out."

THE PLANE LANDED on the runway and from the moment the wheels touched the ground, Kate's shoulders dropped in relief.

Surrey glanced at her with a smile. "You really don't like flying, do you?"

"Not particularly." She unbuckled her seatbelt and peered through the window. "I'm better than I used to be, trust me. It's already getting dark. I was hoping to get here early enough to get a good look at the crime scenes."

"Romero will take us out to the current dig site now, I'm sure. We'll have to wait until morning to see what else is out there." He stepped into the aisle and opened the overhead compartment. "Good thing I packed a bag."

Kate stood up. "Told you."

When they deplaned, Surrey caught sight of Agent Romero ahead. "That's our guy, there." He smiled as they approached. "Vic, my man. How are you?"

"Good to see you, buddy." Romero extended his hand. "Thanks for coming out so quickly." He turned to Kate. "That must make you Agent Kate Reid. Good to meet you. I hear you're one hell of a talented profiler. Even better than this guy here." He tossed a nod at Surrey.

"No question," Surrey cut in.

"Good, then we need you here more than ever." He turned on his heel. "Let's go out there now while we still have a little bit of light."

Kate trailed him. "They're using floods to continue working?"

"Oh yeah." Romero nodded. "They won't stop until they've exhausted all areas of concern."

"Are you still holding strong with your cartel theory?" Surrey asked.

"Buddy, I got nothing else to go by. If you two come up with something better, by all means, I'll be open to hearing it." He stopped at the exit. "My thing is, we've uncovered two sites. Recent kills. If it is the work of the cartels, they're keeping it on the down-low..."

"And that's not how they operate," Kate jumped in. "So, let's see what else we can learn."

As THE SUN lay atop a golden horizon, ready to dip out of sight, Lupe returned inside. "Ma, you want some dinner tonight?" She walked into the old kitchen with laminate counters, cabinets that had been painted about a dozen times, and almond-colored appliances. "I have some pozole leftover. That should be okay for you, huh?"

"No tengo hambre." (*I'm not hungry.*) She sat on the old sofa and turned on the television. "Vangie, tráeme un vaso de agua." (*Vangie, get me a glass of water.*)

"Of course, Ma." The younger sibling joined her sister in the kitchen. "She wants some water."

"She has to eat something tonight." Lupe opened the Tupperware and dumped its contents into a large pot. "Tell her she has to eat. It's not good for her to keep skipping meals."

"You try telling her to eat. You know what she's like."

"Stubborn, like you," Lupe replied.

Vangie smiled but it quickly faded as she reached for a glass in the cupboard. "Why didn't you tell Louisa about the man you saw?"

"Because I don't know who he is or what he was doing," Lupe replied.

"You said you saw him at the Dorado and that he looked like a creeper, just hanging around and shit."

"Yeah, lots of men hang around that bar just waiting for a girl to come stumbling out so they can take advantage. Doesn't mean he chopped up a bunch of people and buried them in the old man's yard," Lupe replied.

"Still, it could help her."

Lupe grabbed Vangie's arm while she filled the glass under the tap. "We don't do that, Vang. We don't help the cops. I don't care that it's Louisa. She's still a cop. They have rules and can come after the people we know whenever they want."

"Fine. Okay. I get it."

Lupe let go of her arm. "Besides, I only seen him the one time."

"If you say so." Vangie returned to the living room. "Here you go, Ma. Lupe says you have to eat, or she'll drag you to the doctor's again."

"I did not." Lupe's voice carried on. "Don't you listen to her, Ma. But you still need to eat."

The older woman rolled her eyes.

The agents arrived at the second crime scene where spotlights shone on the ground and several police cars were parked nearby. The dimming sky was clear and dotted with bright stars.

"This is it." Romero shifted his SUV into Park. "Pretty much out in the middle of nowhere. Got some new homes going in over there." He pointed ahead. "Over there, some retail lot. Nothing much out here."

"What better place to hide bodies?" Surrey opened the passenger door. "And you said it was San Antonio PD running the site?"

Romero joined him. "Yes, sir."

"Why isn't your field office out here?" Kate asked.

"Too many cooks in the kitchen are never a good thing. We're here to guide the investigation and help coordinate between the local authorities." He raised his hands. "Now I know what you're thinking. Y'all being here adds to the chef count, but this? I've worked my share of murder investigations, this kind of thing is all y'all."

Surrey walked ahead and approached one of the CSI officers. "Excuse me. Agent Surrey, BAU Quantico." He turned back and pointed to Romero. "I'm here with Agent Romero and my colleague walking around over there is Agent Reid. You mind telling me what you've discovered so far?"

The woman in the black windbreaker with SAPD emblazoned on it, leaned on her shovel and peered at him. "They got y'all in on this? Well, I'll tell you, Agent Surrey, I've been doing this for almost 15 years and San Antonio's a big city. I've still never seen anything like this before. Not multiple victims like this. We don't even know how many people we got here. Earlier today, we assumed 2, and that's on top of the 4 we found already." She glanced down. "Looks like we got at least one more here." The middle-aged woman who kept herself fit turned to a colleague. "We're going to need more bags over here."

The other officer peered at the body parts. "Damn. I'll get 'em."

When the officer walked away, the woman continued. "Everyone thinks this is the cartel's doing. What about you?"

"We just arrived, but..."

"Hi, I'm Agent Reid." Kate cut in and offered her hand. "I see you've met Agent Surrey."

"Yes, ma'am. I'm Sergeant Harris, SAPD. I have met him. He was just about to give me his thoughts on whether y'all think this is the work of the cartel."

Surrey continued. "As I started to say, I think it's too early to come to that conclusion. I'd like to wait until we get labs back and see if we can find commonality in cause of death."

"Dismemberment isn't enough of a commonality?" Harris asked.

"I suppose it is, but I was thinking along the lines of drugs or a link between the victims that might tie back to the cartels. If we get that kind of information, I think we'll be able to better ascertain whether this is their handiwork."

"I'll keep going then. You let me know if you need anything,

Agent Surrey, Reid. Nice meeting you both." She returned to hand dig around the newest victim. "Hey, Jim, I could really use those bags right about now."

They stepped away to rejoin Agent Romero and Kate surveyed the area. "There's nothing around here but desert."

"That'll change soon enough when the houses Romero mentioned go in." Surrey pointed to the east. "That's where they found the other victims."

"We should get a map and mark the locations. It's only two for now, but there could be more." She turned to him. "And they got this spot on an anonymous tip, right?"

"Someone happened on a woman's bloodied shoe over there. Maybe a construction worker who was scared to give a name. I don't know."

Kate nodded. "Sounds like someone knows more than he wants to say."

"I don't think we're going to get a lot of help from the people around here. According to Romero, they protect their own."

When they reached Romero again, Kate continued. "Are you aware of any other cartel activity in this immediate area? Other crimes, drug-related, or anything like that?"

"I'm not up to speed, but I know who would be. Follow me." Romero started on.

They reached the edge of the grounds where a police officer leaned against her patrol car. Romero approached. "Officer Espinoza, I'd like to introduce you to some people." He turned to them. "This is Agent Jonathan Surrey and Agent Kate Reid. I asked them to lend us a hand and Agent Reid posed a very good question." He gestured for Kate to continue.

"Officer Espinoza, nice to meet you. I was just asking Agent Romero if he was aware of recent crime in this area linked to the cartels. If what has happened is their handiwork, then I'm thinking they might have a bigger presence here."

The young officer appeared hesitant. "The thing about it, Agent Reid, is that if there is cartel crime, it generally goes unreported. Personally, I've spoken to a few of the citizens in the past, oh, six months or so, and there hasn't been an increase in activity from that standpoint. We are a little bit removed from the issues that face the towns farther south, but we do see our share of trouble." She paused a moment. "As far as what's happening right now, I've asked around. No one's saying much."

"Are you from around here?" Kate asked.

"San Antonio. Born and raised. Moved here about 2 years ago. Since we're not far from the city, I might as well be from here," Espinoza replied.

"You must know a lot of people in town pretty well, huh?" Kate pressed on.

"I do, yes, ma'am."

"What do you think it would take to get someone to come forward, assuming they knew anything?"

"I can't really say, but when those bodies are identified, I think the families will cooperate, even if they're scared," Espinoza continued. "That's not to say the victims are all undocumented. I honestly have no idea, but the sooner we find out who they are, the sooner we'll know whether this was the cartel."

Kate nodded. "What about missing persons? Have there been a lot of reports around here in the past several months? Seems to me with at least six victims, families around here would be scrambling for answers if it were their loved ones."

"That's the weird thing, Agent Reid. We haven't had any reports. I don't know who these victims are or where they're from. But I don't think they're from here."

Thank you, Officer. I know Agent Romero is your point of contact, so please reach out to him if you learn anything new."

"Of course, ma'am."

Kate turned to the agents. "I wouldn't mind heading back to the Somerset station. I'd like to do a little research."

Surrey checked the time. "It's getting late, Reid, you sure you don't want to just get settled into a hotel and hit the ground running in the morning?"

"I might have to side with Surrey," Romero cut in. "I have us scheduled to meet with the M.E. first thing in the morning. You two should really get some sleep and we'll catch up at around 7am."

Kate glanced at the work being done and then looked at Surrey. "Yeah, okay. I can do research at the hotel just as easily. Any ideas of where we can stay?"

"We'll have to drive back into San Antonio. Better selection there. Come on. You can hitch a ride with me."

THE ONE THING the FBI hadn't updated was their budget for field agents. While the BAU team weren't exactly field agents, when they traveled, they had to adhere to the financial constraints set forth by the Bureau. That meant, the nearest budget-friendly hotel was where Kate and Jonathan Surrey would lay down their heads for a few hours.

As they emerged from the elevator into the long hotel corridor, Surrey turned to her. "Meet you in the lobby at 6?"

"I'll be there. Good night." She stopped at her door and pressed the card key against the lock to open it. "Get some sleep."

"You, too. Night, Reid," Surrey replied.

As Kate slipped off her shoes and set down her bag, her

thoughts were drawn back to the case in Brazil. Women were murdered and then buried in the hillside. The investigation had put the entire team in grave danger, however, this case felt different. Similarities existed between the two, but the person or persons behind the burial of so far 6 bodies, had different motives. This wasn't some rich guy getting his kicks, thinking he could buy his way out of trouble. This felt like extreme hate, and anger, though it was too early to know whether sexual assault had taken place with any of the victims.

Snacks lay on a tray nearby and she hadn't eaten anything since the airport. "To hell with it. I'll pay the five bucks." Kate ripped open a bag of peanut M & M's and poured several into her mouth.

She sat down on the bed and checked the time. "She'll be up." Kate reached for her phone and made the call. "Eva, it's me. I didn't catch you at a bad time, did I?"

"No. I'm still at the office."

"What? It's 10 o'clock your time. Why are you still there?" Kate asked.

"I guess I didn't want to sit in my hotel room—alone. It seems way too pathetic, and sadly, that's where I'll be until my new place is ready." Duncan sighed. "This whole thing is screwed up, Kate. I knew it would end like this and I did it anyway. Now, I have to deal with it, and I don't want to."

"I'm so sorry you guys are going through this. Cameron loves you, Eva. He wouldn't want you to try to avoid him. Couldn't you just stay with him until you're moved in?"

"No. It would be too hard. It's not like I stopped loving him, so sitting next to him on the couch and watching TV or something like it was no big deal would be—awful. Anyway, what's up? How's it going in San Antonio?"

"We just got into our hotel rooms. I scarfed down a $5 bag of

M & M's and I was just sitting here thinking about the case. We toured the most recent crime scene where SAPD is still digging for bodies. I started thinking about something and I wanted to get your thoughts."

"Why aren't you bouncing ideas off Surrey?" Duncan asked.

"I will but I thought I'd run it by you first. This feels highly targeted to me. The sheer number of victims, all female—we believe. Dismemberment, torture, most likely." Kate sighed. "I don't know. I have some ideas that go against the prevailing theory."

"I'm all ears. Let me hear it."

"The agent here is pretty certain that this is the work of a drug cartel. Given the proximity to the border, blah, blah, blah..."

"Blah, blah, blah?" Duncan asked. "I take it you don't subscribe to the group-think?"

"No. I get that the cartels are a problem in this part of the country, a big problem. But this is something else. I get a prickly feeling under my skin and I just feel there's so much more to it."

"How so?"

Kate stood up and paced the small room with two double beds and a credenza with a TV on top of it. "The bodies have been horribly mutilated in addition to being dismembered. Eva, these women were tortured, by all accounts."

"The cartel is known for that sort of brutality, Kate. That's no surprise."

"I understand, but then I got to thinking about incels."

"Involuntary celibates? Huh, that's an interesting theory," Duncan replied.

Kate stopped in the middle of the room. "If this is the work of incels, the unsub could be getting encouragement from an online group. It wouldn't be the first time. Maybe even one that's local."

"Okay, I can buy that," Duncan began. "How do you want to move on that idea?"

"While we're still recovering victims, can you help with hunting down social media posts from incel groups who are located in the vicinity?"

"Of course I can," Duncan replied. "Most of those guys are harmless, just venting their frustrations, but some have displayed violent tendencies. We've seen it. So, yeah, let me dig around a see what turns up. I'll let you know."

5

Inside the bar, Lupe finished her beer. She noticed the time was almost 11 o'clock. The Dorado was one of only three bars in town. The city had been overrun with fast food places and big chain restaurants recently. It was spillover from nearby San Antonio. But Lupe liked the Dorado because it was run by a local woman named Carmella, who also happened to be her best friend.

That woman stood behind the bar now and peered at her. "You ready to call it a night, Lupe?"

"I guess so. I should go home and get some rest." At only 25, her job in the city was physically exhausting. Lupe worked in a warehouse for one of the largest discount retailers in the country. Everything in their stores was a dollar. People flocked to them and especially in Somerset. Lupe ran a forklift. She was kind of badass like that. It was tiring work, and the commute was tedious, but it paid the bills. Her mother didn't work and Vangie attended community college, so she wouldn't have to work in a warehouse like her older sister.

"I'll wake up early tomorrow and do it all again." She smiled. "But at least I get to come here and drink for free, so there's that."

"The drinking for free part is only because you don't drink much to begin with." Carmella laughed. "Now, if you were like ol' Chuy over there, who can down a fifth of tequila a night, I might not let you off so easily."

"If I was drinking like Chuy, I'd be dead by now." Lupe glanced back at the large man. "He does have about a hundred pounds on me though, so I guess he can take it."

Carmella grabbed the empty beer bottle and tossed it in the trash behind the bar. "I don't think his liver can. But you should go home and get some sleep."

Lupe stood from the barstool. "Yeah, I will. Thanks, Carmella. See you later."

"See you."

Lupe headed toward the door and stepped outside. She pulled her denim jacket tight and walked to her car in the nearly empty parking lot. With her keys in hand, she pressed the remote to unlock her car. The lights flashed and her gaze was drawn to a shadowed figure caught in the brief glare.

She gasped and jumped back. "Hello?" The nearest street-lamp was several feet away and her car was bathed in darkness. The sky was clear, and the stars shone but did nothing to aid her vision. Lupe hurried to the driver's side door and slipped inside. She fumbled with her keys until finding the ignition. "Come on. Come on!" Her eyes darted ahead in search of the hooded figure.

With the key inserted, she turned the engine and relief washed over her. But when her door was yanked opened, the relief was short-lived. "No. No. Please don't hurt me. You can have my purse. Take my car. Just leave me alone." Her voice faltered as she stared at the man in dark clothes.

"Get out," he demanded.

"No. Please." Tears streamed down her cheeks. She glanced back at the bar, praying someone would emerge and see what was happening.

"Don't even think about yelling. No one can save you." He reached in and snatched her denim jacket, yanking her out of the car.

Lupe thrashed her legs and prepared to scream when he slammed his hand over her mouth.

"Don't or I'll kill you right here." He dragged her to his car.

Lupe tried to see the plate number, but it was too dark. She'd learned long ago that she was supposed to make a mental note of the vehicle, the plates, the model. Anything around that might help identify the abductor.

He was a large man, much larger than her 5-foot, 4-inch slender frame. He easily outweighed her by 50 pounds. When Lupe realized he was about to throw her into his car, she noted it was a beat-up older Ford Taurus, with chipped paint and grey Bondo on the back bumper.

"Get in and shut the fuck up or I'll stick you." He opened the rear passenger door and shoved her inside.

Lupe watched him as he closed the door and walked around to the driver's seat. *Go,* she thought. *It's now or never. You'll die here.* The door was still unlocked. The split-second decision to live or die was made. She scrambled to the door, staying low so he wouldn't see her. The silver handle was right there and she reached for it. The click of the lock echoed in her ears. She yanked on the handle, but it was too late.

The driver's door opened, and he climbed in. "Nice try, but you didn't think I'd be that dumb, did you? The child locks are on too, so good luck." He slammed the door and keyed the ignition. "Time to go, Lupe."

A GUST of wind rattled the windows of the single-level apartment where Vangie lay asleep in her bedroom. The noise stirred her and the first thing she did was check the time on her phone. Her blurry eyes read 1 am, and when she glanced at the twin bed next to hers, she noticed it was empty. "Lupe?"

Vangie sat up and turned on her side table lamp. Lupe's bed was still made. She grabbed her phone again and checked for texts or a call. There was nothing. "She probably went to Carmella's." Vangie pressed the Favorites button and called her sister, but it rang straight through to voicemail.

A quick swipe of her phone again and Vangie retrieved Carmella's contact. The line rang and she waited. "Come on, answer."

"Hello?" A raspy voice sounded through the line.

"Carmella? It's Vangie. Is Lupe with you?"

Carmella cleared her throat. "What? No. It's one in the morning, Vangie. I just got home and laid down. What are you doing? Is everything all right?"

"No. She's not home, Carmella. Lupe's not here."

"She's not with me, either. She left the bar at around 11. I saw her walk out myself."

"Well, then where is she?"

"Did you try her phone?" Carmella asked.

"It went to voicemail. Did she leave with anyone?"

"No. She had a couple of beers over like, two, or three hours, and then left. It was quiet tonight, and she didn't talk to anyone but me."

Vangie swallowed down the lump in her throat. "Oh no. With all that's happening around here..."

"Calm down, Vang. It's okay. I'm sure she's fine."

"How can you say that? She should be home. Did she tell you about the man she saw at the bar last week?"

"No," Carmella replied.

"He was some creeper skulking around. I don't know, but maybe he came back." Her breaths grew labored. "What if he took her? Carmella, what if she's already dead?"

"Okay, okay. That's enough. Look, I know you're scared, but your sister is smart. Smartest person I know. Maybe she had car trouble."

"A mile away?" Vangie's voice raised, and she darted a gaze at her bedroom door. "I'm sorry. I'm sorry, I'm just scared. There's some psycho running around out there cutting up girls. Why would she go out at a time like this?"

"I don't know. I didn't think anything about what's been happening. I guess I thought... I don't know what I thought."

Vangie placed her hand on her forehead as her eyes welled. "What do I do? Should I call the police? I can trust Louisa. She'll help me."

"Louisa will help. Call her. In the meantime, I'll go back down to the bar and have a look around."

"No, it's too dangerous. You shouldn't go out," Vangie replied.

"I have to help find her. I'll be fine."

The line went dead. Vangie stood from the bed and threw on her clothes. She hurried to the bathroom in the hall and pulled back her long black hair. For a moment, she stared at her reflection. Her eyes were red and watery, her face, pale from fear. She considered telling her mother, but it would only frighten her. But if she woke up and realized she was alone, that would frighten her more.

Vangie returned to the darkened hall and approached her mother's bedroom. She pushed open the door and regarded her as she lay asleep, a gentle snore sounding from her. Vangie took in a breath and considered the proposition, and the necessary explanation that would surely follow. No. She couldn't upset her that way. Vangie would find Lupe soon enough and there was no point in worrying their mother.

She closed the door, once again, and headed into the living room. Her keys rested in a bowl on the side table, and she snatched them. Just as she reached the front door, Vangie stopped. "Where do I go?" she whispered. Carmella was going to the bar where she last saw Lupe. Where else was there? "Louisa." Vangie peered at her phone as she stepped outside under a bright half-moon. Her breath drifted in a vapor while she made the call. Several rings sounded before the line answered.

"Espinoza here."

It was clear she'd awakened the officer. "Louisa, it's Vangie. Lupe's missing."

"What do you mean, missing?" Her tone sounded more alert.

"Carmella, at the bar, said Lupe left at around 11 o'clock, but I woke up and noticed she hadn't been in her bed. Her car isn't here. I'm scared. There's someone out there killing people. I don't know what to do."

"Vangie, I need you to take a breath, okay? I can go to the bar and see what..."

"Carmella's on her way there now. There has to be something I can do. I have to find my sister."

"I know. I'm going to get dressed now and I'll go to the bar, just in case. That's where we have to start, okay?"

"Can I meet you there?" Vangie asked.

"Yes, of course. I'll see you there in a few minutes. And Vangie, we'll find your sister. I'm sure this is just some kind of mix up."

"I hope so." Vangie ended the call and locked the front door before heading to her car. She slipped onto the seat of her old red

Saturn sedan that was unreliable at the best of times. With her key in the ignition, she turned the engine. After a bit of sputtering, it turned over. "Thank you. I'll never insult you again, I swear it."

The bar was only a mile or so from the apartment building and she turned onto the road ahead that would take her there. She couldn't think of anything except that Lupe was gone and there was no way she could go on without her sister. Their mother would die of a broken heart and life as they knew it, such as it was, would be over. "Stop. You can't think like that," Vangie reminded herself. But it was easy to succumb to dark thoughts given what their family had already been through.

The bar was ahead, and she turned onto the parking lot. Light came from the sign mounted on the building and a couple of streetlamps burned in the parking lot. Vangie spotted Carmella's car parked out front and as she drove on, there it was. "Oh, no." Her lips trembled, and her eyes welled. She pulled alongside Carmella's car, jumped out and ran.

Carmella must've heard her and rushed outside. "Vangie, wait!"

But she couldn't stop. She had to see Lupe's car. She had to know if Lupe was inside. Vangie slowed down and stopped at the driver's side window. She looked to see Carmella approach.

Carmella grabbed Vangie by the shoulders. "I already checked. She's not here. When I left earlier, I went out the back. Jesus, I didn't even see that it was here." Her attention was drawn to the approaching patrol car. "That's Louisa. Please just calm down a minute. Pull yourself together, Vang, I know that's going to be hard, but you have to. Lupe needs you to be clear-headed, okay?"

Vangie nodded.

Officer Espinoza stepped out and walked to Lupe's car where Carmella and Vangie waited. "Can I see inside?"

The women stepped back without a word while Espinoza grabbed her flashlight and aimed it through the window.

"It's unlocked," Vangie said.

Espinoza opened the door with a gloved hand and shone the light at the driver's seat and then moved on to view the rest of the car's interior. Several moments later, she clicked off her light and eyed the women. "I don't see her phone. Nothing appears unusual."

"It was unlocked when I got here. I looked around, but I haven't seen a phone anywhere," Carmella replied.

"Lupe tried to get in or was already inside before..." Vangie began.

"Before what? Vangie, I know you're upset, but we just don't know the whole story yet. There's no blood in here," Espinoza pressed on. "No signs of a struggle and nothing out of place. I don't want to ignore your concerns. We don't know where Lupe's at and that's a problem. But let's take this one step at a time, okay?"

Vangie wiped away a tear. "I know you're trying to make me feel better, Louisa, but you know Lupe. She doesn't just up and leave somewhere without telling anyone. Without her car or nothing. I mean, does she even have her phone? She's not answering it. This isn't normal."

Espinoza turned to Carmella. "When did you see her last?"

"She left the bar around 11 o'clock."

"Who else was here at that time?" Espinoza continued.

"Uh, I guess a couple other regulars. Not many. It was a quiet night. Lupe just comes to talk to me, mostly."

"I know you two have been friends for years. Can you recall who left after she did?" Espinoza asked.

Carmella raised her gaze to the stars. "I think maybe it was Chuy. I don't know. I don't really remember. It could've been Anthony. They were the only ones left inside. But I went into the back for a minute or two. I don't remember if anyone left before or after that point. I'm sorry. I wasn't paying attention."

Espinoza placed her hand on Carmella's shoulder. "It's okay. Why would you be? They were your regular customers, and I don't think either of them had anything to do with wherever Lupe is now, but I'll still talk to them to cover all the bases."

"What can we do now, Louisa?" Vangie asked. "All those FBI people. They're here. Can't they do something? Please, I can't just wait until she shows because I don't know if she will."

Espinoza reached into her jeans pocket and retrieved a business card. "This is one of their cards. Agent Kate Reid. They're staying in San Antonio, but you're right. Too much has happened here lately and if it was under any other circumstance I'd wait, but..."

"Someone is out there killing girls," Vangie pressed on. "I can't let my sister become one of them."

"I'll call her now." Espinoza stepped away a moment while the line rang. When the line answered, she cut in quickly. "Agent Reid, I'm sorry to wake you." She heard muffled sounds in the background as though the agent was getting out of bed.

"Officer Espinoza. Is everything okay?" Kate asked.

"No, ma'am, I don't think it is. I think someone in town is missing."

"What do you mean, 'you think.'?"

Espinoza peered back at Lupe's car. "I'm standing next to her car with her sister and best friend. They called to tell me she hadn't come home, and her car is here at the Dorado bar. It was unlocked and we didn't find her phone."

"Okay, does the car look damaged in any way? Is there blood inside?" Kate asked.

"No, ma'am. I didn't see anything out of the ordinary except that it was unlocked. Her friend, who also owns the bar, saw her leave here at 11 o'clock. No one's seen her since." There was silence on the line for too long. "Agent Reid?"

"Yes, I'm still here. Where are you now?"

"At the Dorado bar on south Acoma Avenue."

"Stay there. I'm on my way." She ended the call and quickly dialed Surrey's number.

"Reid." Surrey cleared his throat. "What's going on?"

"A local woman's missing. Officer Espinoza is on the scene now. We need to get down there."

6

The dark and barren highway toward Somerset left Kate with an ominous feeling about the prospects of finding Lupe Cordova alive. In her mind's eye, she envisioned the woman headless and dumped in a hole in the ground. Burn marks on her body. Deep gashes etched in her chest. The reality of her job sickened her at times, and this was one of them.

"Reid, you all right?" Surrey must've noticed her hypnotic gaze as she drove.

"Huh? Yeah. I'm just thinking," she replied.

The call from Officer Espinoza came unexpectedly and Kate's first thought was to engage Agent Romero or at the very least, let the captain of the Somerset Police in on the situation. Maybe the officer had already done so, but Kate's sense of urgency grew knowing the potential outcome. "Let me ask you something..."

"Shoot," he replied.

"Do you find it strange that no one in this town has been reported missing?" She glanced at him. "That the victims aren't from Somerset?"

"A little, yeah. So where are they from?" Surrey asked. "And why is there now a local woman who has gone missing?"

Kate shook her head. "It's like whoever's doing this knows we're here and is proving a point."

"That he can do what he wants without impunity," Surrey added.

"Maybe. I suppose there's still a chance one or two of the victims are from here. None have yet been ID'd."

"Then why hasn't anyone reported them missing?" he asked.

"The obvious assumption is they're undocumented," Kate replied. "And the families are afraid to come forward."

"No. No way. I don't buy that," he cut in. "As a parent, I wouldn't give a shit what happened to me. I'd tell anyone who would listen to help me find my missing child."

She glanced at him with a curious gaze. "Of course, you have kids. Sometimes I forget that about you. But you're right. If I was a mom, nothing would stop me either. After talking to Espinoza, she said she'd spoken with people who would know if there were families out there afraid to come forward. She didn't get any indication of that."

"Then I don't know what to say." Surrey peered through the passenger window.

Kate pointed ahead. "That's the place. The Dorado. I see cars in the parking lot." She made the turn and drove next to where the women stood.

Officer Espinoza waved at the approaching agents.

Vangie moved toward her. "You're sure it's okay to talk to them?"

"It's fine. They aren't here for any other reason than to help us find Lupe," Espinoza replied.

Kate stepped out and Surrey joined her. As she reached the

officer, she extended her hand. "Thanks for making the call, Officer Espinoza."

"Right now, Agent Reid, we need all the help we can get. And I figured, if the FBI can't help, then no one can." She turned to the women. "This is Carmella Ortiz; she owns the bar and is a close friend of Lupe Cordova."

"She's my sister," Vangie cut in. "I'm Evangeline Cordova."

"Agent Reid, this is my colleague, Agent Surrey."

He nodded.

"Officer Espinoza, have you filed any reports with your department yet?" Kate asked.

"No, ma'am. I came out here as soon as I got the call from Vangie. I thought it would be best to get started right away in looking for her."

"I did put in a call to Agent Romero and expect him here soon," Surrey added. "This is still his jurisdiction. That said, time is not on our side. What can you tell me about your sister, Evangeline? Was she seeing anyone?"

"No. She broke up with Eric a few months ago, but no one since. But there is something." She glanced hesitantly at Espinoza. "She noticed some guy last week hanging around the bar one night. I don't know when, I didn't ask her."

"Did Lupe mention this man to you, Carmella?" Kate asked.

"No. Vangie told me just a little while ago and it was the first I'd heard of it."

"Okay, did she describe this man?" Surrey pressed on. "Any description at all is helpful."

Vangie glanced away. "No. At the time, she didn't think it was important. I asked her yesterday why she didn't mention it to Officer Espinoza. She had no answer for me."

Kate turned to Carmella. "Are there security cameras around here?"

"No. I've never needed them before. I'm sorry."

Espinoza returned a compassionate gaze. "It's okay. None of this is your fault." She turned to Kate. "What do we do now? We see her car is here. Untouched, by the look of it. She's not answering her phone. I should probably call the captain and tell him what's happening. He'll want to know."

"I agree," Kate replied. "And in the interest of time, I think we should move on pulling her phone records to learn who was the last person to contact her." She turned to Surrey. "We can get a list of calls connected to the nearest cell tower from here." Kate considered another approach and looked at Vangie. "Is there anywhere else you can think of that Lupe might've gone to? Another friend, anyone else?"

"She would've come straight home. Carmella says she only had a couple of beers and was there long enough that she would've been okay to drive. And if she wasn't, I would've been the first person she called. Agent Reid, with some killer out there, you're wasting your time looking for phone records or calling her friends." Vangie glanced at Espinoza. "I know this town. I also know sometimes people pass through here on their way to look for work in San Antonio."

"We do get a lot of travelers," Espinoza replied. "Mostly they keep to themselves."

"Is there anyone around here who might be helping these travelers navigate their way to the city?" Kate asked.

"I might know of someone," Carmella jumped in. "I have a friend I can talk to."

"Will this friend cooperate with the FBI?" Surrey asked.

"Under the right circumstances, I believe so," she replied.

Surrey regarded Kate. "You should take them to the station. I'll stay here until Romero arrives. We need to search the grounds for tire tracks, or anything that will point to an abduction."

"It's too dark. You'll have to wait until daylight," Kate replied.

"There's no time. If we don't do what we can now, we'll be too late."

THE SUN HADN'T YET RISEN when Kate returned to the Somerset Police Station with Espinoza and the two women desperate to find Lupe Cordova. Under a pre-dawn sky, they stepped out of the patrol car and headed toward the entrance.

"Captain Brown said he'd be here. We have to talk to him." Espinoza pushed through the entrance.

Kate let the officer lead the way, already knowing that there was nothing more the captain could do than what they had already done. No BOLO could be issued. They had no car to look for. No Amber Alert because Lupe was an adult. They had no persons of interest to question, other than an unknown creepy man no one else had seen except for Lupe. Espinoza was about to learn how hard this job could be and how helpless an officer could feel at times like these.

Kate stopped at the lobby and grabbed Espinoza's attention. "Maybe it's best if Vangie and Carmella wait here a moment while you speak to the captain."

Espinoza glanced at the women. "Sure. That's probably a good idea."

It appeared that Vangie was about to object when Carmella took her arm.

"It won't be for long. I promise." Kate hurried to catch up to the officer and followed her to Captain Brown's office. Since arriving only hours ago, she hadn't been acquainted with him. Her arrival might come as a surprise.

Espinoza reached his office. "Excuse me, Captain?"

Brown stood from his desk and regarded her. "Louisa, thank you for calling me. I just arrived. Tell me exactly what's happened." He turned to Kate. "You're the FBI agent?"

"Yes, sir. Kate Reid. I'd met your officer out at the crime scene with Agent Romero on our arrival just a few hours ago. My partner and he are at the bar where Lupe Cordova was last seen. Officer Espinoza asked that I get involved. I hope I'm not over-stepping."

"Not at all," Brown replied. "I don't complain when help has arrived. But you say the other agents are at the bar?"

"Yes, sir. As you know, in cases like these, time is against us. So, they wanted to start immediately in hopes of finding something that might point to a direction the abductor traveled," Kate replied.

"Captain," Espinoza cut in. "Everyone's afraid of what's happened to Lupe. They know why the FBI is here. I did speak with Carmella. Lupe had mentioned to her sister that a strange man was seen at the bar about a week ago. Carmella is going to ask around in hopes she might know of anyone who had seen this man. Whether he was passing through, I don't know, but she wanted to do more than wait."

Brown nodded. "I'm sure. But Agent Reid, you're the expert here. It is no coincidence Lupe Cordova is missing at a time like this."

Kate glanced away. "No, I don't believe it is. That said, it's my understanding that no one has reported any missing persons here in Somerset. It's not lost on me that it has happened now, after the FBI has gotten involved."

"Almost as if to draw your attention," Brown replied.

"Possibly. My partner and I are trying to wrap our arms around this at the moment. We're exploring a number of theories. Very early stages, of course. Technically, we're here to offer assistance to Agent Romero and I should get with him to put together a plan of action, but I want you both to know that we'll do whatever we can to help you as well."

Brown sat down again. "Romero is of the belief this could well be the work of the cartels. The look on your face makes me think you're not on board with that?"

Kate raised her shoulders in uncertainty. "It's just too early to know for sure. As I said, we're looking at all possibilities right now. I really wish I had more for you. I think finding Lupe Cordova is going to jump to the top of the list of priorities."

JUAREZ. THREE YEARS EARLIER.

The woman inside the checkpoint booth appeared worn out and it was only 6 am. She motioned for the man to approach. "Sir?"

The busy port of entry had lines that were a mile long and the understaffed facility brought huge delays for those who worked across the border but lived in Mexico.

"Sir? You're next," she repeated.

"Sorry." A man in his mid-30s, wearing baggy jeans and a graphic t-shirt, approached the booth.

"Your passport, please." She waited while he retrieved it from his back pocket. "Thank you." The woman opened it to the photo and studied it for a moment. She looked at him and again at the photo. "Your work visa?"

"Here you are," he replied.

After a thorough review, she returned to him the documents. "You should know your visa expires in 2019, six months from now. Have a nice day, sir."

"Gracias." He continued through to the other side on foot.

Juarez, Mexico was near the El Paso border. Travelers passed over the Bridge of the Americas, along with three other entry points by the thousands every day. The largest city in the state of Chihuahua, it was easy to disappear in this city, whether one wanted to or not.

A factory near the border employed many who lived both in El Paso and in Juarez. And in 2018, it employed Xavier Medina. He walked inside the massive building and headed toward the employee's back room. He punched his time clock and returned to the floor to start work. The twelve-hour days were long, but Xavier was young, and strong, and the labor hadn't bothered him.

As he pulled the lever to punch the steel plate on the conveyor, his attention was drawn to the young woman who walked by. She was new. He smiled as she glanced over her shoulder at him.

"You don't stand a chance, ese."

He turned to the man who spoke and glared at him before returning to his task.

Before he knew it, the time reached 7pm and his shift was finished. Without a word, Xavier walked to the back and clocked out. He grabbed his backpack from the locker and walked out into the warm summer night air. The city was shrouded in purple and orange light from a setting sun.

Xavier walked along the fractured sidewalk and headed back toward the bridge where he would stand in line for at least 2 hours before he could cross back into El Paso. Cars drove by, the occasional gunshot sounded in the distance, and a few bystanders nodded as he walked on.

The dangers of walking alone on these streets were nothing he hadn't faced every day. But he kept his head down and didn't talk to anyone.

As the sun lowered in the sky, he heard voices in the distance. Female, or at least one of them had been. The narrow streets were lined with old, rundown buildings and alleyways in between. It reeked of garbage in this part of town.

The voice grew louder, and the woman screamed. Xavier stopped in his tracks and looked around for anyone who could help. His pulse raced and panic imbued in his eyes. He forced his legs to move and they carried him quickly along the path toward the noise. He looked sideways at the alley and saw the man with a knife in his hand. The woman was on the ground, and he slashed at her.

The man must've felt eyes on him as he whipped around. Xavier locked onto his gaze. He was frozen for a moment until he finally broke free and ran. He didn't look back but heard the man yell at him.

"Mantén la boca cerrada, hijo de puta. Te encontraré." (*Keep your mouth shut, mother fucker. I'll find you.*)

He made it to the bridge, still peering over his shoulder. Medina had worked in Juarez long enough to know that sticking his nose into matters that hadn't concerned him was a good way to wind up dead on some back street where no Mexican cop would care, and an American cop couldn't find.

SAN ANTONIO, PRESENT DAY

The time on the wall clock showed 2:30am. Xavier Medina's shift wasn't even half over yet. But when the gurneys started rolling in, he knew something was up.

An attendant hurried through the corridor. "Coming through. Make way."

Medina grabbed his mop and bucket and stepped out of the hallway while staff pushed the gurneys through to the exam rooms. The medical examiner's office was usually busy, but this was different. He worked the night shift, and that was always when the bodies rolled in, but as he watched them enter, what he hadn't known was what lay inside the covered bags. They didn't look like bodies. "What the?" He stepped forward again and caught the attention of a staff member. "Hey, what's going on?"

The man looked at him. "Dude, you don't want to know. It's bad. I'll just say that." He continued on.

Medina had grown curious now and waited a moment until the workers disappeared. He walked into the hall again and toward one of the autopsy rooms into where the gurneys disappeared. He peeked through the window and spotted one of the doctors unzip a bag. "Holy shit." Medina jumped back and spun around to check whether anyone had seen him. He swallowed hard and his eyes were wide. After regaining composure, he walked back to his mop and went back to work.

SURREY AIMED his flashlight at the edge of the parking lot of the Dorado. "Hey, I think there could be something here."

Romero joined him. "What is it? It's so damn dark out here, I feel like we're wasting our time."

"Maybe not." He squatted low and again trained his light onto the asphalt. "Right here." He used his index finger to outline the spot. "A skid mark. It's well defined here, but then as it goes along, it's less evident."

"It's like the car skidded to a stop at the edge of the lot, stopped to look for oncoming traffic, and continued," Romero replied.

"Leaving a decent track mark for us," he added.

"This could be from any car in the last two weeks."

"Not a chance. That's fresh rubber." Surrey stood up again. "Besides, do you have anything better?"

"Not at the moment." Romero took out his phone and photographed the mark. "I can send this to my lab when we get back to the station and have those guys get started on cross-referencing it with the vehicle database."

"Any chance we can bump up our meeting with the M.E. this morning?" Surrey asked. "If there's any hope he can ID those victims, it might help us find Lupe Cordova."

7

The search for the missing local woman had stalled before it even began. Officer Espinoza had already made calls to her friends, none of whom had seen her. No one had heard from her. Kate had received a text message from Espinoza with the update and all she could do was to reply, *"keep trying."* What the hell good was that going to do?

It was barely sunrise and the meeting with the medical examiner had been pushed up to 6 am. With the missing woman at the top of her mind, Kate hoped the M.E. could reveal something—anything about these victims that might help with finding Lupe. Going back to the idealistic young cop empty handed was the last thing Kate had wanted.

She stepped out of the shower and donned fresh clothes. Standing in front of the hotel bathroom mirror, Kate pulled back her long brunette hair into a ponytail. For a moment, she hadn't recognized the face staring back at her. While she was only just 35, the lines on her forehead were a little deeper. Her crow's feet, a little more prominent. No doubt a job that entailed witnessing humans' capacity for violence might have had a physical effect. A half-smile appeared on her lips at the thought of the young optimist she'd once been while working for the victim's advocacy group before the discovery that she had been a victim, herself.

That life seemed so long ago. Before Marshall, before Nick. And yet both of those men had forever changed the trajectory of her life in a way so meaningful, she couldn't have known the impact it would have on her. Except for the damn wrinkles on her face now. And that spark of enthusiasm was all but diminished. What was left was a woman who had survived much, and knew her life's calling was to do exactly as she had been doing—chasing monsters.

When the knock on her hotel room door sounded, Kate was brought back to the present. Back to the reality that dismembered women lay waiting for justice, and another woman lay waiting to be rescued. God willing, it wasn't too late.

Kate dabbed a tissue under her eyes to soften the concealer and walked to the door. "I'm ready. Let me grab my bag."

Surrey walked inside. "How'd you sleep?"

"The three hours we got? Not bad. You?" She slung her laptop bag over her shoulder.

"About the same," Surrey replied.

She made her way to him. "Well, then, I'm glad we're both wide awake and refreshed."

He snickered. "You seem to be in good spirits this morning, all things considered."

Kate walked through the door and held it for him. "Good spirits might be putting too light a spin on it. Let's just say I've come to realize that this is exactly where I'm supposed to be."

They walked along the hall and reached the elevators. Kate stepped inside and pressed the button to the lobby. "Did you read my text last night?"

"About the incels?" He nodded. "I did. Sorry I didn't reply, but it was late."

"I know. I just wanted to throw it out there. Maybe it's something. Maybe not," she added.

"It's an interesting idea, though I'd really like to rule out the cartel theory first."

"Without the luxury of time, we should pursue both." When the doors opened, Kate stepped out into the lobby. "I attended a seminar about a year or so ago. In fact, it was led by a profiler I used to work with. A woman who I greatly admired at one time."

"Who was that?" Surrey asked as he walked alongside her.

"Doesn't matter now. What matters is that this was back when a recent spate of men associated with incels in Japan, England, and the US, went out and murdered women for the hell of it. Because they were women. She explored the notion that these incels find camaraderie online but tend to act alone with some encouragement from their online cohorts. To do what we've seen done to these current victims would have taken an individual a lot of time, patience, and isolation. The first site on the property of Mr. Ortega was fairly secluded in that his neighbors were few and far between. And to be honest, I'm not sure the killer knew he was on someone's land. It was far enough away that he might've thought it was a vacant lot. The second location was a large construction site out on the edge of town. Not many people around there either." Kate pushed through the lobby doors.

"So why here? What's so special about Somerset?" Surrey asked. "What's the connection to this place if these women were not from around here?"

Kate regarded him a moment. "I wish I knew. But right now, we have one woman who could still be alive. She's from here and a lot of people know her."

"Not the same M.O," Surrey replied.

"No, sir." Kate stepped into the driver's seat and pressed the ignition.

Surrey buckled his seatbelt and closed the passenger door. "Did I mention Romero's meeting us there?"

"You did." Kate pulled out onto the road and headed toward the highway. "You've known him a while, huh?"

"We worked together on a joint investigation when I was in Denver, and he worked in Boulder. He got transferred to San Antonio a year or two after that."

"Oh yeah? What kind of case was it?"

He turned away and gazed through the passenger window. "The kind that didn't end well."

Kate kept her eyes on the road ahead. "I'm sorry to hear that."

"Yeah, well, it happens. We all know that." He took in a breath. "It was a child sex trafficking case. A state-wide investigation that brought in a lot of various law enforcement, though it was spearheaded by my office."

"And you were the lead?"

"I was." Surrey hesitated again. "A young boy from my daughter's school was kidnapped. They were in the first grade together."

Kate's lips parted as if to say something, but she thought better of it and waited for him to continue.

"We didn't find him in time." He looked away again. "It changed how my daughter looked at me. Like I had failed her, and I had. It's part of the reason I'm divorced now. Not all, of course." He pointed ahead. "This is the place. Romero said to park on the west side. That's where law enforcement enters."

"Yeah, okay." Kate didn't know what else she could say. There was usually nothing to say in this kind of situation. She wasn't a mother but could empathize with him. She'd lost plenty and had seen similar looks in the parents of the victims she'd had to face. It wasn't the same, no doubt, but she was grateful he'd opened up to her. Slowly, but surely, the two had grown closer. It was a necessary part of this job. They had to trust one another.

When she parked and stepped out, Kate thought it best to change the subject. "So how's the house treating you?"

He turned to her. "You know what, it's great. Thanks for putting in a good word for me with the son. He said if it wasn't for you referring me, he probably would've sold it rather than renting it out again."

"I'm glad it worked out." Kate walked through the entrance. "You said Romero was here?"

Surrey glanced at his phone. "Yep. I just got a text from him. He's waiting for us at the front desk."

"There you are." Romero walked toward them. "Thought you two might've slept in."

"Not a chance," Surrey replied. "Is the doctor ready?"

"Ready and waiting." Romero waved his hand and they followed him back to the autopsy room. "Dr. Bauer. Appreciate you coming in early to talk to us."

"Not a problem at all, Agent Romero. I see you brought company."

"Yes, sir. These are the Bureau's finest. Agents Surrey and Reid. Quantico," Romero replied.

"Good to meet you, Doctor." Surrey offered his hand.

"Same here." He turned to Kate. "Agent Reid. Pleasure."

Kate accepted his hand. "Nice to meet you, Dr. Bauer. I know we've rushed you in here this morning, but we're hoping you might have some new information for us regarding the identities of the victims."

"Right to the point. I like that." He turned to the refrigerated cabinet and pulled open one of the drawers. "This woman here was our best shot at returning an ID because her remains were, well, the most complete. We tried dental records, but nothing came back. Prints aren't in our system either."

"But you found something," Surrey pressed on.

"Yes, sir." He pulled down the sheet to expose her torso. "A couple of things we found, actually. Come take a look." The agents drew in and the doctor used his index finger to point at her side. "This scar here is from a kidney transplant. Well, I should clarify that to say she donated her left kidney."

Kate eyed him. "Donors are on a database."

"That's right," Dr. Bauer continued. "But since we didn't know her name, we needed more details."

"Her labs. You can find her blood type and run those parameters through the database," Kate added. "But you'd still need a date or a name."

"Yes, ma'am. And we had neither. That said, I was able to home in on an approximate date simply by the look of the scar and the tissue inside when it was removed. It appears that the removal of her kidney happened in the last year, maybe two. So I was able to narrow that down and with her blood type, zone in on it even more."

Surrey appeared to grow impatient. "Doctor, I appreciate you giving us the rundown, but we have another victim who may still be alive. Identifying this woman could help us find her. Please, can you tell us who she is?"

"Of course. I don't mean to drone on."

"It's okay, Doc," Romero cut in. "Agent Surrey's anxious. We all are."

"Sure, I understand. This woman is Lisa Gutierrez. 27 years old."

"Is she a US citizen?" Kate asked.

"Yes, she is," the doctor replied. "I haven't notified next of kin for positive ID but based on the information in the database." He walked to a laptop on the counter. "This is her."

Kate approached the doctor and viewed the screen to see a stunning young woman with long black hair and wearing a smile.

Bauer peered at her. "This all came to light in the wee hours, and I wanted to make y'all aware of it first."

THE BRIGHT MORNING sun shone in Lupe's eyes, stirring her from what had amounted to a half-conscious sleep. Exhausted, dehydrated, and scared, she squinted in the light and tried to make clear her surroundings. It was the smell that she recognized first, like she stood in one of those restaurants with sawdust on the floor. Wood. It smelled like freshly cut wood. And as she blinked to clear her vision, her senses hadn't betrayed her. Sawdust lay on the concrete floor. A few woodworking machines were stationed along the walls. It took another moment to realize that she was on the concrete floor, laying on a blanket with a small pillow under her head. The room was freezing, and the light came from a small square window near the ceiling along a front wall.

Lupe tried to sit up, but when her arms wouldn't move, she looked down to see that they were tied to a metal ring clamped to the concrete floor. She was shackled to the ground and as she grew more lucid, her surroundings grew clearer. "No..."

"Good morning, Lupe."

She turned her attention to the man who approached with a cup of coffee in his hand. He spoke with a heavy Mexican accent. "Who are you? Let me go." She tugged her arms and the ring clinked against the ground.

"Like I told you last night, I won't hurt you as long as you don't give me any trouble." He sat down on a metal stool nearby. "Figure out where you are yet?"

"My father's cabinet shop," she replied. "How did you get in here?"

"The place has been empty for—let's see." He cast up his gaze. "Your dad died about 2 years ago, wasn't it? Shame what happened to him."

"You didn't know my father. Don't you dare talk about him," Lupe replied.

He leaned closer. "You're in no position to demand anything, Lupe."

"How do you know my name? How do you know my father? Did you kill all those women at Mr. Ortega's house?"

"Lots of questions for a girl who has her hands tied," he replied. "So, let's get back to why you're here. I know you work at the warehouse of the discount store in San Antonio. I know you hang around the Dorado, too. But what I didn't know was that your dead dad used to work for one of the homebuilders in San Antonio. He was a cabinetmaker. Makes sense considering where we are. Too bad he was murdered on his way home that night."

"Stop. You don't know what you're talking about," Lupe said. "Why are you doing this?"

He looked around. "I thought you'd appreciate being back here. Your dad had a long history back in Juarez."

"I wouldn't know. I wasn't born in Mexico," Lupe replied.

"Oh, I know that. I will tell you one thing, Lupe. I think it's time you learn who your father really was."

KATE STUDIED the body of Lisa Gutierrez, or what remained of it.

"Doc, can you tell me whether she died of asphyxiation, or had she lived through her limbs being sawn off?"

Surrey looked at her with a knitted brow before turning back to the doctor. "Have you determined cause of death, yet?"

"Not yet, however her limbs appeared to have been severed after she died, just based on the condition of the surrounding tissue. I'll also be able to give you some idea of the type of knife used as I get into the reporting. At first glance, I concluded a straight-edge, at least for the flesh, most likely a saw used on the bone, but I need to continue to process the details."

"Why was there no blood found on the ground?" Kate asked. "Where they were dug up. Could it have been due to a length of time? Did it just absorb into the soil?"

"There would still be traces," the doctor continued. "It could be a case that the victims were moved to the site where they were eventually found."

"So, he what, lets them bleed out and then moves them?" Kate asked, rhetorically. "Maybe he didn't want to get his car messy."

"These are things we'll need to explore," Surrey cut in. "But for now, Doc, how soon do you think you'll be able to get us IDs on the rest of these victims?"

The doctor glanced at his technician. "They won't be as easy to identify. We don't have much to work with, I'm afraid. I've already run fingerprints. We just don't have enough yet."

"We'll start with Lisa's background. Find her family, friends. Anyone who can tell us what she was doing before she went missing and how long it had been since anyone had seen her," Kate replied.

Romero had been fairly quiet while Kate prodded the doctor. He turned to Bauer. "We just need something that's going to help us find Lupe Cordova and fast."

"Let's check with the sister, Vangie," Surrey replied. "See if she or Lupe knows Lisa Gutierrez. That would be the best place for us to start."

Kate nodded. "Maybe Lisa worked with Lupe? Do we know where she worked?"

"We need to find out," Surrey replied.

Romero paced the room. "Hey, I'm all on board with you wanting to find a link between this victim and Lupe Cordova, but we need to jump on this shit like now. You both know as well as I do that if we don't find the missing within about 48 hours, the chances we will..."

"We know," Kate folded her arms and turned on her heel for a moment. The door behind her had a small window in it and she caught sight of a man walking by. He darted away his gaze and she returned her attention to the doctor. "So what I'd like to run with..."

"Hang on," Surrey interjected. "Reid, I don't mean to cut you off, but what if we cross-reference the timeline from when Ms. Gutierrez disappeared, assuming we get that nailed down, and then look for others from the San Antonio area who've gone missing around the same timeframe. I don't want to think it'll be that easy to figure out who these women are, but what if it is?"

"It's worth looking into for sure," Kate replied. While we check out Gutierrez's life, Agent Romero, maybe you could run a missing persons' report for the metro area? Surrey might be right. If our first victim is from here, maybe the others are too. We can be ready with that information as Dr. Bauer learns who these victims are." Kate turned to the doctor. "We appreciate your time, Dr. Bauer. You have a lot of work ahead of you."

"I'll head back to my office to get the ball rolling," Romero began. "We need to notify next of kin ASAP, though. That has to happen before we can start talking to the victim's friends and family. In fact, I'll stick around here until Doc makes that happen.

I'll see to it they know what's going on. Then I'll meet y'all back at the Somerset station and we can huddle up to see where things stand." He turned to the doctor. "Keep doing what you're doing, Doc. Appreciate the effort."

"Of course," he replied.

"Thank you, Doctor." Kate opened the door and walked into the hall while she waited for Surrey and Romero to file out. The hall felt 20 degrees warmer. She glanced around the corridor and spotted the same man from earlier.

He pushed a broom at the end of the hall, perpendicular to her. He must've felt her stare because he glanced back.

Kate noticed a look of fear in his eyes. It was subtle, like he'd been caught staring. "Excuse me?"

Surrey entered the hall. "What are you doing, Reid?"

"Excuse me, sir?" Kate started toward him and quickened her pace. "Hello? Can I ask your name, sir?" When she reached the end of the hall, the man scurried away. "Hey?" She glanced back at Surrey and waved him over. "Hey, hang on a minute," she continued to speak to the man, who had almost reached the door that led outside.

Surrey quickly caught up to her. "Reid, what the hell are you doing?"

When the man opened the door and the light shone inside, her eyes stung for a moment. He pushed outside and when she and Surrey reached the door, he was already in his car and the engine turned.

She stopped and looked at Surrey. "Why the hell did he run?"

8

I t took a moment to learn his identity, but the woman behind the desk handed Dr. Bauer a slip of paper. He eyed the agents. "His name is Xavier Medina. He's worked here for about 8 months."

"Why would he take off like that?" Kate asked. "Last I checked, we weren't wearing FBI jackets. He wouldn't have known we were federal agents. Even if he did..."

The doctor turned to her. "It's possible he submitted fraudulent documents to work here. He could have a record, or he could be illegal. I just don't know at the moment, but we can certainly find out."

Romero widened his stance as if at attention. "Do you have an address for him?"

Dr. Bauer looked to the woman at the desk. "Would you pull that up for us?"

"Of course." She typed on the keyboard a moment. "Here it is. He's at 12469 W. Desert Vista Road. Apartment 207 in Somerset. At least, that's what we have on file."

Kate's brows raised. "Somerset? What a coincidence."

"Our plates are full with Gutierrez at the moment," Surrey replied. "What do you want to do? I mean, he ran from you. He didn't pull a gun on you."

Kate nodded. "You're right. Still, I'm getting a weird feeling about him. You know what? I'll ask Espinoza to run by and see if he's at his home. We stand a better chance of her getting through to him rather than us."

"If she finds him, what do you want her to do?" Romero asked.

"Ask him why the hell he shot out of here like that. Something's not right there. I have to listen to my gut on this one," Kate replied.

Surrey raised his hands in surrender. "Far be it from me to keep you from listening to your gut. Check with Brown first. I know those guys are looking for Lupe just as hard as we are. He might have other plans for Espinoza. If not, then it can't hurt. People don't act squirrelly for nothing."

"No, sir, they do not," Romero added.

"Thanks again, Doctor. We should get moving." Kate started ahead and Surrey quickly caught up to her.

On the way out, Kate reached for her phone. "I can call the captain now."

Surrey slipped behind the wheel and when Kate closed the passenger door, he continued. "I'll admit it's odd that man just took off like that, but I suspect he somehow figured out who we were."

Kate buckled her seatbelt while he pulled out of the parking lot. "I don't know. All that he accomplished was drawing our attention to him. He made it worse for himself, if that was his reasoning."

~

LUPE HAD HEARD THE RUMORS. She and her sister ignored them. Their mother insisted none of it was true. The girls' father had been a good father. Kind and loving. He worked hard to support his family. He even had his own business and thrived doing the work that he loved.

This place—his place—had been his pride and joy. Five others had worked for him. He believed in second chances and often employed those with a criminal record or a scant work history.

So when this man, this person who had abducted her, insisted Lupe hadn't known the truth about her father, she knew he was lying. It was to scare her into submission. To control her. Lupe knew better.

"You're wondering if I'm telling you the truth," the man said.

"No, I'm not. You're lying. I don't know who you are or why I'm here, but I do know that you're a liar," Lupe replied.

On a table next to his stool rested a manilla envelope. He opened it and retrieved several photos and tossed them in front of her on the ground. "You think I'm lying? See for yourself."

Lupe returned a sideways glance at the pictures.

"You don't want to look?" He bent over and picked them up again. "Then I'll show you." He held in front of her a picture of a dismembered body. "This was in Juarez almost 3 years ago. She was 18 years old. Just a girl."

Lupe closed her eyes, refusing to cast her gaze on the photo for a moment longer.

"Do you want to know who did that to her?" he asked. "I'll tell you, but you won't like what I have to say."

"No." A tear streamed down her cheek.

"Eduardo Cordova. Your father. She was just one of his victims."

"You're lying!" Lupe shouted. "You're thinking of someone else. You have to be."

"Eduardo Cordova was part of a group in Juarez. I don't know how many they murdered, but I do know that she was among them." The man leaned closer and gripped Lupe's face with his hand. "I am that girl's father, and you will tell me what I want to know."

I T W A S N ' T long before the agents returned to Somerset and as Kate and Surrey walked inside, Espinoza hurried toward them.

"Agent Reid. You both are back," she began. "What did the M.E. say?"

"He ID'd one of the victims," Kate replied. "Romero was slated to talk to the family and friends. Her name was Lisa Gutierrez. She lived in San Antonio. Does the name ring any bells?"

Surrey retrieved a photo from his suit coat pocket. "This is what was found online." He held up the photo.

Espinoza took the picture and examined it. "I don't recognize her. You say she lived in San Antonio, but she was found here."

"That's right," Kate replied. "We were hoping you might be able to tell us something."

"I wish I could, Agent Reid, but I don't know this woman. I'll ask Vangie if she or Lupe knew her."

"There is something else we'd like to ask," Kate continued. "The apartment building on Desert Vista Road. Did Captain Brown ask you to check it out for us?"

"He hasn't been in yet. There was some big meeting with top brass at SAPD about all this. He didn't mention that to you?"

"I left him a voicemail earlier," Kate replied.

"Oh, okay. Well, what's this about?" Espinoza pressed on.

"A man by the name of Xavier Medina lives there in unit 207. He works at the M.E.'s office and we'd like to talk to him, but I think being FBI, we might scare him off. I don't know what his story is, but could you check him out for us?"

"Yeah, sure. If he knows anything about this stuff, or where Lupe is, I'll talk to him. No problem. Do you think there is a connection?"

"We don't know, but he seemed jumpy around us. Didn't set right with Reid. Me, either, actually," Surrey replied.

"What happens if I talk to him? Should I bring him in?" Espinoza asked.

"No, just give me a call right away," Kate said.

Espinoza peered at them and nodded. "I'll do what I can."

LOUISA ESPINOZA HAD BEEN a cop in Somerset for nearly 2 years. In that time, the number of occasions she has had to confront a suspect could be counted on one hand. It wasn't that the town had no crime, it was just that she hadn't been the one to answer the calls when they came. The other, more experienced, officers handled the serious offenses. So when the FBI asked her to track down a person of interest, her nerves stood on end.

She arrived at the Desert Vista Apartments on the south end of town as midday approached. The two-story complex consisted of 4 different buildings, painted cream with a stuccoed finish. Xavier Medina resided in unit 207, according to the agents.

Espinoza stepped out of her patrol car and checked her weapon. The parking lot was nearly empty as she would've expected on a Tuesday afternoon. Agent Reid sent her the details of Medina's car and right now, it was nowhere to be seen. Nevertheless, she had to confirm if he was inside his place and started up the wrought iron staircase that led to the second-floor units. His was near the end of the walkway and she stood in front of it.

Espinoza knocked. "Mr. Medina, this is Somerset Police." She waited a moment. "Mr. Xavier Medina, Somerset Police. I'd like to ask you a few questions, please."

Footsteps sounded behind her and when she turned, a man stood several feet away. His eyes widened and his lips parted. "Excuse me, are you Mr. Medina?"

He was frozen in place, holding a bag of fast food. He dropped the bag and spun around, jogging back down the stairs.

"Mr. Medina? Damn it." Espinoza ran after him. "I just want to talk to you, sir. Stop!"

He reached the parking lot, and she was quick to catch up to him. "Mr. Medina, stop. Now!" She placed her hand on her gun, ready to unsnap the case. But she knew once that happened and she decided to draw her weapon, things could turn ugly in a hurry. "Please, I'm asking you to stop. Don't make me..."

He halted on a dime and with his back still turned from her, raised his hands. "Don't shoot. Don't shoot me."

"Turn around—slowly." Espinoza trained her weapon on him until he faced her. "Why did you run?"

"I don't know."

"Are you Xavier Medina?" she asked.

"Yes, ma'am," he replied.

"And you work for the Bexar County Medical Examiner's office?"

"Yes, ma'am," he continued. "Have I done something wrong?"

"You tell me. I just came here to talk to you." She peered around. "Maybe we could talk in your apartment unless you want the neighbors listening in. I'm going to lower my weapon now."

Medina nodded and lowered his hands. "We can talk in my place. It's at the end of the hall."

"Lead the way, Mr. Medina." She stood ready with her hand on her holster while he walked by her and headed back up the steps toward his apartment door. As he keyed the lock and stepped inside, Espinoza tightened her grip on her weapon and surveyed the room.

"Please, come in," he said.

She followed him inside and continued to eye her surroundings. "Mr. Medina, the reason I'm here..."

"I know why you're here, Officer," he replied. "I have ID I can show you."

"That's not why I'm here, actually. I was sent by the federal agents who were at the M.E.'s office early this morning. Apparently, when one of them caught your attention, you ran. Why was that, Mr. Medina? Do you know something about why those agents were at your place of business?"

"I guess I don't trust them much. I got scared and ran. That's all it was," he replied.

Espinoza regarded him a moment. "Somehow, Mr. Medina, I think you know why they were there. It's no secret what has been found here in Somerset. And now another woman is missing. People are scared and they're right to be. So if you know something—anything—about those found buried in Mr. Ortega's property or at the construction site, now would be a good time to say something."

Medina was quiet for a moment and peered down at his feet.

"Mr. Medina, please. If you know something that can help us find the missing woman..."

"I know that I have seen this before." His tone was soft, and he kept his gaze aimed at the floor.

"Where?" Espinoza sat down on an old recliner across from him. "Where have you seen this, Mr. Medina, and when?"

He grew visibly shaken before he raised his eyes to Espinoza. "Juarez. I used to work in Juarez when I lived in El Paso. I worked in a factory. I saw a lot of things happen there."

"Things like what's happening here now?" she pressed on.
"Maybe."

"Then why did you run like you were guilty of something? Those agents are here to get to the truth." She continued to gauge him as he looked terrified to speak. "Agent Reid, the one you ran away from, she asked if you would talk to her. It sounds like maybe you should, Mr. Medina. She and her partner are at the police station. Would it be okay if I took you there now?"

"I don't know who did those things if that's what you're thinking," he replied.

"You can only speak about what you know. And right now, every little bit helps. We're searching for another possible victim as we speak. She could still be alive, so if you can help, wouldn't you want to do that?"

"What if they find out?" he asked.

Espinoza returned an inquisitive gaze. "What if who finds out, Mr. Medina?"

VANGIE CORDOVA HADN'T LEFT the police station since arriving with Officer Espinoza in the middle of the night. She lay slumped low in a chair inside the lobby waiting for answers. Waiting to learn where her sister had gone. Now, as the sun shone high in the sky, no one knew anything more than they had in the early hours before dawn. Lupe was gone and no one could find her.

The doors opened and Officer Espinoza walked inside with a man Vangie hadn't known. She pushed off the chair and called out as Espinoza walked by. "Louisa? Louisa, do you know anything yet about my sister?"

Espinoza stopped and touched Medina's shoulder. "Hold on a moment, please." She started back to Vangie. "We're doing everything we can to find Lupe, Vangie. I promise you. I don't know anything more yet, but we are working to find her. The captain has everyone out there talking to Lupe's co-workers, her friends."

Vangie glanced at Medina. "Who is he? Is he a suspect?"

"He's here on another matter. You should go home and get some rest. Your mother will need you right now. I promise you, I will call if anything changes."

Vangie watched Espinoza and a man she hadn't known continue down the hall. But when she spotted Agent Reid, whom she'd met hours earlier, and another man stop Espinoza in the hall, she waited and tried to listen in on their conversation.

"Why did you run from me?" Kate asked Medina.

Vangie stepped closer to the hall as the agent spoke.

"Do you know anything about the victims at the M.E.'s office?" Surrey continued.

Medina trembled. "I already told her. I got scared. That's all. I didn't do anything. I don't know anything."

Vangie continued to listen. Her eyes narrowed as she homed in on the man while the agent spoke.

"I came here because Officer Espinoza asked me to. I can try to answer your questions, but I'm telling you, I don't know anything."

Vangie hurried into the hall. "Where is she? Where is my sister? Did you take her?" She marched closer to Medina.

"Whoa, hang on, Vangie." Espinoza used her hand to stop the young woman. "I already told you this man doesn't know anything about Lupe."

Vangie eyed him. "Yes, he does. You know, don't you? You know where she is!"

Medina's eyes widened with confusion as he shook his head. "I don't know who you are."

"Okay," Kate stepped in. "Vangie, I know you're upset, but

we're just talking to people and trying to get a handle on the situation."

Espinoza took Vangie by the shoulders and turned her around. "Let's get you a ride home, okay? You need sleep."

Vangie struggled to free herself from the officer and spun back around, marching again toward Medina.

This time, Kate stepped between them and squared up with her. "Vangie, please do as Officer Espinoza asks. Please go home."

Vangie's breath was heavy, and her eyes were full of anger. "Arrest him. He knows something. I can see it in his eyes. He knows where my sister is." She began to sob.

"Let's go, hon." Espinoza glanced back at Kate before taking the young woman once again and leading her back into the lobby.

Surrey drew in a breath and peered at Medina. "Well, she seems to think you know something, at least about her missing sister. So, do you, Mr. Medina?"

9

It had already been an hour and still the BAU agents got nothing from the man who worked for the medical examiner in San Antonio. Kate paced the office in frustration while Surrey sat at the table across from Xavier Medina. Sweat beaded on Medina's forehead and his thin brown hair looked damp. He chewed his lower lip to the point that it bled.

Kate walked to the table and stopped in front of the men. She burrowed her gaze into Medina's eyes, but he only returned a worrisome look. Distress crossed his face like a shadow in the sun's rays. "Cut him loose."

Surrey shot her a look. "What's that now?"

"He doesn't know anything." Kate looked at Medina. "Of course, if you did and kept it from us, you'd be committing a crime and would definitely go to jail for obstruction of justice."

"I don't know how many different ways I can tell you that I don't know anything about what happened to those people you found," he replied.

Kate squatted to meet his gaze. "I'd be more apt to believe you had you not run away when you saw me at the M.E.'s office. Do you understand what's at stake, here, Mr. Medina? People are dead and more will likely follow. Why won't you help us?" When he remained quiet, she stood up again. "What do you know about a group known as 'incels.'?"

He returned a curious glance. "What?"

"Involuntary celibate," Surrey cut in. "You know, guys who can't get girlfriends and blame women as the reason they're alone. You've never heard of them before?"

"No," Medina replied. "Sounds made up."

Kate scoffed. "I assure you, it's not. They can be dangerous and especially when they're encouraged by others in the group to act out against women as some sort of revenge tactic. It's far from made up."

Medina held her gaze. "I've never heard of them. I'm sorry."

Their attention was drawn to the door when Captain Brown walked inside.

"Pardon the interruption. I just thought I'd share some information that might help." He continued inside and handed Kate a file folder.

"What's this?" she asked.

"I have a few friends on the other side of the border. After you brought in Mr. Medina and made mention of what happened, I asked around." He turned to Medina. "You said you worked in Juarez a few years ago and lived in El Paso."

"Yes, sir." His demeanor shifted.

Kate opened the file and laid it on the desk in front of Surrey as they both read it. A moment later, Kate's eyes shot up at Brown before returning to Medina. "You have a record in Juarez."

He closed his eyes a moment. "I didn't do anything wrong. You don't know what it's like there, Agent Reid. Especially for Americans coming there for work."

"You wouldn't think that happened a lot," Surrey cut in.

Medina shot him a glance. "You know nothing of Juarez, then, Agent Surrey. The jobs there are many and when the US had no jobs, I worked in the factories in Juarez. I crossed the bridge every day. It took hours, but I did what I had to do."

"Then what happened?" Surrey asked. "Why were you arrested for assaulting a woman?"

Medina shook his head. "It wasn't assault. I was protecting her. A man was attacking her, and I tried to stop it, then I was arrested. I knew the man was probably a cop or part of a cartel and that was why the police arrested me and charged me. I spent 6 months in a jail cell. After that, I wasn't allowed to work in Juarez anymore."

"Is that when you moved to San Antonio?" Kate asked.

"Yes."

Kate handed back the folder to the captain. "Thank you for looking into this. Could we get a copy of this for our files?"

"Of course." Brown turned on his heel, but not before eyeing Medina. "You better hope they believe you, son."

"Is there a way to find the woman you helped to have her corroborate your story?" Surrey asked.

Medina looked away. "No. That's not possible."

"Huh, convenient. And why is that?" Kate asked.

He eyed them. "Because she's dead."

INSIDE THE CABINET shop Lupe's father owned before he died, she waited at the hand of a man she hadn't known, but who had known her. "I already told you, my dad was a good man. He worked hard to build his business and raise my sister and me." Her eyes welled. "You're talking about someone else."

The man pushed off the chair, knocking it over. "I'm tired of this. You know who he was. How could you not?" He rushed toward her and squatted to meet her eyes. His lined face was marked with scars. His grey hair was disheveled and unclean. "When he didn't come home until late at night, didn't you wonder why? Weren't you curious?"

Lupe sobbed. "I don't know what you're talking about. Please let me go. Please. I promise I won't say anything. I won't tell the police, just let me go."

He pulled back his hand as if ready to hit her but stopped. "Give me the names of his friends."

Her hands were still bound to the metal ring and so she tried to blink away the tears that blurred her sight. "Whose friends?"

His eyes darkened. "Do not test me. I don't want to hurt you, but I will in order to get what I need. Now tell me who your father's friends were."

Lupe cleared her throat. "I—I don't know...maybe I know one or two."

"Then tell me who they are," he demanded.

She studied him for a moment. "I'm sorry about your daughter, but I know my father would never have hurt anyone."

"No? I found his shoe prints at the scene." He leaned in toward her. "Tell me the names of his friends and I promise you, you'll never see me again. Isn't that what you want?"

This was going to be her only way out and while she hadn't spoken to any of her father's friends since the funeral, she knew them to be good men. None of this made any sense to her. Why her and why now? "He's been gone for over two years. Why are you doing this now?"

"Because it's taken me that long to track him down and when I learned he was dead, I had to keep going to find the others responsible for murdering my daughter."

Lupe swallowed down the lump in her throat and closed her

eyes while a tear streamed down her cheek. "Michael Garza, Rich Ceballos, and um, I can't remember who else..."

"That's not enough. Give me another name or I swear that you won't leave this place," he said.

"Um," she began to cry again. "Samuel... I don't remember his last name. I swear it." She looked at him as he wrote down the names and caught sight of his wallet that lay open behind him. Her brow drew in at what she saw, but when he returned his attention, she averted her gaze.

"I know you're afraid, but I had no choice." He leaned in closer. "I will tell you this. If I look into these names and it turns out they aren't who you say they are, I will return. Do you understand me? I will return and I will take your sister. I might not treat her as well as I've treated you. And if I feel like the cops are onto me, you won't survive the day."

Whatever she said, it had been enough. He talked like he was going to let her go. "Okay. I understand."

THE INFORMATION CAPTAIN Brown returned had been useful, but Medina continued to deny any wrongdoing. Kate stood inside the captain's office with Surrey at her side. "We have to get him to submit to a DNA swab. Given what you discovered, Captain, we'd be crazy to let him loose without that."

Surrey pursed his lips and groaned. "Right now, we have zero on this guy. He raised the hairs on the back of your neck because he took off, but there's no indication he could even remotely be a suspect. That said, if he agrees to a swab, then great, but I wouldn't hold my breath."

The captain regarded the agents. "First of all, I'll grant you that we have nothing to hold Medina on. Although, the fact he was imprisoned in Mexico for assault against a woman does raise an eyebrow. That doesn't mean he's the one we're looking for. You two are the experts, here. Ask him and see what he says. If it's a hard 'no', then you have no choice but to let him walk."

"Yeah, you're right," Kate replied. "If he doesn't want to cooperate, we might want to rethink whether he's telling us the truth. Sadly, we can't ask the woman involved. Still, I'm not sure I trust his story." She started into the hall toward the interview room.

Surrey caught up to her. "Hey, look, I get it. You want to know what Medina's connection is. And even I don't buy his whole 'I ran because I was afraid' routine. What the hell was he afraid of? He didn't know who we were. It sure as hell wouldn't have been the first time he'd seen law enforcement in the M.E.'s office."

"He knew what we were there for with Dr. Bauer. How could he not? He lives in Somerset. Everyone knows and they're all afraid," Kate replied.

Surrey stopped. "Hang on. We have no legs to stand on at the moment, so if you want to take a run at him, we'll only get the one shot and see what sticks. Until the medical examiner identifies these other victims, or Romero learns more about Gutierrez, we're flying blind. It'd be a good idea to have Medina's DNA for future reference, but we sure as shit have no legal right to it. So our best bet is to politely ask for his cooperation and make him aware we'd like it in order to exclude him. We stand a chance that he'll go for that."

"Fair enough. We'll see if he bites." Kate opened the door. "Mr. Medina, sorry to keep you waiting."

He shrugged. "I'd like to go home now if it's all right with you and call my boss asking if I still have a job."

"I understand that Dr. Bauer might be thinking twice about you because you ran from us," Kate began. "There is something that we can do to help sway him to the notion you got spooked and that this was all just a big misunderstanding."

"It *was* a big misunderstanding," he replied.

Kate pulled out a chair to sit while Surrey remained standing. "It sounds like it, but we're happy to show the M.E. just how cooperative you've been. If you submit to a DNA swab so that we can eliminate you as a person of interest, that will go a long way to proving the point."

"Fine," he replied. "I told you I have nothing to hide. If this is what it will take to show you that, then so be it. I just want to get out of here."

"I'll go get a kit." Surrey left the room.

Kate eyed him for a moment. "You said the woman who had been assaulted in Juarez, you said she died. What happened to her?"

"The same thing that happens to a lot of women over there."

"Which is?" Kate pressed on.

"Agent Reid, you asked me about these people; these—what did you call them—incels?" He shook his head. "I don't know what the hell they are, but in Juarez, women are murdered by the hundreds year after year. And what's happening in this town now with the cut-up bodies? That looks a lot like the kind of stuff I seen when I worked in Juarez."

"Are you saying you believe it's the same thing that's happening here in Somerset, now?"

"I don't know, but maybe you should focus your efforts on figuring out why so many women there are killed because it could be happening here too. The Mexican Guard don't give a shit. Maybe no one here does either."

∽

WHEN HE SPED AWAY, kicking up dust in Lupe's face, she removed the bandana from her eyes and screamed. She'd just been dumped on the side of the two-lane road and watched the vehicle disappear in the plume. Thirsty, hungry, and scared out of her mind, Lupe couldn't call anyone. The man had taken her phone. Based on the position of the sun, her best guess was that the time was somewhere between 1 o'clock and 3 o'clock.

She peered left and then right, uncertain which direction would take her home. The industrial park where her father's cabinet shop lay was about half a mile from the high school. But as she looked around, the school was nowhere in sight. In fact, nothing was in sight. "50, 50, chance I'll get it right." Lupe started back in the direction the car had bolted, figuring that was her best shot at returning home. Maybe she would happen upon a payphone and could call Vangie. Her sister must have been terri-fied and God only knew what was running through her mother's head. After their father was murdered, she believed they weren't safe. Turned out, their mother had been right.

As Lupe walked along the edge of the asphalt, she replayed the terrifying events. Never once had the man identified himself, but he sounded Hispanic and spoke of a time in Juarez. Yes, she knew her dad had visited there, but it was long ago. This man claimed her father had been a murderer. She knew nothing of what he was saying. He was lying, that's what it was.

The men's names she had spouted had been his friends. She only recalled them because of the funeral. Her father had never had much time to spend with their family, let alone friends. In fact, she wasn't sure if they were friends at all, but she had to give that man something.

Lupe squinted toward the distance when the sun's rays reflected off something. "A car. Oh, thank God." She smiled with relief and waved her arms in the air. "Hey! Hey, over here!" She jogged ahead, still waving and flailing her arms. "Hey! I need help."

It appeared that the burgundy compact car had slowed. It looked like it could have been a Honda Accord. "Hey!"

When it reached her, the car stopped, and the passenger window rolled down. Lupe rushed to the window and peered inside. "I need the police..." she stopped cold a moment. "Actually, I just need a ride home. My stupid boyfriend and me got in a fight and he told me to get out of the car. Can you give me a ride home?"

The woman behind the wheel regarded her with suspicion.

"Please. I have no water. I'm not even sure exactly where I am or how long it would take me to get home. I live in Somerset. Can you please help me? I don't have any weapons." She held out her arms. "See? Nothing."

The woman pressed the button to unlock the door. "Get in, mija. I'll take you home."

10

Vangie opened the front door and her lips trembled at the sight before her. "Lupe. Oh my God, you're okay." She swung her arms around the neck of her older sister and pulled her close. "Where have you been? Everyone's been looking for you."

Lupe tried to choke back her emotions but was so relieved to see Vangie again. "I wasn't sure I'd ever see you or Ma again." She pulled back from the embrace. "I'm sorry I scared you. I started walking. Just thinking and walking and I got lost." She wiped away her tears and chuckled. "Can you believe it? The one time I forget my phone, you know?"

Vangie regarded her in disbelief. "What? You got lost?"

"I know. It's so crazy. Where is Ma? I should see her." Lupe noticed the look in her sister's eyes. She hadn't believed the story. "We should go inside. No one else needs to overhear our business."

Vangie closed the door as they entered. "I don't understand. You went for a walk from the bar without your phone in the middle of the night when there's some crazy person out there killing people."

"I know. I was just feeling overwhelmed, I guess." Lupe continued inside and started into the hall. "Is she asleep?"

"She wasn't a few minutes ago when I checked on her." Vangie followed her into the hall. "Did you take drugs or something, Lupe?"

"What? No, of course not." She stopped at the door of their mother's room and peeked inside. "Looks like she's resting now. I won't wake her."

Vangie stood frozen in the hall while Lupe walked by and returned to the living room. A moment later, she made her way back and planted her feet in front of the television. "Lupe, we have to go to the police station. They're looking for you. I went with Carmella, and we reported you missing. Even the FBI knows."

"What?" Lupe asked. "What do they know?"

"That we've been searching for you. Everyone's been worried sick thinking you were dead like the others." Vangie walked to Lupe's side and sat down. "I thought you were dead."

"I'm so sorry. It was stupid, I know. So, so stupid." Lupe teared up again.

"I'll drive. We have to get to the station." Vangie stood again and grabbed the car keys. "I hope you're telling me the truth, Lupe."

INSIDE A SPARE OFFICE in the Somerset Police Station, Kate peered through the window and held her phone to her ear. "And you weren't able to find any recent meetings, or anything planned for the near future in the area?"

"Not from what I could see," Duncan replied. "That doesn't mean anything though."

Kate nodded. "Right. I'm not ruling out anything. This guy's record doesn't bode well for him."

"Maybe that's the place to start," Duncan continued. "His time in Juarez and the jail stint. If the arresting officer is still around, see what you can get from him. Considering what you've got your hands on right now, Medina's looking like he fits your profile."

"It was more than two years ago, but who knows? You're right that we can't dismiss it out of hand. So, we've got the theory about the cartels, involuntary celibates, and now, what, femicide?" Kate replied.

"It's been happening for decades in Juarez," Duncan added. "It's not inconceivable the trend has moved north. It may not be anyone from Juarez, but an admirer of the work. You've got a head start with Xavier Medina. I'd run with that. Listen, I'll keep looking into this on my end. Let me know if we need to get in touch with friends on the other side of the border."

"I will. Thanks, Eva. Speak soon." Kate ended the call and returned to the captain's office where Surrey awaited.

Surrey stood on her return. "We got the swab."

"Really? I thought we'd get pushback from him."

"Maybe he is telling the truth," Surrey replied.

"Where is he now?" she asked.

"On his way home, I imagine," Captain Brown cut in. "We can't keep him. But Agent Surrey put in the call to Dr. Bauer and let him know what happened. Like us, he was perplexed as to Medina's reasons for fleeing. But aside from that, we'll have to wait until DNA comes back and cross-reference it with whatever he's found on the victims." Brown removed his reading glasses and eyed the agents. "Where does that leave your investigation? And for that matter, we still haven't found Lupe Cordova. I've had my officers knocking on doors, but no one knows anything."

Kate regarded Surrey a moment. "I don't know if it'll help us find her, but Romero should be working on speaking with the Gutierrez family and friends. I don't know..."

Their attention was drawn to the door and the captain jumped to his feet. "Lupe. Oh, my Lord. You're okay." He glanced at Vangie. "What, where?"

Vangie ushered Lupe inside. "She was lost, and a woman picked her up from the side of the road and brought her home just minutes ago."

Kate approached her. "Ms. Cordova, I can't tell you how good it is to see you right now."

"I'm so sorry I got everyone worried," Lupe began. "Like I told Vangie, I went for a walk without my phone and got lost. It was so stupid, I know. I shouldn't have worried everyone this way, especially with..." she trailed off. "Vangie said everyone was out looking for me, and that we needed to let you know I'm safe now."

Kate studied her body language. Something was off. Lupe fidgeted with her fingers, averted her gaze, and her voice cracked. She recognized the signs. Before her stood a woman who was afraid for her life. "Lupe, how about I take you to the kitchen and get you a glass of water. You can sit down for a minute. Would that be okay?"

Vangie nodded. "Yeah. Lupe, you should get some water."

Kate revealed a tender grin and ushered Lupe from the office and into the hall. "It'll be good for you to sit for a moment and then we can talk about how all this came about. Just to get a statement for the police. Then you can go back home with your sister and get some rest." She continued on until they reached the breakroom. "Have a seat. I'll get you a glass of water."

Lupe sat down at a small table and watched the agent retrieve a glass from the cabinet and hold it under the water dispenser. On her return, Kate took a seat next to her. She gulped down the water and wiped her mouth with the back of her hand. "Thank you."

"Of course." Kate held her gaze. "You must've been pretty scared out there knowing what's been happening in town."

Lupe nodded. "I guess I just had one beer too many and figured I'd go for a little walk. Next thing you know, I was lost."

Kate nodded. "You've lived here for several years, right?"

"Yes, ma'am. But like I said, I drank a little too much and got myself turned around."

"You couldn't have walked all night. Did you find a place to lay down and close your eyes? A park or something like that?" Kate pressed on.

"Well, I don't know exactly where I was, but I did find a little playground. I laid down on a bench for a while, but I didn't stay long. It was getting cold."

"And you don't know where this was?" Kate asked.

"No, ma'am. I wish I could remember."

Kate reached for Lupe's hand and took hold of it. "I know you're scared. I can see that. But you're safe now. No one can hurt you." She drew in a deep breath. "Lupe, I need you to tell me what really happened last night and today."

Lupe's chin trembled and her eyes reddened. "I can't," she whispered.

"Why not?"

"He said he would come back and take Vangie." Lupe raised her gaze. "He said he would hurt her."

～

A BEAT-UP CAMPING trailer was parked under the sparse shade of a Palo Verde in the middle of the desert. A dirt road had been carved between the cacti and prickly shrubs to the spot where it sat. Former Juarez Police Lieutenant, Armando Guzman, hadn't been the only one to claim the site. He'd been at this a long time and had made many an ally along the way. One, of whom, had known this camp well and offered up the refuge.

Red dust billowed from Guzman's old Ford Taurus as he drove along the narrow path and made his way to the trailer. He stepped out of his car and climbed the metal stairs to the door. Upon opening it, the heat had built up inside the tin box, even in winter, so he left the door open. With only a small generator, he hadn't wanted to bother with the power until night arrived.

Guzman knew he'd crossed a line. A line that could see him inside a Texas prison cell should he fail in his effort, or even if he succeeded. Kidnapping Lupe Cordova had gone against everything he stood for as an officer. Even Mexican police had their limits. He knew what kind of reputation they had but he wasn't like many of the others. He didn't take cartel money to look the other way. He didn't take bribes from politicians. And now that he was on this side of the border, searching for those who murdered his daughter, he may have committed the only crime in his life.

Armando Guzman had seen what had been happening to the young girls and women in his city. But when it happened to his own daughter, his entire life upended.

Now, Guzman hunted them all the way to San Antonio. News of Eduardo Cordova's death had been a blow, but he persisted, even going so far as to find whoever had killed him. That effort hadn't lasted long, so he returned to the hunt. Only now, he'd kidnapped a US citizen. What were the odds the young woman wouldn't talk? No doubt, they would come for him soon, and it wouldn't be that hard to find him. Lupe Cordova would've seen his car as he left her on the side of the road.

His phone rang in his pocket, and he answered the line. "Hola." (*hello.*) He listened as the caller spoke. A brow raised slightly, and his lips tightened. "No. Debo quedarme hasta que sepa más." (*No. I must stay until I know more.*) He swallowed hard and shook his head. "Estoy cerca ahora. No pierdas la esperanza todavía, mi amor." (*I am close now. Don't give up hope yet, my love.*) Guzman ended the call and closed his eyes.

It was a high-wire act that Kate had taken on plenty of times. Pressuring Lupe Cordova to discuss what happened could see her clam up completely. She had to take her time, one foot forward, to ensure the young woman knew that Kate was there to help. "How about I get you something to eat? A bag of chips? A candy bar? There's a coffee shop nearby. I can get you a sandwich."

With her gaze still directed down, Lupe replied, "I'm not hungry, but thank you."

"Okay, then, I just need to step out a moment. I'll be right back." Kate walked into the hall and returned to find Surrey inside the empty office. "She's scared out of her mind. Whoever it was threatened to come back and take her sister if she talked."

Surrey shoved his hands in his pockets and pursed his lips. "Shit. Do you think you can convince her that we can protect her?"

"I'm going to try. I just want to give her a minute to think about it before I go back inside." Kate sat down on a side chair and peered at Surrey while he perched on the desk. "This person who took her...he's not the killer."

"She wouldn't be here otherwise," Surrey replied. "So who was he and why did he take her in the first place?"

"She doesn't know Gutierrez, the only victim we have a name for at the moment. According to Vangie, no one else they know has been reported missing. There's still the so-called 'creeper' who she'd seen at the bar. There could be something there."

Surrey nodded. "Possibly, because I don't know why else she would've been targeted. What do you think about the idea she was taken to send a message to us? Consider the timing of this."

"A threat to our investigation? Maybe. That, to me, suggests we're right on track and I have a feeling that means there are more bodies in the ground we aren't supposed to find," Kate replied.

Surrey pushed off the desk and meandered inside the office. "The only way this girl will feel safe is if we can assure her we'll keep her family safe too. What if we offer her those assurances?"

"Such as?" Kate asked.

"Well, she's afraid for her sister, that much we know. What do you know about the rest of her family?"

"Their father was murdered a couple of years ago. That raises a big red flag. Their mother doesn't get around well and can't work. Lupe works to support the family," Kate replied.

"Yeah, I'd say the dad getting knocked off could be something. Maybe he was affiliated, and someone was looking to get back at the family for something. But why now, just when we arrive?"

Kate stood up again. "The only way we're going to figure that out is to get her to talk. You mentioned assurances. Well, I say we get the family out of their apartment temporarily. Get them someplace where Lupe feels safe."

"The city?" Surrey asked.

"That could work. I don't know if they'll be willing to leave, but with what's happening here in Somerset, I don't know why anyone would want to stay."

"Then let's get with the sister and Captain Brown. I may have to get Romero to help coordinate this, but we can get them in a safehouse for a while. Maybe then, Lupe will feel comfortable enough to talk."

"If you can run on that," Kate began. "I'll get started on learning more about the Cordovas. The kidnapper is connected to the family somehow, and probably the father. That's where I'll start."

11

S till in the throes of a devastating cyber-attack, Senior Unit
Agent Nick Scarborough remained at Quantico coordinating efforts between the Bureau and the CIA officers
who were familiar with Russian and Chinese hackers. The trains
were still down in most major metropolitan areas along the east
coast creating a transportation nightmare nationwide. He hadn't
slept. No one on his team had since it happened yesterday in the
early hours of the morning.

"Agent Scarborough?" A woman, who appeared in her thirties,
with short blonde hair and a fitted pants suit entered with an
outstretched hand. "I'm Candice Morgan, Information Ops."

Nick stood from behind his desk and accepted the greeting.
"Yes, I remember you from this morning's briefing. The CIA's
Critical Infrastructure Protection group. What can I do for you,
Ms. Morgan?"

"As you know, we've been working side-by-side with DHS and
NSA to narrow down our list of groups capable of taking out the
trains."

"Yes, we've been waiting on that. Is it available?" he asked.

"That's what I've come to speak to you about." She glanced around a moment. "May we speak in private?"

Nick closed his door and returned to his desk. "Go on."

"While our best minds continue to work to bring the systems back online, I understand your team has been analyzing the origins of the breach."

"That's been our only goal. Based on what we've learned, similarities to other attacks have been uncovered. The results shouldn't come as a surprise to anyone," he replied.

Morgan hesitated a moment while she sat down across from Nick. "It's obviously very early in the process, but I'd like to know what your team has learned so far. Have you identified a country of origin?"

"Not definitively, as I stated in this morning's intel briefing," Nick replied.

"I know what you said this morning. I was there. Now, tell me what you really know."

He pressed his lips together and inhaled deeply. "Okay, but this stays between us until I can be absolutely certain. The last thing I want is for the president to make a call prematurely."

"Fair enough," Morgan replied.

"As I said, the attack has similar markings to other recent attacks. Specifically, the pipeline, and likely the Israeli water systems attack last year."

She nodded. "Which attempted to spike chemical levels to disrupt the water supply. So, you're telling me it's the Russians."

"Again, I don't want to speak out of turn. This is just what we've uncovered so far. We still need to cross-reference our leads with that of DHS and your people." Nick focused his gaze. "Why the rush to pinpoint a source before we're certain?"

"The president is anxious," Morgan replied. "It's the second major attack on his watch and he doesn't like it. He wants to know who's responsible."

Nick's phone buzzed on his desk, and he looked at the caller ID.

"Do you need to take that?" she asked.

He pressed the button. "No. I'll call them back."

LEVI WALSH ENDED the call as he peered at Fisher and Duncan. "I got Scarborough's voicemail. I imagine he has his hands full with the train situation."

"No doubt." Fisher chewed on his toothpick. "I hate to bother him with this, but I know he's investigated these groups before."

"We can dig around for the files," Duncan added. "But it would be helpful if he gave us the names. I need to give Reid something. She and Surrey are considering three different scenarios and exhausting them on their own isn't doable. Not when they have this many bodies turning up and who's to say there won't be more?"

"As I understand it, they've ID'd one of the victims and both are working that lead now," Walsh replied. "Let's get on the horn with our people and offer to jump in the water with them."

"It's still Romero's case," Fisher added. "If anyone's going to jump in, it'll have to be on his authority."

Walsh dropped down onto a side chair. "They need more boots on the ground. I feel like we're leaving them out there flapping in the wind."

Fisher pulled up to his desk. "Might as well make the call now since we're all here. Let her tell us what she needs." He made the call and placed the line on speaker.

"Reid, here."

"It's Fisher. I've got you on speaker and the whole gang's here."

"Afternoon, everyone," Kate replied.

"We're calling to get a feel for how things are progressing down there in San Antonio," Fisher continued. "We know you asked Duncan to scratch up some intel for you."

"I did and she came through as always," Kate replied.

Duncan leaned closer to the speaker. "Reid, we know you have a lot of bodies piling up and not a lot of leads. We wanted to get your take on the situation and see what we can do to wade in if you need us."

"I appreciate that, guys. We did have an interesting development just about an hour ago. A woman was kidnapped last night and released early this afternoon. She's scared to talk, so Surrey and I were about to get her and her family someplace safe in hopes she'll open up about what happened. Agent Romero's on board with the idea."

"She was taken by the unsub and released?" Walsh asked.

"This couldn't have been the unsub, not after what we've seen him do to his victims. No, Surrey and I agree there's another connection to this woman and we think it's her father. But she's scared. She won't give us any details about her abduction."

Fisher regarded the others a moment. "What's the plan, then, Reid? Your plate appears to be overflowing. We're reaching out is all I'm trying to say."

"Give me tonight," Kate began. "Let me see what I can get from this woman. We're already getting reporters sniffing around town. If we don't contain it quickly, we're going to have an even bigger problem on our hands. I'll keep you updated."

"Fair enough. Let's touch base in the morning. Stay safe out there," Fisher replied.

"Will do. Thanks, guys." Kate ended the call and looked at Surrey. "That was interesting."

"You think Fisher's feeling heat from above?" Surrey asked.

"Maybe. The story's getting out there. Mass grave sites found in quiet suburban community. Makes for a good headline."

"So, we see what we can get from Lupe Cordova this evening and go from there?" he continued.

"That's our plan." Kate started toward the door. "Romero's waiting at the safehouse. He spoke with the Gutierrez family already. They reported her missing about 6 months ago. SAPD is still working through the friends and acquaintances. We don't have a choice but to convince Lupe to open up to us. It's the only way we move forward on this case right now."

The agents headed into the bullpen to find Vangie Cordova sitting at Espinoza's desk.

The officer peered at the agents. "Is it time?"

Kate nodded. "Vangie, are you ready?"

"Yes." The younger sister stood and eyed Espinoza. "You're coming, too, right?"

"I'm right behind you."

"Then we should go." Kate took the lead with the younger Cordova. They continued into the hall and toward the breakroom where Lupe had been waiting.

Vangie walked inside. "We're ready to get Ma if you still want to go with the agents, Lupe."

Lupe regarded Kate. "And you can protect our family?"

"Of course we can. This is the best possible solution for all of you, Lupe. Everyone will remain safe."

"He won't know?" she pressed on.

"No," Vangie replied. "No one will know where we are."

Lupe closed her eyes. "Then I'm ready."

Levi Walsh was the closest thing to a brother Kate had. Their friendship grew immediately on her arrival at Quantico. And he loved her like a sister. So when he saw Kate flinch with a weapon trained on a suspect months ago, he knew she needed help. And he called her out on the plane ride home. Now, months later, she had been back on track, and he couldn't have been happier.

And as far as Fisher and Duncan, well, he trusted them with his life. Nevertheless, that same trust hadn't been fully extended to Jonathan Surrey. He was different than the others on the team. Aloof, almost. And he was all Kate had at the moment to back her in San Antonio on a case that was only going to become more intense. She'd already been betrayed by a member of the team, who was long gone now. It nearly destroyed her and her career.

Surrey had turned his back on Kate once before, albeit he thought it had been for the right reasons. Maybe. But it was something Walsh couldn't quite forgive him for. He worried that Surrey wouldn't have Kate's back this time around if things went south, which they somehow always managed to do.

Walsh arrived at Nick's office and stood in the doorway. "Hey, man."

Nick peered up at him. "Walsh, come on in. Hey, I'm sorry I didn't answer your call earlier..."

"Don't sweat it. Couldn't be worse timing on my part. I'm sorry about that." He continued inside and sat down. "I, uh, I don't want to keep you. Just needed to ask you some questions about an old case you worked on back at the WFO."

"Sure, yeah. I might have to search my memory banks on that."

"You mentioned it once upon a time and Duncan wanted to pull the files, but we don't have enough to make the request to

WFO. Figured you could throw in a good word with your buddy. What was his name, Jameson? He's the head honcho over there now, right?"

"Right, yeah, he is. Great guy. I miss him." Nick regarded Walsh. "What was the gist of the case?"

"Involuntary celibates, incels, for short. Making online threats against women. I don't remember what else it entailed," Walsh replied.

"Oh shit." Nick pulled back. "I remember that case. Had some kid posting about killing women. He called them out online and we worked with the women to track him down."

"Glad it rings a bell. Kate thinks that could be what she's dealing with now in San Antonio."

"Really?"

"It's one of the theories," Walsh replied. "She's proposed three. These so-called incels, then you got your drug cartels, and possibly a situation that plagues Juarez, Mexico."

"Which is?" Nick pressed on.

"Femicide. Women being murdered just because they're women."

"I'm familiar. Big problem there, and other countries too." Nick raised his gaze to the ceiling as if thinking on the matter. "Drug cartels make the most sense, given the proximity to the border."

Walsh nodded. "Uh-huh. Except for the fact all the victims are women. Bludgeoned, dismembered."

"Geez." Nick looked away.

"Yeah. So while it's a possibility, Kate was thinking about this other group, given their appetite for hating women," he replied.

"And what about the femicide? It's not usually one killer. It's multiple killers, which is part of the reason why it's been so hard to get control of in Juarez," Nick replied. "Any idea why she's leaning on that theory?"

Walsh shrugged. "You know Kate. She gets a hunch..."

"Yeah, I know." Nick rubbed his smooth chin. "I can make a call to WFO. It'd be nice to talk to my old friend. Now isn't the best time for me, but I'll do my damnedest to squeeze it in."

"We're plugging away at the other theories, but a helping hand from you would sure be appreciated. I hate like hell to even ask considering what you've got on your plate right now," Walsh replied.

"Don't worry about it. Like I said, I'll do what I can."

Walsh pushed off the chair. "Gotcha. You got a job to do here. Probably more than you expected when you took the gig, huh?"

A smile raised from the corner of Nick's mouth. "A little. I got the president breathing down my neck now."

Walsh's brow raised. "No shit?"

"No shit."

"And I thought Unit Chief Cole was tough." Walsh started toward the door. "Thanks, bud. And if you don't mind, keep this between you and me?"

"Why's that?" Nick asked.

"You know your wife. She doesn't always like to accept help she hasn't asked for," he replied.

"She does like to figure things out on her own."

"Don't I know it. But this one?" Walsh shoved his hands in his pockets. "This one's gonna be big, my friend. Bigger than Kate realizes."

SWEAT DRIPPED DOWN HER CHEEK. Her face ached from the bandana tied around her head and lodged in her mouth. She was surrounded by darkness and the constant drone of tires on the road. An occasional bass drum sounded from the car's radio. With hands tied at her back and ankles, she peered into the darkness, but there wasn't even a sliver of light from inside the trunk. The sun had beat down on the trunk lid to the point that it heated the interior like a sauna. How long she'd been in here was unknown, but the constant motion made it feel like it had been hours.

He never revealed his face—her abductor. She only felt a hand over her mouth and a tight grip on her waist. He whispered, "don't scream," and threw her inside the trunk. A strike to her jaw caused her to lose consciousness, which made it pretty easy for him to tie her up. When she came to, they were already on the road.

Marissa had been on her way home from work. She'd offered to take the early shift for a friend who hadn't been feeling well and headed to the bus stop in the late afternoon to go home. She lived in the border town of Laredo, Texas and worked in a chain restaurant as a server. The 19-year-old had always felt safe here, until now.

There hadn't been much point in screaming. The bandana muffled most of the sound. She couldn't kick her way out. She already tried. Tears streamed down her face again as she writhed inside the small trunk and shook the vehicle. Marissa knew she was never going to see her family again. Not her mother, or father, or even her stupid little brother. Not her boyfriend. No one. She knew she was never going home again.

More time went by with no end to the horror in sight. That was, until the car slowed and finally came to a stop. Was it another traffic light? Too early to tell. Marissa waited for the vehicle to move again, but it didn't. Then, the car door shut. Her eyes widened. This was it. They weren't moving anymore. Wherever she was would soon be revealed.

The afternoon light burned her eyes when the trunk lid opened. A shadow stood before her and Marissa squinted to clear her vision. Still, she couldn't see her abductor, but knew he was a man. His strength easily overpowered her and his voice, as he whispered in her ear, was deep. The shadowed figure was square shaped, and it looked like he wore a baseball hat, but she couldn't tell whether his hair was short or long. His jacket appeared over-sized and thick, like a bomber jacket. But the sun was behind him and the shadow he was in left much room for interpretation. He was a faceless, colorless figure.

Marissa moaned and tried to speak, but the words wouldn't form and even if they had, they would be inaudible.

"I don't want to hurt you again, but if you fight me when I pull you out, I won't have a choice. Comprende?"

He sounded like an American trying to speak Spanish. No discernible accent, except a hint of a Texas drawl so minor it was hard to pick it up. She tried again to speak.

"Don't bother. Now, are you gonna cooperate, or do I have to hit you again?"

Marissa nodded.

"Good." He reached for her arm that was tied around her back.

She moaned as he tugged because one of her arms had fallen asleep from this position. The pins and needles burned.

"Take it easy, now." He reached into the trunk and slipped his arms beneath her body like a forklift.

Marissa was pulled out and he held onto her like she was his new bride, and he was going to carry her over the threshold. She looked around, desperate to figure out where the hell she was, but recognized nothing. There were no houses nearby, just the one straight ahead. They were surrounded by desert.

As he carried her in his arms, the thought of wriggling out of his grip crossed her mind. But what would happen if she fought back while she was tied up like an animal? She would drop to the ground and lay there until he beat her senseless. If Marissa wanted to find a way out of this, she would have to play along. No matter what.

12

T he FBI's safehouse, operated by the San Antonio field
office, was situated in a quiet neighborhood on the city's
outer loop. As evening arrived, so had the Cordova
sisters and their mother. Agent Victor Romero made the arrangements and opened the home for them.

Kate followed the sisters as the younger Vangie ushered Lupe
inside. She looked at Surrey, who walked beside her. "We need to
get her to open up tonight. Whoever took her isn't likely to hang
around."

He touched Kate's shoulder. "Hold up a minute, would you?"

She stopped in her tracks and turned to him. "What is it?"

"Did you get anything yet on Medina's background?"

"We'll have to ask Romero. He ran it through his office. Why
do you ask that now?"

Surrey folded his arms and watched as the others walked
inside. "I'd like to know who Medina's friends are. Where else he
worked in the more recent past. There are still a lot of unanswered
questions about him."

"Pending the DNA results, we have no reason to suspect Medina's involvement in the current murders. If he had anything to do with Lupe Cordova, I'm not so sure he would've been willing to submit to the swab, and the timing doesn't work. Look, all of us being here right now is a waste of our resources. We don't have time to wait for more bodies to turn up." Kate glanced at the door where the women had just entered. "I'll handle the Cordova family. You and Romero can pursue Medina's connections."

Kate continued inside and regarded the sisters. "You're safe here. Agent Romero's team will be just outside. They aren't going anywhere. I'll be sticking around with you." She thumbed to Surrey and Romero. "These two need to keep searching for answers, so they're going to head out."

Vangie glanced at Lupe and then at Kate. "Do you believe what happened to Lupe has something to do with the buried bodies?"

"We don't know, but that's what they're going to try to find out." Kate sat down across from them. "While your mother is resting, I think it would be a good time to talk about what happened to you, Lupe."

Romero approached them with his hands in his pockets. "I can't imagine what you went through, Ms. Cordova, but know that you and your family are safe here. There is nothing to fear anymore."

Kate glanced at Romero. "I think we'll be okay. I'll take good care of them. You two should go."

He nodded. "Then we'll get to work."

"If you need anything." Surrey turned to her.

"I know." Kate waited for them to leave and stood again. "How about I get you two some water?"

Vangie sat next to her sister with her arm resting on Lupe's thigh. "Thank you, Agent Reid."

Kate walked into the kitchen and heard the two whispering but couldn't distinguish their words. She hoped it was Vangie attempting to talk sense into Lupe. The case was at a virtual stand-still without DNA or identifying the rest of the victims. Now was Kate's opportunity to extract information from the frightened woman.

She returned with glasses of water and set them on the table. "I'm sure your mother must be exhausted."

Lupe took the glass into her hands. "She'll be okay. She's been through much worse."

"Worse than worrying over her missing daughter?" Kate paused a moment. "You mean, with your father?"

"It was hard on her when Dad died, Agent Reid," Vangie replied. "I know our mother was worried for Lupe, but it was one of many times."

Kate peered down a moment. "I'm sorry to hear that, but now that we've gotten you here, Lupe, It's critical that we understand what happened to you last night and this morning. Who took you and did he tell you why you were set free?"

THE SMUDGE of blood on the bomber-style jacket wasn't rubbing off. "Son of a bitch." It would have to be burned now along with all of Marissa's clothes. "Fuck!" He slammed the trunk and plunged Marissa into darkness once again. Only this time, she had no cause to fight back. She was already dead.

He tore off his jacket and threw it onto the back seat before slipping behind the wheel. Daylight had faded and left behind an orange sky as the desert dust floated in the air. It was time to place Marissa alongside the others. The others no one had yet found.

The headlights shone on the single lane road when he neared

Somerset. The sky had gone completely dark now, though the stars were bright this evening with no clouds obscuring the view. The people here were afraid and had every right to be. It made things that much easier as he traveled the streets. Few were brave enough to step outside their homes. They held onto their daughters tightly.

In the distance was the carefully chosen spot; the backside of the inert landfill. No one lived nearby and the rock, concrete, and landscape trimmings offered protection from exposure to the highway it fronted.

The car stopped and he turned off the headlights. "They're waiting for you, Marissa." He stepped out of the car and opened the trunk.

Next to her body lay a shovel. He went for it first, leaving the girl exposed to the cold night air, naked, and in pieces. It had taken time to prepare her. The house contained the necessary tools, the plastic, everything he needed to complete the job in an orderly manner. Mistakes were uncovered in the details, and so he overlooked none.

With the shovel in his hand, he pierced the dirt and created a hole adjacent to one that had been there for a while. Perspiration built around his neckline even in the cool night air. He was a fit man, but it was hard work, nonetheless. The shovel hit something soft, and he squatted low, pulling away the dirt with his fingers. "Best not to disturb the others." He stood again and kept digging.

THE FORMER LIEUTENANT stepped outside the camping trailer and took in the brisk air. The feeling that at any moment, police would roar up the dirt road and find him, lingered. He used to be a cop. A damn good one. It was hard to be a good cop in Juarez. But when his daughter went missing, everything changed. Now, he had no one, except for his still-grieving wife who had pulled away from him, likely never to return. His son hadn't wanted to see him. He was alone and consumed with finding those responsible for killing his daughter. It was time to hunt down the men whose names were given by Lupe Cordova, daughter of a known murderer. Whether she knew it or not hardly mattered.

Armando Guzman was no longer a cop, but he hunted for justice, nonetheless. He walked down the steps toward his old beige Ford Taurus. He would hunt at night to avoid detection. Relying on Lupe Cordova to keep her mouth shut was too risky. The police would convince her she was safe and that her sister was safe. Guzman had no intention of going back to that girl or her family. The father was dead, and he got what he needed. Still, he couldn't risk them knowing who he was. He'd been careful but even the most careful of people slipped up. He only hoped his slip-ups wouldn't be discovered until he was back on the other side of the border.

He keyed the ignition and turned around the old car on the dirt road. Plumes of dust wafted in the night air as the tires rolled along the powdery earth. The highway was ahead on the other side, and Guzman was going back to town to find Cordova's friends.

With the window rolled down, he took in the fresh air and soon spotted the highway's entrance on the other side of the road. As Guzman continued on, a glint of light caught his eye on the south side of the single-lane road, near the approaching landfill. Nothing else but desert surrounded him. In fact, from here, he could see the back of the landfill as he drove. "Must be glass." But with no sun, how would glass reflect? He peered up to see a half-moon. The light from it was scarcely enough. Then he saw it again. "The hell?" His gaze narrowed and tried to focus on the flicker of light as he drove near the landfill and its small mountain of dirt and debris.

He slowed down and turned off the headlights. The movement and light ahead were a good couple hundred yards away. "A car?" Guzman came to a stop on the side of the road and cut the engine. He reached for his pistol that rested on the passenger seat and checked the clip.

He opened his car door and stepped out into the darkness. Light from the inside of the car flickered but quickly extinguished upon closing the door again. Guzman tucked the weapon into the back of his pants at the waist and started into the desert. Town was still about 3 miles away. His cop instincts kicked in and whatever was out there, no doubt, wasn't going to be good.

Guzman's boot prints left impressions in the silty earth as he walked deeper into the desert. Creosote bushes brushed against his worn jeans, and he was careful to avoid the few barrel cacti in the area. The darkened skies made the journey precarious, but he pressed on toward the flickering light in the distance. A tremor in his hand, which had plagued him for years, worsened as he moved in. For a cop, it was a sign to call it quits. For Guzman, it meant he was onto something big.

A faint sound that resembled a grunt reached his ears, though he still saw nothing but an outline of what looked to have been a car. The flicker of light must've come from the car's interior. Guzman pulled out his gun and held it at his side. With several more feet to go, he still hadn't had a plan. He'd seen much during his tenure in Juarez. Horrors the likes Americans could scarcely understand. So whatever awaited him now, he would go with his gut, as always.

When the shadows grew into shapes, Guzman saw him. A dim light inside the car's trunk cast a small halo around the area. Something lay on the ground, though he couldn't tell what it was. Pieces of wood? Rocks? He stopped and now saw exactly what was on the ground. He aimed the gun at the only thing that moved and flipped off the safety.

The click of the weapon drew the attention of the shadowy figure that spun around. "Who the fuck are you?"

Guzman saw the body parts as clear as day. It had been a woman, maybe just a girl. "Step away from the body and keep your hands where I can see them."

Deep growling laughter sounded from the man. "You're making a mistake. It's best you turn around and head back to wherever you came from."

"I don't think so, jefe." Guzman steadied his hand and kept his gun trained ahead. "Turn around with your hands up and walk backwards towards me. Now."

"This is your last chance to walk away, my friend. I suggest you take advantage of it." He slammed the lid of the trunk. "There's nothing for you here."

"I think we both know you ain't letting me walk away. I ain't letting you." Guzman's mind raced for a solution. He couldn't tell if the man was armed, but the assumption was in the affirmative. "You don't sound like you're from Mexico."

"I'm not from that shithole excuse for a country," the man replied.

The corner of Guzman's lips raised into a smile. "It is what it is mostly because Americans are nothing but drug addicts. So we can sit here and play politics, or you can come with me now and I'll turn you over to the authorities. I have a feeling they'll be very interested in you." For a moment, he considered the notion that this man could have been one of Cordova's associates. Maybe he'd just gotten lucky enough to happen upon him in the middle of the gruesome scene.

"Shit." He watched as the man darted behind his car. Guzman

quickly fired. The move was quick, but his aim wasn't. The bullet struck the car. There was no place to take cover and he was exposed. He laid down more fire and turned to run, shooting behind him while he ran as fast as he could. But when a bullet struck his calf, Guzman fell to the ground. "Pendajo!"

The man laughed again in a deep voice. "You're the asshole, my friend." He stood over Guzman. "Who the hell are you?"

"The motherfucker who's going to kill you." Guzman raised his gun.

The man fired at Guzman's head, striking him between the eyes. "Well, shit. You really screwed with my night, pal."

KATE LISTENED while Lupe relayed the details of her abduction. While it hadn't pointed to a potential suspect in the current rash of murders, there was no doubt the situations were related. "Thank you, Lupe. You're doing the right thing." Kate grabbed her phone and walked outside where two agents flanked the entrance. A nod to the men and she stepped away to make the call. "Surrey, it's me. Where are you?"

"At the Somerset station with Romero and Brown. What's going on? Did you get her to talk?"

"Yes. Can you get Brown to issue a BOLO for an older model Ford Taurus, tan, four-doors? Plates are from Chihuahua."

"Juarez?" he asked.

"She said the man claimed to be from Juarez. He was smart enough not to give his name. But he's older, mid-50s, around 5-feet 7-inches and weighs roughly 160 pounds."

"On it. Anything else?" Surrey pressed on.

"He insisted Lupe's father had a part in murdering his daughter back in Juarez a few years ago. She said that wasn't possible, but he claimed to have proof, though he didn't show it. And apparently, once he learned Lupe's father was dead, he decided to go after her father's friends with the belief they had been involved too. She had no choice but to offer up the only names she could recall. It was the only way he would let her go."

"Jesus. Now we're going to have to find these people before he does."

"Yeah," Kate replied. I still don't know if any of this is tied to our case unless Lupe's father had been involved in the murders here. Some of the bodies we've uncovered had been in the ground a while. Oh, and he held her at her dad's cabinet shop near the old airstrip. One final thing, Lupe caught a glimpse of the guy's wallet and noticed an ID badge. She couldn't see the name, but Surrey, the man's a Juarez cop."

"Okay, I did not see that coming," Surrey replied. "Does she know the plate numbers on the Taurus?"

"Yes, I'll text it to you. But if he is who she thinks he is, I have a feeling he's probably back on the other side of the border. My guess is, he'll come back in another vehicle and try to find these associates," Kate replied.

"We have a Mexican cop looking for vigilante justice, and several bodies in the ground. No way these aren't connected, Reid. Not with Medina's Juarez connection too. So, what about the mom? She must know whether Mr. Cordova had a shady history."

"The woman's not in good shape. She's been resting," Kate replied. "You could be right and that's something we'll have to explore."

"Let me get with Brown on issuing the BOLO. What's your plan for tonight?" Surrey asked.

"I'll stick around here, and I'll keep my phone on."

"Got it. Let's keep in touch." Surrey ended the call and returned to Brown's office where Agent Romero waited. "That was Reid. We have details on the abductor's car and where Lupe Cordova was taken."

"Finally. We have something we can sink our teeth into," Romero replied.

The phone on Brown's desk rang through. "Sorry. Let me take this a moment." He answered the line. "Captain Brown. Okay." He paused a moment and knitted his brow. "Damn. No, send whoever's on duty. Chihuahua plates, you say? No. Thank you. I'll handle this one. I'm on my way." He hung up the phone. "An abandoned car was spotted along the highway headed north into town about three miles away, near the landfill. Dispatch said someone called it in as a courtesy and offered the plate number for reference."

Surrey regarded the men. "Did I mention the abductor's car had Chihuahua plates?"

"Are you shitting me?" Romero cut in. "What the hell are the odds of that?"

13

What Surrey said about the mother hounded Kate's thoughts as she sat alone in the quiet house while the Cordova family slept If the father had been involved in the murder of the cop's daughter, would the mother have known about it? Even worse, had he been tied to any of the bodies they'd found so far? And who the hell killed him? The man had been dead for two years.

It forced Kate to reevaluate her theories, and all but disproved her notion that the murders were committed by someone tied to the incels. It didn't, however, dismiss the idea of femicide, or even cartels, though that had seemed less likely now.

As the hour approached 11 o'clock, Kate's attention was diverted to her phone that buzzed on the couch cushion. She answered the call. "Surrey, what is it?"

"We found the car."

Kate pulled up at attention. "Where is it? Do you have the driver in custody?"

"Hold on. A call came into the Somerset station. Romero and I wanted to get out here and take a look before I alerted you."

"What's going on?" Kate heard him sigh through the line. "Surrey, what happened?"

"The driver is dead," Surrey replied. "Shot in the head at close range about 50, maybe 100 yards from where he left the car."

"Who shot him?" she asked.

"We took a walk out farther into the desert and found what looked to be a fairly large hole in the ground. Not unlike to the ones uncovered already."

"Oh, no."

That's not all we found," Surrey continued. "Body parts were nearby laying on some thick plastic. A woman. I think if the driver is the same man who abducted Lupe, then he came up on the killer while he was in the process of hiding the body."

"And the killer fled?" she asked.

"Looks that way. Reid, this is actually good news for us. He left the scene unfinished."

"Meaning he might've left behind evidence that could lead us to him."

"Yep. Listen, I need you out here. Romero's team can handle the Cordovas."

"I'm on my way." Kate ended the call and gathered her bag. She walked outside where the agents sat on a couple of camping chairs. "Something's come up. I have to get to the highway. They found the abductor's car. You two can look after the family?"

"We'll keep watch, Agent Reid. You need a ride, don't you?" The agent reached into his pants pocket and retrieved his car keys. "Take mine. There's another here if we need it."

"Thank you." Kate nodded. "I'll have Romero keep you posted." She started ahead and stepped behind the wheel of the Chevy

Tahoe. A moment later and Surrey sent a pin to her phone to mark his location.

It took about 45 minutes to get from the safehouse outside San Antonio to the edge of Somerset. The red and blue patrol car lights were pretty hard to miss, not to mention a spotlight in the middle of the desert. Kate stopped the SUV behind one of the cars and jumped out. She noticed Surrey ahead speaking to Agent Romero. Their faces reflected the flashing lights.

She made her way toward them. "The Cordovas are being looked after by your team, Romero. So tell me, what did I miss?"

"Probably easier to show you." Surrey walked ahead. "Come take a look."

She followed the agents into the desert and noticed the landfill in the distance. "What are the odds the guy who took Lupe happened to be traveling on this single-lane road and spotted the killer near this landfill?"

"Not as great as you might think," Romero replied. "Brown's officer took a drive down that road and spotted a camping trailer near it about two miles away. They're searching it now while we secure this scene."

"So he was staying there. Still, the unsub chose this spot?"

Surrey pointed ahead. "The highway is on the other side over there. I'm thinking the killer thought the landfill would keep him hidden. Guess he didn't figure someone was camping out a couple miles away down that road."

Kate nodded. "So are we sure the abductor wasn't part of this? Maybe he was helping the unsub and things went sideways. He told Lupe he was here to find his daughter's killer. It's possible he was lying and only wanted the names of her father's friends for whatever reason."

"You're getting into a scenario we just can't be certain of right now," Surrey replied.

They reached the well-lit area and Kate peered into the hole and then back at the body that lay on the plastic.

"My God." Kate examined the horrific scene. "He would've buried the parts at random, like the others." She peered out near the hole again. "Which means this could be another burial site."

"That's why I wanted you out here," Surrey began. "It's a damn strong possibility."

Romero turned around. "Over there is where the abductor's body was left. It's been loaded in the truck already."

Kate stepped toward the spot that wasn't far from the vehicle. "Why would he leave the abductor's body? Why not put them both in the ground when he had the chance? He all but pointed us to his burial site."

"Could be he felt exposed, not realizing there was a road over there. I just don't know," Surrey replied. "But like I said, I'm sorry as hell we got two dead bodies here, but this is an unfinished scene. He left something behind."

"Now we just need to find it," Kate added. "How long before we can get the CSI team out here to search the area for more victims?"

"Brown's coordinating that now," Romero said. "We might also get some answers depending on whether they find anything in the man's camping trailer."

Kate squatted down next to the exposed body. "There's not much blood here. He didn't do the wet work here, that much is certain."

"Well, that answers one of our questions. You wanted to know why there was no blood found near the victims. So where is he chopping up these women?" Surrey asked.

Kate stood up again, feeling slightly nauseated by the sight. No matter how often she came onto scenes like this, it never got any easier to stomach. "I have no idea and we aren't going to know more until we learn who she is. I don't think this is random. I think these women are being targeted. He knows them. They know them."

"They?" Romero asked.

"Could be more than one. We don't know anything about the dead cop in the truck except for what he told Lupe. That could've been a load of crap for all we know," she replied. "His dead daughter? Maybe, but we don't know that either."

Romero peered down at the body. "With the car and the plates, Brown's contact in Juarez will be able to ID him. That should open up something for us."

Kate looked again at the dismembered body. "There aren't any lacerations or contusions on the body, except for the blade used to cut off her limbs."

"Not like the others who appeared to have been beaten first," Surrey replied.

"Right. Did she know him? She didn't fight."

"Uh, I don't mean to be ghoulish." Romero walked to where the head lay. "There's a bruise here on her cheek. It looks like he hit her."

"Okay. Well, there goes that idea." Kate drew in a breath. "But maybe not. She's still different from the others. Some of the bodies were too decomposed, but on others, a struggle clearly took place, and the wounds were far more aggressive and violent." She looked at Surrey. "Yeah. Definitely a 'they' situation. I'm certain of it."

THE LIGHT from the television reflected on Cameron Fisher's face as he watched the late-night talk show. He should've gone to bed an hour ago, but when members of his team were in the field, he never really slept. And it had gotten even harder to sleep now that

Eva was gone too. He had insisted they could weather the storm. That Human Resources couldn't do squat about their relationship because it had started before he was promoted. Then Eva reminded him that he had still been the senior agent on the team, and technically her boss, when they started dating. It was a no-win situation.

He missed her more than he ever thought he would. Seeing her every day at work and pretending he was okay was hard as hell. But he was a big boy. He ran Unit 4 now. He'd gotten everything he'd wanted, except for her.

Fisher was drawn to the light from his phone as it lay on the side table next to his bottle of beer. He swiped open the screen and answered. "Reid, what's going on?"

"I didn't wake you, did I?"

"Did you need to ask that question?" he replied.

"I guess not. Look, I think it's time we get everyone down here."

He pulled up to the edge of his sofa. "What happened? Earlier, you wanted me to give you the day."

"I did," Kate said. "But that was before we found another burial site. More dead bodies. One left out in the open, and a dead kidnapper."

"Jesus." Fisher rubbed his forehead.

"Yeah, that sums it up pretty well. We need the manpower and especially from our people. Romero agrees. We're going to be up against an even more frightened community and the media is going to hit hard."

"Do you feel that you're in over your head?" he asked.

She chuckled. "This time? Maybe. I know I need input. Surrey and I have been running through the various scenarios. Each one is going to take time to rule out or run on. We can't do it alone."

"Okay. I'll gather the troops and we'll head out first thing in the a.m."

"Thank you. SAPD has just started excavating the newest site. Romero is overseeing that as we speak. Surrey and I are about to search the kidnapper's camper. We have a lot of moving parts here," Kate said.

"I hear you. We'll be there in the morning. Try to catch some rest until then if you can." Fisher ended the call and rubbed his hand over his thick head of hair that was turning grayer with each passing day. He glanced at the time and made the call. "Walsh, hey, Reid and Surrey need us in San Antonio first thing tomorrow."

"That was fast. What happened?" Walsh asked.

"Too much to go through now. I'll brief everyone on the plane. Get some sleep if you can. Pack a bag and be ready to go at first light."

"Will do."

"I'm out." Fisher pressed the end call button and pulled up Duncan's contact. Her line rang and she answered. "Hey, are you asleep?"

"I was just heading to bed. Is everything okay?" she asked.

"Reid called. It's time to get to San Antonio. The intel you've been gathering for her, bring it. I'll charter the plane for first thing in the morning."

"Walsh know about this?" she asked.

"I just told him. They have an unknown number of victims. Reid said they uncovered another burial site. It's bad."

"Yeah, okay. I'll be ready. See you in the morning."

"Hey, Eva?"

"Yes?"

"You know you don't have to stay at that hotel till your new place is ready."

"I know. I'm fine here. It's only for a little while," she replied.

"Okay, if you're sure." He sighed a moment. "I haven't told HR yet. It isn't too late to go back to the way things were."

"I know you think that, Cam, but it is. Our jobs are our lives. They always have been. And neither of us should put our careers at stake."

"But we can make it work just like Scarborough did."

"Cam, he didn't. In case you've forgotten, he doesn't work in our unit anymore. He let his relationship with Kate get in the way. It almost ruined her career and his."

"That's not the same. They had Quinn to deal with..."

"It's close enough," she cut in. "I don't want that kind of drama or any drama for us. I'm so sorry, Cam. I love you, but..."

"Not enough."

"Don't. Please. You know that's not true. We have to get past this. Can we?"

He rubbed his forehead. "Yeah. Sure. I'll see you in the morning, Eva. Get some rest."

THE CAMPER TRAILER was nearly impossible to see as Kate and Surrey made their way toward it. The hour approached 1 am and she felt the strain of the case bear down on her shoulders. Having to reach out to Fisher wasn't ideal, but Kate knew her limitations and remembered she wasn't an island, as Surrey had recently reminded her.

With flashlights shining around the camp, Kate tried the door. "Unlocked."

"Guess he figured no one would come out here," Surrey replied. "Brown's guys found it this way. They weren't able to learn his identity, but it's best we have a look around."

She stepped inside the dark and musty trailer. "Did he have a generator?"

"Let me check." Surrey stepped outside.

Kate continued to use her flashlight. A couple of dirty paper plates lay on the small kitchen counter. Pizza boxes and some Chinese takeout containers lay nearby as well. A moment later, the lights came on and Surrey returned inside.

"We have power," he said.

"That should help. She turned off the flashlight. "Looks like he'd been here a while."

Surrey moved toward the sofa. "Not much of a place, but I suppose enough to give him some shelter."

Kate walked down a narrow hall and pulled back the curtain. "Bedroom's back here. I'll take a look." She had to turn sideways to get around the unmade double bed. The headboard was also a bookshelf, and she examined the items that lay on it.

She spotted a photograph that was tucked between a notepad and a book and picked it up. Her eyes softened at the sight of a teenaged girl smiling for the camera. It looked like it had been taken at a zoo. A cage was behind her and what looked like an animal habitat. "Hey, I found something."

Surrey walked back toward her. "What is it?"

She held up the photo. "A teenage girl. Could be the daughter."

Surrey carefully stepped around the bed toward Kate and peered at it. "Yep."

Kate still gazed at the picture. "What the hell does Eduardo Cordova have to do with her death? I think it's time we learn more about him."

"The abductor? Yeah, of course."

"Him, yes. But Cordova, too. Someone killed him, and then this cop comes here looking for Cordova's friends."

"Like they also had something to do with his daughter's murder," Surrey replied.

"Right. Let's keep looking here, but I just can't believe that the man who killed this Juarez cop and the woman in the desert doesn't have something in common with Eduardo Cordova."

"There is one commonality that seems a little more relevant now," Surrey began.

"And that is?"

He held her gaze. "Xavier Medina."

14

The call to bring in the rest of the team left Kate apprehensive. As morning arrived and she made her way to the hotel lobby to meet Surrey, a part of her wondered whether he saw the move as a sign of her uncertainty. But as usual, Kate had a nasty habit of second-guessing herself.

She noticed Surrey on one of the sofas in the lobby holding a cup of coffee. Another sat on the table, and she hoped it had been hers.

"Morning."

Surrey rose from the couch. "Hey, I got you a coffee. Figured we both could use a pick-me-up this morning considering how late it was when we got back."

"Thank you. You have no idea how much I need this." Kate took a sip from the paper cup.

Surrey reached for the car keys in his pocket. "We should probably head out. The rest of the team will arrive at the San Antonio field office in about an hour. I'll drive."

"Yeah, fine." She walked beside him and took another sip of

coffee. "As long as we get there in one piece. I'll let you take the wheel this time."

"This time?" He laughed as he pushed through the lobby doors.

Kate slipped onto the passenger seat and waited for Surrey. She scrolled through her phone while he turned the engine and pulled away. "How'd you sleep?"

"Meh. You?" He glanced at her.

"Meh."

"I did speak to Captain Brown just before you met me in the lobby," Surrey began. "I told him we wanted to take a look at the investigation into Eduardo Cordova's murder. He was going to have the files ready for when we get back."

"Good. Did he ask why we wanted them?"

"He made mention that it was an open case. No killer found, so he wasn't sure what good it would do to spend time reviewing the files, but I told him that with the Juarez cop and his search for Cordova's friends, there was a good chance of a connection somewhere along the line."

"And to Xavier Medina," Kate continued. "I should've pressed him harder. Nobody runs from the feds without a reason. His good faith effort at submitting to a swab might've been an attempt to keep us from taking a deeper dive into his story." She reached for her phone. "I'd better check in with Romero's team at the safehouse. "Good morning, Agent Reid here. How'd everything go last night?"

"A-okay, here. No activity. The family slept through the night, as far as I can tell. What's the plan for today?" he asked.

"We're headed back now to meet at your field office. Given what happened last night, I'll meet the Cordovas there at the house when the meeting is finished and get them back home."

"You got it. I'll give them a heads-up."

"Thank you." Kate ended the call.

"It was still the right move; getting the Cordovas to a safe-house," Surrey added.

"It was the only move we had, and it gave us insight as to who took Lupe. Too bad he turned up dead. But there's still hope the captain can get us a name."

He kept his eyes fixed on the road ahead. "There could still be one thing to consider."

"What's that?" she asked.

"I don't want to lose sight of Cordova's associates—the men who Lupe named. I know the cop is dead, but if there is a chance of a connection to Medina and whoever else, those men could still be at risk."

"Understood. Better to be safe than sorry." Kate eyed the building ahead. "Here we are."

Surrey pulled into the parking lot. "Well, Reid, it's gonna get real cozy with all of us here now."

Kate stepped out of the car and joined him as they walked to the entrance. "Maybe so, but if it means getting this situation under control fast, then I'll live with it. Hey, can I ask you something?"

"Sure."

She peered at him. "What would you have done?"

"About what? The Cordovas?"

"No. I mean, would you have requested that the team join us," Kate added.

He stopped and turned to her. "Look, Reid, you're the one in charge here. Not me. I like working with you. And frankly, I've seen you pull rabbits out of hats before when it comes to a case. But that doesn't mean any one of us could do our jobs alone. We are still a team and the fact that you recognized the need for the expertise of the rest of our team shows me that you should be in the position you're in." He started on again. "If I could make one suggestion?"

"What's that?"

"Stop looking to others for approval. You don't need it. You never did." He opened the door for her. "After you."

She returned a smile. "Thank you"

Romero approached them in the lobby. "Bout time y'all got here. Needed your beauty sleep, did you?"

Kate thumbed back at Surrey. "I think he could use a little more. Didn't take the first time."

"You're a funny one, Reid. Gotta love a girl with a sense of humor." Romero chuckled as he spun around on his heel. "Come on up. Your people are already here."

The agents followed him to the communications room used for task forces and special operations. He opened the door. "Look what the cat dragged in."

"And the cavalry's already here." Kate walked inside and approached Walsh, offering a light embrace. "Good to see you, Levi."

"Glad to be here," he replied.

Fisher offered his hand. "Reid. You and Surrey have done well to get this far. Don't think your work has gone unnoticed."

"I appreciate that." Kate glanced at Duncan. "And Eva, thank you for jumping in on a lot of the background already."

"You got it. Hey, that's why I'm here."

Surrey pulled out a chair after greeting the others and sat down. "You all know most of what's been going on down here, but last night we had some new developments. Reid and Romero can fill you in on the specifics."

Kate walked to the head of the table. "Late last night, I sent over the new details on this investigation. A third burial site was found, among other things. And I know you all had access to the rest of the files, so I'm sure you got up to speed on the flight over. I won't waste your time rehashing anything, but I will say this, for as long as I've been on this team, I've never seen anything like what's happening here in the suburbs of San Antonio. I've expressed my theories, but I need you here so we can home in on a direction and run with it."

"What are we talking about here, a single unsub, or multiple?" Walsh asked.

"That all depends on how we want to frame last night's shooting death of a man who looked to have been a Juarez cop," Kate replied. "Captain Brown with the Somerset Police is working with his contact in Mexico to get an ID on him, so we know just who and what we're up against."

"He was the kidnapper," Fisher added.

"Yes, sir, which added a whole other element to this situation. We considered the possibility that he could've been lying to his victim, Lupe Cordova, to get what he wanted. Suggesting he was there to avenge the murder of his daughter. The circumstances surrounding his death seemed too coincidental for him not to have a connection to the recent murders." Kate looked back at Surrey a moment. "However, after we searched the camper where he was holed up, we found a picture of who we believe was his daughter." She retrieved the photo from her carrier bag and handed it to Duncan. "It gave us pause. Maybe he was telling the truth and it was just dumb luck he happened across the killer in the middle of the job."

"I believe in dumb luck about as much as I believe in coincidence," Fisher replied.

"I get that," Surrey added. "And I'd be with you except that this burial ground had clearly been there for a while. Possibly longer than the camp. We don't think this unsub realized a road existed on the backside of the landfill. The camper was only two miles down that path that was hardly a road at all."

"I don't want to paint the kidnapping cop as a good guy," Kate continued. "Whatever his reasons for being there, he took Lupe Cordova and threatened her and her family. I can only assume he spotted a light near the landfill as he drove along the dirt road and grew curious. He also had a weapon and fired it when he came across the unsub at the landfill. Gunpowder residue was found on his hands. It's hard to say whether his bullet hit the unsub. We found little to no blood except near his body. A few casings were found at the scene that will need to go to Ballistics."

"There's still too much uncertainty surrounding what happened," Surrey jumped in. "But it's entirely possible, given what we found in his trailer, the chance encounter was just that. And what it did was open up new possibilities for us in this investigation. Going back to your question, Walsh, based on what we observed on the body of the female victim found near the landfill, we think there could be a second unsub doing the same thing but with a different method."

"The M.E. did a quick comparison of the cuts on the victim's limbs. They appear slightly different than what he found on Lisa Gutierrez, our only known victim," Kate said. "The M.E. is still going through the autopsies. And the victim we found last night didn't have the same injuries. Fewer bruises, lacerations. It appeared almost as though she hadn't wanted to fight back. Of course, he could've drugged her too. That'll show up on the labs."

"Speaking of the M.E., where are we on the rest of forensics and lab work?" Fisher asked. "It's imperative that we learn who these victims are as well as when they died."

"I can try to answer that one, at least, partially." Romero stepped in. "The victim from last night is currently being identified as we speak. Her body, though hacked all to hell, was in one location. It's likely we'll get an ID on her today. You already know of Lisa Gutierrez, the first victim to have been identified. The rest we're still working on, but we're hoping for results soon."

"It's time to divide and conquer," Kate interjected. "Work our way to a single theory and move on. People in this community are afraid. Women have been slaughtered. The time for suppositions is over."

A SOMERSET OFFICER hurried down the hall and stopped at Captain Brown's doorway. "Captain? I have the Chihuahua police commander on the line for you."

"Thank you." Brown picked up the call. "Comandante. ¿Qué puedo hacer por ti?" (*Commander. What can I do for you?*) He listened while the head of the Chihuahua State Police spoke to him. "Yes, sir. It is very unfortunate, and we are processing the body now so that he may be transferred back to the Mexican authorities." Brown pulled back in his chair and his brow knitted. "I see, a former lieutenant. Very unfortunate circumstances. I assume his visit to my city was not an official visit." He nodded. "Of course. So he'd been retired for some time. Thank you for the information, Comandante. Would it be possible for you to send me what you have on Lieutenant Guzman? This could aid in our investigation. Yes, sir." He cast down his gaze. "Thank you, sir. I'll keep my eye out for the report. Muchas gracias." (*Thank you.*) Brown returned the phone to its receiver and leaned back in his chair. He took in a breath and rubbed his eyes.

Espinoza appeared in his doorway. "May I come in, Captain?"

Brown opened his eyes again and nodded. "What is it, Louisa?"

"I was just wondering when I could go and get Lupe and

Vangie and bring them back home. Have you heard from Agent Reid?"

"She and her team are at the San Antonio FBI office. I expect to hear from her soon and I'll ask. I'm sure they have people who can handle that, though."

"I know. It's just that—they know me. They trust me. I've worked hard to build that trust with the people in our community. I just want them to know that I haven't abandoned them," she replied.

Brown displayed a gentle smile. "You were meant for this line of work, Louisa. I am grateful to have you here. Just as soon as I hear from the FBI, I will let you know, and you can meet them at the location."

"I appreciate that, sir. Thank you." Espinoza turned to leave.

"Louisa?" Brown called out.

"Yes, sir?" She turned around and peered at him.

"You still haven't heard any rumblings about what's happening around here, or whether anyone knows who these victims are?"

She lowered her gaze. "I wish I had, sir, but no." She set her eyes on him again. "I do know they are afraid. And that was before word of what happened last night comes out. If we don't do something to calm their fears, we're going to have people walking around town with their guns loaded and their eyes open."

"And fear in their hearts. That's never a good thing." He sighed. "Thank you, Louisa. I'll keep you in the loop."

She nodded and left his office.

The captain peered through this office window onto the road ahead and the medical offices on the other side. Now he knew who Armando Guzman was. But why was the former lieutenant hunting down associates of the deceased Mr. Cordova, and why was he willing to commit felony kidnapping in another country to find out where they were?

He reached for his cell phone and made the call. "Agent Reid, good morning."

"Good morning, Captain. We were just wrapping things up here at the field office and I was planning on picking up the Cordovas soon."

"That's good news. But I'm calling on another matter, though not unrelated."

"Okay," Kate replied.

"I just got off the phone with the Chihuahua State Police commander. Agent Reid, Armando Guzman was the man found last night—the man who took Lupe Cordova. He was also a retired police lieutenant in Juarez."

Kate stopped in her tracks as she stood in the hall of the San Antonio field office. "Retired?"

"Yes, ma'am. Left the force around the time of his daughter's murder. The commander said Guzman hadn't been on the radar since then. Agent Reid, you don't pursue a dead man's associates unless you have damn good reason to."

GOING BACK to work at the Medical Examiner's office after what happened yesterday seemed a risk. But Xavier Medina had to go back to cast away any lingering suspicion that he had anything to do with the dead bodies turning up all over Somerset. They would look at him regardless. They would all wonder why he fled.

As he arrived, he sat in his older model Chevy Impala and let it run. It was a cold morning, by his standards, and heat from the vents warmed his hands that clung to the steering wheel. The only way he was getting out of this was to go inside and do his job, despite the inevitable conversation he would have with his boss.

Medina finally stepped out of his car and closed the door,

locking it with a press of the key fob. The stocky man with short black hair and a thin mustache walked inside at a slower than normal pace while he worked out what he would say. He opened the back door and entered the long and narrow hallway. His tennis shoes squeaked on the white tiled floor. As he reached the doctor's office, he held his breath as if that would make him invisible.

"Xavier?" Dr. Bauer walked into the hall and called out again. "Xavier?"

Medina stopped and closed his eyes. A moment later, he turned around. "Good morning, Dr. Bauer."

"Xavier, would you come in here for a moment. I think we should discuss what happened yesterday."

"Yes, sir." Medina shuffled back toward the doctor's office.

"Please, sit down." Bauer returned to his desk. "I was informed by the federal agents here yesterday that they tracked you down at your home to learn why you ran from them."

"Yes, sir, they did. I explained everything. I was told that they would speak to you about it," Medina replied.

"I did receive a call from them. However, I find it hard to believe your reason for doing what you did," Bauer added. "And I'd like to hear the truth from you now."

"Dr. Bauer, I didn't lie to the FBI if that's what you think..."

"I don't think you lied." Bauer pressed his fingertips together. "I do think you may have left certain elements from your story."

"No, sir," Medina replied.

Bauer pulled up in his chair and leaned over his desk. "Xavier, I've worked here a long time. I've seen more dead bodies than I care to remember. So let me just say this, whoever you're afraid of, you need to tell the FBI. You see what's been happening in Somerset, right?"

"Yes, sir," Medina replied.

"If you know anything, anything at all, you need to come forward."

"Doc, they must've told you about my history," Medina said.

"I'm aware. And it's something that should've been disclosed on your job application. However, you've worked here for more than 8 months, Xavier, and in that time, I've seen only hard work and dedication from you. But please don't distract from the question at hand. You ran for a reason. I need to know what that is."

Medina fidgeted with his hands and swallowed the lump in his throat. "I didn't say anything more to the agents because I don't have any names or any real information."

"Then what? What do you know?" Bauer asked.

"I know that I have seen this before. And if it has come here, then I'm afraid there will be no stopping it."

15

It was the brief spark in Agent Romero's eye that caught Kate's attention. While he spoke on the phone with the medical examiner, it appeared the spark had been ignited by news about the victims. She mirrored his enthusiasm and regarded the team while they waited inside the FBI field office.

Romero returned his phone to his pocket. "Bauer is sending the reports now. Two of the first set of victims have been identified, in addition to Lisa Gutierrez. He was also able to identify the woman found last night."

A tremendous weight lifted from Kate's shoulders. "Okay, so that leaves only one unidentified from the initial site on Ortega's property. Still waiting on the three from the construction site. And then two more from last night in addition to the woman found on scene."

"Yes, ma'am. Ten, in total. Four, now identified." Romero refreshed his laptop screen. "Here we go. Just got the email. I'll send it to the wall monitor."

The team awaited the results and set their eyes on the monitor.

Kate moved in next to Walsh. "If what we know about Lisa Gutierrez ties in with the other victims, I can start putting together a comprehensive profile. Narrow down our operating theories."

"That's the goal." He peered at her. "How you doing, anyway? We haven't had much of a chance to catch up."

"Me? Fine. In light of the nature of this investigation, I'm feeling all right. Really."

"No doubt this is a doozy of a case," Walsh added. "I'm glad we're all here. Not that you haven't been doing a bang-up job on your own."

"I appreciate the kudos, but Surrey's done his part," she replied. "I'm glad things have worked out the way they have with him. He's provided a good balance for me, Levi."

The email appeared on the wall monitor. "Let me open the attachment." Romero clicked on it and the image popped up. "Here's the summary. Looks like this is for last night's victim. Says here, 19-year-old Marissa Padilla, Laredo, Texas."

Kate read on. "Blunt force trauma and mutilation were not the main causes of death. It was palmar strangulation." She glanced at Surrey. "He used his hands, same as Gutierrez."

Surrey raised a brow and grunted his acknowledgment. "Hey, Romero, can you scroll down? I want to see the description of the knife, wounds, etc. Reid, you're of the belief that a different M.O. was used on Padilla, suggesting two killers. Let's see if that rings true."

Romero scrolled down to the section. "Here it is. According to the M.E., the unsub used a 4 ½ inch blade, roughly 2/10 inch thick, serrated edge on Padilla's flesh and muscle. Upon reaching bone, a hacksaw was used. All of this was done post-mortem." He typed on his laptop. "Let me pull up the Gutierrez report. Here we are. Okay. I can put this up on the screen if you want, but it indicates the blade used to sever the flesh was a 4-inch blade, about the same thickness." He peered up at Surrey. "Thin, straight edge. But a hacksaw, again, was used on the bone."

"And no additional lacerations, just a bruise on her cheek." Surrey looked over at Kate. "You may be on point. Different knives, different wounds. Sounds like different people."

"It makes sense there are two of them out there." Fisher studied the report on the wall monitor. "What would make it clearer would be knowing when these victims were murdered. We have to know what kind of timeframe we're dealing with."

Romero again perused the reports. "I don't have any indication here, but let me call the M.E. That could be information he's still working on." He stepped out of the room to make the call.

Fisher pulled out a toothpick from his shirt pocket. "What we need to know, too, is whether these women were connected in any way."

"That's going to be key to breaking through this wall," Kate added. "But it's also critical that we understand why this killer was in Laredo, took Marissa Padilla, and then drove her to Somerset. Why go through the trouble of driving all that way? And does this mean the other victims could be from different parts of the state? Gutierrez was from San Antonio." She approached Duncan. "Romero said there were two other reports he received."

"Right," Duncan pulled the laptop toward her. "He had the email up. Let me see if I can open the attachment. Here we are." She broadcast it to the screen. "Angela Freemont. 22 years of age. Same cause of death—strangulation. Let me find the weapon details." A moment later, the information appeared on the screen.

Kate set her sights to the monitor. "What do you know? Same as Gutierrez. That tracks considering they were found in the same location."

"And finally, we have Jennifer Martinez. 20-years-old," Duncan scanned the information. "She lived in Austin. Appears to have been the same cause of death and the same type of knife. So, without knowing the identity of the other victim on the Ortega property, the three victims found there died from strangulation, post-mortem shows the same type of knife used to cut away flesh and muscle, same type of saw to sever the limbs. Marissa Padilla is the outlier, suggesting a second killer. As they identify more victims, this theory should come into greater focus."

Kate walked to the white board and grabbed a marker. "Laredo, Somerset, and Austin. What about Freemont? Where was she from?"

Duncan reviewed the information. "The most recent address was in San Antonio."

"Okay, so we also have a former Juarez cop and a janitor at the M.E.'s office who did time in Juarez. We know that we currently have ten victims, six of them are still unidentified, and three different cities," Kate replied. "But why Laredo then? I get the other two. They're not that far from here. But Laredo? That's what, an hour and a half, two hours from here?"

"Hold on, let me see." Duncan returned to Marissa's file. "No, I don't see anything other than an address in Laredo. But that doesn't mean she hadn't lived somewhere else."

"Of course," Kate began. "It could be she lived in one of the other cities. Now that we've ID'd her, a background should tell us that."

Walsh gazed at the white board. "The connection could be that these women knew one another in San Antonio, or someone in San Antonio knew them. I think that makes it all the more important to learn exactly when these victims died."

Kate continued to study the board. "I still maintain the unsub or unsubs know Somerset well. They'd have to. No one could've chosen those locations otherwise."

Romero walked inside again. "Sorry about the delay. Here's

the deal. Dr. Bauer hasn't firmed up the dates, but I pleaded with him to give us some sort of time frame. Best he could figure with what he knows right now, pending labs, Gutierrez has been dead roughly 6 months. Freemont, around 4 months, Jennifer Martinez died roughly 4 months ago, and of course, we know Marissa Padilla was murdered in the last few days."

Kate drew in a breath and eyed the ceiling for a moment. "The killers aren't wasting time. These women are being abducted and then murdered likely within days. So I think it's safe to rule out any notion the women are being held captive somewhere. I'm willing to bet the remaining victim from the Ortega property was also murdered around the timeframe as the others found there." She returned her gaze to the team. "Five or six months ago, that construction site where 3 others were found would've looked much different. In fact, there probably wouldn't have been any park carved out yet. That makes me think the victims from the construction site had been murdered more recently."

Surrey and Kate traded a knowing glance when he continued. "They're moving on to new locations. Different killers using different weapons and new burial grounds."

Fisher stood from the table in a huff. "Christ, what the hell are we talking about, people? Is this going to be a whack-a-mole situation? We find one site and another one pops up?"

"Reid, you said last night that you didn't think this was random," Surrey began. "That these women were targeted. How so?"

"These were not crimes of opportunity. An opportunist wouldn't take the time to do what's been done to these victims. They were targeted, hunted, by who I also believe were multiple perpetrators. What I said before about this possibly being the work of an incel..." She shook her head. "This isn't the work of one. It's the work of a group. We'll need to scrutinize what Duncan's found so far with online activity in this part of the state. And Surrey and I should head to Laredo and speak to Marissa Padilla's friends and family. Find out where she was last seen and when she'd been reported missing. I believe she's the most recent victim and the trail of her disappearance is still fresh enough that it could lead us to where we need to be."

"We can work with the local authorities on the other victims identified," Romero added. "See where we can find some overlap among these women."

"Good." Kate turned to Fisher. "The Cordovas are still at the safehouse. While I can't see where they fit into this yet, or Armando Guzman, any immediate threat to them is over now that Guzman's dead."

"You don't think they could still be a target?" Walsh asked.

"No one from Somerset has been reported missing or identified as a victim," Kate began. "If Guzman had been part of the group, Lupe Cordova would be dead. Honestly, I think the safest place for them to be is back in their home. Brown can step up patrols around the area, if necessary. That said, the Cordova mother could hold answers as to why the cop was here and what her husband was involved with. She should be questioned. If a connection is discovered, we'll discuss what it means for our investigation and ensure they're protected."

"Duncan and I can handle that," Fisher replied. "Romero, if you'd like a hand, Walsh can run on the inquiries into the other victims with you, for the sake of time."

"I'm good with that," Romero replied.

Kate turned back to the white board a final time and scribbled the words. *Multiple killers. 10 bodies so far.* "In case we all forget. This investigation has hit social media and local news. In the next 12 to 24 hours, it'll be a national story. We'd better be prepared."

As KATE DROVE to the city of Laredo, about 140 miles away, Surrey regarded her from the passenger seat. "You know, what I said earlier about not seeking approval from anyone?"

"Yeah." She kept her eyes on the road ahead.

"I see you took my advice."

Her cheeks raised in a smile. "What do you mean?"

"You kicked ass back there in the meeting. For a minute, I thought you were the senior unit agent, not Fisher."

"Did I come off that strong?" A brief uncertainty crossed her face.

Surrey raised his hands. "Hey, don't backpedal now. You did what you thought you needed to do. And guess what? People listened. Fisher listened. I've noticed that he gives his people enough rope to do with what they will..."

"And you're saying I haven't hung myself with it yet?"

"Not yet." He returned his gaze to the road. "No, I'm just saying, you did good back there. Exactly as you should've done. It was impressive, that's all."

"Thanks. Now I just need to back it up, huh?"

"Well, that's another story." He laughed.

It wasn't often that Surrey opened up to Kate, but it had become a little more frequent over the course of this investigation. He'd even gone so far as to mention his kids. "You know, I forgot to tell you that I got an email a while back from the owner of the house you're in."

"Oh yeah?" Surrey asked.

"The son emailed me. I hadn't heard from him since I recommended you for the place. Anyway, he just reached out to say how nice it was that you fixed the back deck and didn't ask to be paid for it."

"Oh, that. Yeah, no, it was nothing." Surrey swatted away the comment. "It's a nice place. And I think my kids will be coming to see me for Christmas soon, so I'm happy to have a house for them to run around in."

Kate drew in her brow. "You don't say much about them."

"My kids?" he asked.

"I knew you were divorced, and of course, you mentioned the case about your daughter's schoolmate. I mean, you are kind of a closed book, but I try not to hold that against you." She smiled at him. "But it's great. It's great they'll be coming to see you. Two kids? How old are they?"

"One of each. My son, Elijah, is 12, my daughter Emma is 10. Emma and I still struggle to get closer, but I hope as she gets older, that'll change."

"Elijah and Emma. Those are nice names. I'm sure Emma will grow to understand what this job entails. I imagine it's not easy for a kid to get it," Kate replied. "If they do come out, you should bring them by the office. I'd love to meet them."

"Thanks. Maybe I will if it all works out. I have to settle a few issues with the ex, but fingers crossed. Do you and Scarborough plan on having kids?"

Kate glanced down for a moment.

"I'm sorry. That's none of my business." He turned away.

"No, no, it's fine. I just asked you about your kids. It's just funny because I don't really know a lot of agents, well, in our office, at least, who have kids."

"This kind of work tends to get in the way, which is why I'm divorced. But anyway..."

"Well, to answer your question, no. We don't plan on having kids. Don't get me wrong, we like kids, but they're not for us." She smiled, though underneath her grin was the truth that she couldn't have kids, not that she hadn't wanted them. It had been a long time since she talked about having children. That part of her life simply no longer existed.

"Understandable," he replied.

And that was it. He didn't speak on that subject or any other. The awkwardness between them lingered for a few more moments until Kate cleared her throat. "So, we agree that we'll meet with the family first, right?"

"Uh, yeah. I know the Laredo police have already spoken to the parents. Romero said they know we're coming and have agreed to sit with us at the police station."

"Good." She drove on, cursing herself for dismissing his attempt at strengthening their friendship. She enjoyed Surrey's company. She had wanted to be closer to him. Well, that wasn't going to happen today.

Duncan had once told Kate that she thought the two of them had formed a unique bond and played off each other's strengths. She was right. Of course, Kate had often given into the notion that she and her partners had special connections. That rang true when she worked with Nick, and it had developed into a marriage. Noah Quinn? Not so much. Their budding partnership went down in flames, but initially, Kate thought the two shared a similar bond. It hadn't lasted long. But this? What she and Surrey had together was different. Duncan picked up on it and Kate wondered if the others had too.

"We made good time." Kate eyed the *"Welcome to Laredo"* sign on the side of the highway. "How far is the station from here?"

Surrey opened the map on his phone. "About three miles."

Kate exited the highway.

On their arrival, Surrey stepped out of the car and waited for Kate to catch up. "How do you want to approach these people?"

She walked beside him as they reached the entrance. "Their daughter was just murdered, they aren't going to want to hear a bunch of BS about how hard we're working to find her killer. They want to know what we know."

"Which is?" Surrey pulled open the door.

"Not much. And we have to be honest about that. But with their help, we could learn more," she replied.

"My two cents? I'd leave out the possible Juarez connection. It may not be relevant in any case," Surrey added.

"I agree. No need to muddy the waters." Kate stepped inside where an officer approached them.

"Afternoon. I'm Detective Walker. You must be Agent Kate Reid. Agent Romero said I should be expecting you." He offered his hand.

Kate accepted the greeting. "That's me. This is my partner, Special Agent Jonathan Surrey."

"Agent Surrey." The detective extended his greeting. "I appreciate y'all coming down here to speak with the parents directly. I am damn sorry this situation seems to involve a whole hell of a lot more than their daughter, Marissa."

"Which is why any help the parents can offer will be greatly appreciated," Surrey replied.

"Are they ready for us?" Kate asked the detective.

"Yes, ma'am. If you'll follow me. They're in my office." Detective Walker, a beefy man, headed down the hall until he stopped at his door. "One more thing, from what Agent Romero told me, a man was shot down at the place where the killer was about to bury Marissa."

"That's right," Kate replied. "We believe the killer was confronted and after he shot the man, fled the scene. It's frankly the only reason their daughter was found when she was."

"Yes, ma'am." Walker opened the door and stepped inside. "Mr. and Mrs. Padilla, these are the FBI agents I talked to you about. Agent Kate Reid and Agent Jonathan Surrey. They've come all the way from D.C. to assist us with your daughter's investigation."

"Mr. and Mrs. Padilla, I'm very sorry for your loss." Kate pulled out a chair to sit down. "I'm sure you're tired of hearing that, but the fact of the matter is, there really are no words that offer the kind of comfort you need. For that, I'm truly sorry."

Surrey took a seat next to Kate while the detective moved in next to the parents.

"Thank you, Agent Reid," Mrs. Padilla replied. "It sounds like you're no stranger to loss."

"No, ma'am, I'm not. Would you mind if we ask you some questions about where your daughter was before she went missing?"

The parents eyed one another when the father turned to Kate. "Marissa worked at the Chili's not far from our home. She went to community college during the day and worked most nights at the restaurant, though on that day, she had covered an afternoon shift for a co-worker."

"Does she have a car to get her to and from?" Kate asked.

"No, ma'am. She walks mostly. Sometimes if it's raining, she'll catch a bus. But like I said, it's only a couple miles and she was a young, athletic girl." He wiped away a stray tear.

"Of course. Do you know if any of her coworkers watched her walk from the restaurant that day?" Kate asked. "We plan on speaking with them too, but for the sake of time..."

"Yes, well, I don't think so. Most of the staff drive. They would've all gone out back while she left through the front," Mrs. Padilla replied.

Kate turned to Surrey. "We'll be sure to get any security footage from the restaurant."

He nodded.

"May I ask you something, Agent Reid?"

"Yes, ma'am. Of course."

Mrs. Padilla swallowed hard. "Why did he take her to Somerset? That's so far away. And how did he do it?"

Detective Walker stepped in. "Mrs. Padilla, we don't know all the specifics just yet. But I will be working closely with the agents here and we'll learn a lot from the forensics analysis once it's completed."

Mr. Padilla reached for his wife's hand. "She just wants to know if our baby suffered, that's all. Did he...did he hurt her before he drove, or..."

As the detective was about to speak again, Kate jumped in. "We suspect he acted quickly. It would've been difficult to drive that distance with a young woman, who I'm sure would've been hell-bent on escaping." She eyed the detective who appeared grateful.

"I see." Mrs. Padilla looked down. "At least she didn't suffer for long."

"Your family, have you always lived in Laredo?" Surrey asked.

"Oh, yes, sir," Mr. Padilla answered. "The wife and I grew up round here. Wanted our kids to do the same."

"Well, there was that time," Mrs. Padilla cut in. "That time Marissa lived in San Antonio with a friend from high school. It didn't last long, some months maybe. The two ended up at odds over something or other. I suspect a boy. Marissa came back home shortly after that."

Kate and Surrey exchanged a glance before Kate asked, "Can you remember about when that was?"

The parents looked at one another as if it helped them to recall. It was Mr. Padilla who spoke up. "Just last year. Over the spring, if I recall correctly. She'd gone to see the friend over Spring Break, because, you know, Marissa went to college too. Anyway, she called us all excited about the big city and said she wanted to stay awhile. Me and the wife weren't too keen on the idea, especially since it would put a damper on her schooling, but what are you gonna do? She was 18 at the time. Can't exactly tell your adult child what to do, now, can you?"

"No, sir," Kate replied. "But she came back not long after?"

"Yes, ma'am. Got a job up there and all, but it ended up being for nothing. Came back, got back into school and that was that," Mr. Padilla replied.

That was the connection. Marissa had lived and worked in San Antonio, same as the other victims, except for the woman who lived in Austin.

Kate offered her hand. "I want to thank you for talking with us today, Mr. and Mrs. Padilla. I understand Detective Walker has already spoken to Marissa's friends, so we'll go over what he learned. And of course, we'll speak to her co-workers. But we have learned a lot today, so thank you for that." She stood from the chair. "If you have any questions, please don't hesitate to get in touch with Detective Walker. We'll be in constant contact with him until this is over."

"Thank you, Agent Reid," Mr. Padilla said.

"Thank you, sir." Kate nodded and walked out of the room, not noticing Surrey trailed her. She doubled over and placed her hands on her knees.

"Hey, you all right?" He gripped her shoulders.

"Yeah. I'm fine." She returned upright. "It's never easy, you know?"

"I do know. But you did great in there. Better than I could've done."

"I doubt that." Kate regained her composure and noticed the detective approach. "Thank you for letting us speak to them."

"Any time, Agent Reid. You helped put their minds at ease, at least somewhat. I mean, it ain't gonna help anyone knowing the finer details now, is it?"

"Sometimes it doesn't," Kate replied. "I'd like to speak to the restaurant owner and see what they have on their security cameras."

"Let me make the call now and I'll arrange it." He picked up his phone. "Excuse me a moment."

After he walked away, Surrey looked at Kate. "We found the connection."

She grinned. "We found the connection."

16

Inside the restaurant where Marissa Padilla worked, it appeared that news of the young woman's death had already made the rounds. And when Kate and Surrey arrived, they were greeted with forlorn gazes and an atmosphere clouded with sorrow. It seemed their presence was immediately noted by the girl at the host's station.

"You're here about Marissa, aren't you?" she asked.

Kate retrieved her credentials. "We are. Was she a friend of yours?"

"Yes, ma'am. My best friend." She cleared her throat and dabbed at her welling eyes.

"I'm very sorry for your loss. We're with the FBI. We'd like to speak with the manager, please."

The girl nodded. "I'll go get him."

Only moments later, the young woman returned with a hefty man at her side who wore a black button down and khaki dress pants. He offered his hand to Kate. "I'm Mike Ingram. You're here about Marissa?"

"Agent Kate Reid." She took his hand. "This is Agent Surrey. Yes, I'm sorry to say. We're assisting the Laredo police with their investigation. We'd like to examine your security footage from the day she disappeared."

"Yes, of course. Please follow me." The large man shuffled to the back and into the kitchen. "My office is back here. I was told by local police y'all would be helping out because it has something to do with a bigger case you're working on."

"Yes, sir, that's part of it. May I ask how long Marissa had worked here?" Surrey asked.

"About 6 months or so, maybe a little longer. She was one of my best employees. I could always count on her to help close up at night and she never complained about her shifts. Not once." He opened his door. "Please, come in."

"Thank you." Kate walked into the cramped office. "Did she close up a lot and was she usually alone in that?"

"Oh no. We keep three on staff for closings, though I understand Marissa was working the afternoon shift the other day; the day it happened." Ingram sat down at his desk. "I'll pull up the footage here. Corporate keeps everything on the Cloud, so it'll only take me a moment to retrieve it."

"Who were the others on shift that afternoon?" Kate pressed on.

"Uh, let me see." He cast his gaze upward. "Travis and Emanuel, for sure. I'd have to check the schedule for the others." He returned to Kate. "They're expected in later today if you'd like to speak with them."

"Let's see how far we get with the footage and go from there," Kate replied.

"Fair enough." Ingram turned around his laptop. "This is it, here."

They leaned closer and viewed the footage. Kate knitted her

brow. "This is inside the restaurant about, what, an hour before she clocked out?"

"Yes, ma'am. As you can see, it was a fairly quiet afternoon. Mid-week and all."

Kate pointed her index finger at the screen. "Who's this guy right here? He's got his back to the camera."

Surrey studied the image. "He's alone at the bar. Got a few more over there at the tables..."

"But they're in groups. He's the only single patron," she added.

"Ma'am?" Ingram cut in. "We get a lot of single persons, men in particular, who sit at the bar and watch sports on the televisions."

Kate nodded. "Of course. Do you know if this man is a regular?"

"Can't say for sure, to be honest, but I can ask my employee who was working the bar at the time," Ingram replied.

"You would have receipts from this man, too, right?" Surrey asked.

"Sure would, unless he paid cash, of course." Ingram stood up. "I can go find that out for you here real quick, if you'd like."

"Yes, please. That would be helpful," Kate replied. "We'll keep looking through this."

Ingram left the agents to retrieve the information. Kate pressed play again as they both viewed the footage.

"It's now twenty minutes before Marissa clocked out and that man is still there," Kate said.

"Funny, but I don't see her anywhere. Do you? What about the exterior footage?" Surrey asked.

"Got it." Kate pulled up the files. "Where do the staff park?"

"Must be around the back. I see a few cars out front," Surrey replied. "See if there's another camera at the back."

Kate examined the file folders. "This could be it here. Yep.

This is the rear of the building. Three more cars. Marissa walked to the bus stop or home if it was clear."

"It was a clear afternoon, by the look of things. Let's just see how this plays out." After several more minutes, the staff was seen exiting the back. "Here we go. That's a couple employees there."

"They're getting in their cars. Nothing looks odd and I don't see anyone around. Let's take a look at the front." She clicked to open the other file. "Okay, wait, hang on. Where's our guy from the bar? Did you see him leave?"

"Back up the video. Let's see if we missed it," Surrey added.

She reversed the files and played it again. "There he is. I see him. He's walking to his car out front. Damn it, I can't see his face."

"He's wearing a hoodie and no sign of Marissa," Surrey replied.

"Not yet." Kate continued to view the footage. "That's her. Right there."

"And she's walking. She'll be out of view in a minute. The guy from the bar is gone. The other employees are gone."

"It's just her now," Kate replied. "And we know how this ends." She pulled back and stopped the video. "Damn it. I thought we might get something."

The door opened and Ingram walked inside. "Good news. The guy at the bar paid by credit card."

Kate reached out her hand. "May I take a look at the receipt?"

"Yes, ma'am." Ingram turned it over.

The signature was scribbled and illegible, but the name on the credit card was printed clearly, and it seemed the agents quickly realized the importance of the find as they regarded one another.

"Is this a joke?" Kate's face masked in a fusion of anger and bewilderment. "You gotta be kidding me."

"Xavier Medina gets around," Surrey replied. "I'll give you one thing, Reid. You called it. This guy runs from us and now I think we know why. The thing is, we saw him leave. He might've been there, but it doesn't look like he took her."

Kate peered again at the receipt. "We both know this is no coincidence. He's a spotter. Son of a bitch is a spotter."

Surrey regarded her. "If that's the case, and he didn't take her, then who the hell did?"

THE APARTMENT COMPLEX where the Cordova family resided came into view. Officer Espinoza transported the mother and daughters home while Agents Fisher and Duncan followed. They'd left it to Espinoza to get the girls to warm to the idea of letting the agents talk to the mother. The more they could glean about the father's murder, the more they could understand the connection, if any, to the former Juarez cop and his run-in with the killer.

The collection of scattered theories and "what ifs" had so far hindered the investigation, which was why the rest of the team had been brought in. Cameron Fisher, as leader, had to get his arms around the situation before the press took it and ran with it, truth be damned.

He pulled up behind Espinoza and turned to Duncan, who was in the passenger seat. "How's your Spanish?"

"About as good as my French," she replied. "So, not good at all."

"The daughters may have to help, or Espinoza, if she's fluent." Fisher stepped out of the car and trailed the officer.

Espinoza glanced back. "Agent Fisher, would you give me a minute with them inside?"

"Yes, of course." He stepped back and waited for Duncan to catch up.

"What's going on?" she asked.

"Espinoza wants a minute alone with them." Fisher watched as they walked inside and closed the door. "Did the captain forward Eduardo Cordova's file to you, by chance?"

She checked her email. "Yes, actually. Here it is. I'll forward it to you and we can take a look."

They opened the file and began to read the officer's notes.

"He had been leaving his workshop. Killed in his vehicle on the way home," Fisher said.

"They suspected road rage," Duncan added. "No one had seen a vehicle. Ballistics showed a bullet from a 9-mil killed him. No other leads."

"Shit, that's it? That's all they got after a man was murdered on his way home from work?" He looked at her. "Why the hell is this file so light?"

"That's a damn good question," Duncan replied.

"Excuse me, Agent Fisher?" Espinoza stood at the front door of the apartment. "You can come in now."

Fisher started ahead. "If that's all they told his wife, we might be wasting our time here."

"Let's not count her out yet. The wife always knows something." Duncan followed him. "And she might have a damn good reason for not opening up about it."

The agents entered the small apartment where Lupe and Vangie stood in the kitchen and their mother sat on the reclining chair in the living room. Lupe approached Fisher. "She's agreed to speak to you, but you should know, her memory isn't what it used to be. She suffered a mild stroke shortly after our father was murdered. She hasn't been the same since."

"And you're okay with this?" Fisher asked. "We understand with what you've been through..."

"I'm fine. I want the truth. Vangie isn't exactly okay with it, but I have to know why that man took me and why he said those things about my father. Ma doesn't talk about him. Not ever."

"Thank you, Lupe," Duncan began. "We'll take care not to upset her as best we can. Would you like to be the one to translate? We understand she doesn't speak English as well as you do. I'm sure Officer Espinoza can sit in, if you'd prefer."

Lupe eyed them with resolve. "It should be me."

"Okay." Fisher started into the living room and sat down on the sofa. "Mrs. Cordova, my name is Cameron Fisher. This is Eva Duncan. We're with the FBI." He paused a moment while Lupe sat next to her to translate. "We know you've been through a lot over the past few days with your daughter, and please know that we're here to get to the bottom of what happened and why." He stopped again while Lupe interpreted for him.

Duncan regarded Fisher a moment and he nodded for her to continue. "Ma'am, we know your husband was murdered about two years ago and we received his file from the Somerset Police. It's our understanding that he was shot by an unknown assailant in his vehicle on his way home from work." She waited again for Lupe. "The information they have isn't much, to be honest, so we were hoping you might know if he'd had any concerns in the days leading up to his death."

While Mrs. Cordova spoke, Lupe prepared to relay the information. "She says Dad had talked about a man he thought was bad."

"Bad?" Fisher asked.

"Yes." Lupe turned to her mother while she continued to speak. "Uh, Ma says that when Dad traveled to Juarez years ago to see his brother, one time he came back all beaten up. He stopped going after that."

"Can you ask her when that was?" Duncan said.

Lupe relayed the question. "Okay, she says that was about a year before he was killed." She listened again while her mother spoke. "After that, Dad stayed at work a lot at night. He tried to build his business. Ma says she always thought there was more to it than that."

Duncan regarded her. "Did she ask him about it?"

"Uh, no. She says it wasn't her place." Lupe turned to Duncan. "That's old school, you know? My parents are very traditional. The man works, the wife stays at home to raise the children." She turned back to her mother while she spoke. "She's saying that my dad had become concerned about some men he knew. That he thought they were the bad people. One, in particular."

"And this was more than two years ago," Fisher added. "I'm not sure how valid this will be, but if she recalls a name, that would be very helpful."

"Ma, do you know the man's name?" Lupe asked in Spanish.

The mother set her eyes on Duncan. "El diablo gabacho."

Duncan looked at Lupe for translation.

"El diablo is devil. Gabacho is what Mexicans call white people from the U.S. It's more derogatory than gringo," Lupe replied. "She's basically saying Dad called him the white devil."

Duncan raised her brow." Well, that narrows it down."

"I'm sorry, Agent Duncan. My father wouldn't have wanted Ma to know about any of this, so if she says that much, then this is all she knows. I don't know if it will help you. But one thing is for sure, my dad was a good man. He was murdered and no one did a thing about it. Now, a man who kidnapped me claimed my father killed his daughter in Mexico. I don't believe that. I hope you don't either."

"There's a lot we don't know about the man who took you, Armando Guzman, and now that he's dead, we won't know the truth." Duncan cast down her gaze a moment. "This white devil, do you think he could have been a business associate of your father's?"

"I don't know. We don't have much left of Dad's work files. His workshop still has some things in it. Agent Duncan, Armando Guzman's daughter was murdered, and he believed my father and his friends had something to do with it. Now you've heard from my mother. Do you believe Guzman was telling the truth?"

"I believe he thought he was telling the truth. I think it's time we find these friends." Duncan stood from the chair. "Agent Fisher? We should let her rest now."

"Of course." He joined her and turned to Lupe. "Please tell her how much we appreciate her help. And that we will do our best to learn not only what's happening in this town, but to get to the bottom of what happened to your father."

Lupe nodded. "I will. Thank you both."

The agents stepped outside and walked back to their car. Duncan slipped onto the passenger seat while Fisher got behind the wheel. He peered at her. "One of our killers could be a white man."

"Reid was pretty sure these people were from Somerset," Duncan replied.

Fisher's phone rang and he looked at the caller ID. "Speaking of Reid." He answered and placed the call on speaker. "Were your ears burning?"

"What's that?" Kate asked.

"Nothing. I'm just sitting in the car with Duncan and we were about to leave the Cordova house. Turned out, the mother knew a few things, but not a whole hell of a lot that's going to help us."

"What did she say?" Kate continued.

"That Eduardo Cordova feared a white man," Fisher continued. "A devil, as she called him. The father had traveled to Juarez to see his brother a few times. Came back once, beaten all to hell. Stopped going back about a year before his murder, and then I don't know what changed. That part is still unclear. But he was certain a bad white man was after him. Could be the guy who shot him."

"No name, huh?" Kate asked.

"Now, that would make our jobs far too easy, Reid."

"I have another name for you," Kate cut in. "Xavier Medina was at the restaurant where Marissa Padilla worked on the day she went missing. We didn't see her get into his car. In fact, it appeared he left before she had. But the point is..."

"Medina was there." Fisher shot a glance to Duncan.

"That would be one hell of a coincidence, and we all know how you feel about those," Duncan said. "Reid, what do you want to do about this?"

"Maybe Cordova's friends, the names Lupe offered up to Guzman, maybe they know who this white devil is."

Fisher turned the engine. "While you two head back from Laredo, we can start to hunt them down and we'll get with Brown regarding Xavier Medina. You mentioned he'd submitted a swab. We'll work on our end to get an update on his situation. And we'd better figure out quick what part these so-called friends of Cordova's are playing in this game."

17

I t would be a couple of hours before Kate and Surrey returned from Laredo. A good opportunity to home in on Cordova's associates, Richard Ceballos and Michael Garza.

Fisher walked inside the Somerset stationhouse and held the door for Duncan. "We'll brief the captain on what we learned at the Cordova house, then we pull every detail available on these two men."

"I'm on it." She continued inside and walked toward Brown's office. "Captain?"

"Ah, Agent Duncan. Where is your..." but before he could finish Fisher appeared in the doorway. "Good. You're both here. I hope you were able to get something useful from Mrs. Cordova."

"Whether it's useful to us remains to be seen," Duncan replied. "Before we get into that, any chance you could follow up with the lab on Medina's DNA?"

"I reckon I can. Why's that?" Brown asked. "I thought y'all felt pretty comfortable he wasn't involved in any of this."

"He was at the restaurant where Marissa Padilla worked the

day she went missing," Duncan continued. "Video shows he left before she did, but no chance that's a coincidence. If there's a DNA match, we'll have him, so let's see what the M.E. can do on that front first."

"And if he doesn't have it back yet?" Brown asked. "Sounds like it could be time to put a tail on him."

"Yes, sir," Fisher cut in. "If he's involved, he could lead us to the person who did take her. It's possible we have enough to hang onto him for a while, but I don't want to blow our shot at learning who he's associating with. And as far as Mrs. Cordova goes, well, she didn't say much except something about a white devil her husband had mentioned."

Brown slowly nodded. "Mrs. Cordova has spoken of something similar when we conducted our investigation into her husband's murder. But we never did learn who this white man was, and without a name, it was a fairly broad description not easy to nail down. No one saw a car lingering around the shop. No one saw anything, which is why the case is still officially open. It appeared to be a random shooting. Maybe road rage, we still just don't know." He sighed. "I'm sorry. I had hoped she would disclose new information."

"I do still think it's relevant, and could be a piece of the puzzle," Duncan began. "It'll be up to us to figure out where it fits. So here's what we'd like to do."

"Lupe gave Guzman two names," Fisher jumped in. "These people could prove important, so while we await the return of the rest of our team, Duncan and I planned on running down these two men if you're good with that."

"Sure thing," Brown replied. "Let me know what you need to find them, and I'll make it happen."

"Just a place to hang our hats for a while and we can handle the rest," Fisher replied.

"You got it. I have a spare office you can set up in. Follow me." Brown led the way into the hall and toward the empty office. He switched on the light. "Will this do?"

"Yes, sir. Thank you." Duncan walked inside. "We'll get started then."

Fisher joined her. "Appreciate it, Captain. We'll come see you if we have any questions."

"Let me get to work on Xavier Medina. If this som' bitch is part of this mess, it's best we get to the bottom of it now." Brown took his leave.

Duncan grabbed her laptop and logged into the database. "I'll pull a background on Ceballos first." She keyed in several commands and waited for the screen to populate. "Okay, here's something. DOT records show one Richard Ceballos, 50-years-old. Legal resident of Somerset. No traffic violations. No criminal record noted." She glanced at him. "The guy's clean."

"Check his passport. See if he travels back and forth to Mexico. Specifically, Juarez. It seems a lot of signs are pointing in that direction," Fisher replied.

Duncan got back to work and reviewed the data that returned. "According to State Department records, the last time he left the country was 4 years ago."

"Tell me he traveled to Juarez," Fisher replied.

"He traveled to Juarez, but that was long before Cordova died. And before Medina served his time."

Fisher placed his hands on his hips. "Okay, uh, let's pull an address on this guy. We still need to talk to him. He could be in danger. Maybe from Medina, I don't know, but I'm starting to believe these people are connected. I just can't figure out how. And let's run his name against the incel groups you uncovered for Reid. I'm still not convinced of her theory, but we can't ignore it."

THE APARTMENT BUILDING came into view and Fisher drove into the complex. "This is Ceballos's place. What was his apartment number?"

Duncan glanced at the address. "Building C, Unit 148. Looks like that's the C building on your left."

"Got it." Fisher turned toward the building and pulled into a parking spot. "Do we have the make and model of his vehicle?"

"Yeah, according to his motor vehicle records, he owns a 2012 grey Ford Expedition."

Fisher surveyed the area. "I don't see a Ford SUV anywhere." He pointed ahead. "Hold on. I spoke too soon. What's that right there?"

"Looks like the SUV," Duncan replied. "He might be home." She opened her door and stepped out of the car. The bright sun warmed her face as the weather dipped below 60 for the first time since her arrival. Compared to what she was used to in D.C., this felt like a warm spring day.

Fisher joined her and checked his weapon. "I'd like to think this guy is going to cooperate, but we need to be prepared. There could be a lot more here than what we know."

"Understood." Duncan checked her gun and returned it to its holster at her hip. "Looks like the unit is on the first floor. Bad news for us."

"Yeah, he can't jump off a second or third-story floor, but he can hop out of the first-floor window fairly easily."

"Then again, according to his background, the guy's 5-feet 10 and a hefty 230." Duncan smiled. "We'll keep our fingers crossed he's a slow mover."

Fisher started ahead and Duncan joined him. He glanced at her a moment. "This sort of feels like normal, you and me."

"Yeah, it does. That's a good thing, right?" she asked.

"I think so. Hang on, this is his apartment." Fisher knocked on the door. "Mr. Ceballos? This is the FBI." He peered at the olive-green door with a small gold knocker in the center and waited a moment. He tried again. "Mr. Ceballos? FBI. We'd like to have a word, please."

Duncan stepped toward a front window. "I can't see past the curtains. I don't think he's here, Cam."

"Then we go in."

Duncan's brow raised. "Without a warrant? Are you kidding me?"

"Welfare check. We'll find the manager and have him let us in." Fisher turned on his heel and started back.

Duncan hurried to catch up to him while he reached the door to the manager's office.

He stood ready to walk inside. "We'll tell them the Bureau is concerned for his safety. Eva, the guy's truck is here and he's not answering."

"Yeah, okay," she replied.

He walked inside. "Afternoon. FBI. I'm Agent Fisher. This is Agent Duncan. We're looking for Richard Ceballos, a tenant here. We'd like to conduct a welfare check."

The older woman behind the counter shifted her gaze between them. "Uh, okay. Let me get the key." She turned away a moment to reach for her keys and walked around the counter toward the door. "I don't know the man well. He pays his rent on time and stays out of trouble. Those are the best kind of tenants as far as I'm concerned."

As they walked through the breezeway, she fiddled with the keys and retrieved the one she needed. On approach, she knocked. "Mr. Ceballos? It's Nancy, the assistant manager. Uh, sir, the FBI is here to speak to you." A moment later, she turned to Fisher. "No answer."

"Yeah, we tried."

"Of course." She inserted the key and unlocked the door. Upon opening it, she stepped inside slowly. "Mr. Ceballos? It's Nancy. Are you here, Mr. Ceballos?"

Fisher walked inside and Duncan pulled up the rear. He placed his hand on the woman's shoulder. "Nancy, would you mind if we had a look around? Something doesn't seem quite right here. Might be a good idea for you to step outside."

"Sure thing. I'll wait just out here," she replied.

After she left, he surveyed the living room. "I don't like this, Eva."

"Good God. Either he was a complete slob, or someone tossed the place," she replied.

Fisher retrieved his gun and readied it while he continued into the hall. A single bedroom and bathroom lay near the end. As he entered the bedroom, he lowered the gun. "God damn it."

Duncan stepped inside next to him. "Someone got to him before we did. Bullet to the head right where he sleeps. Why? Guzman's dead. Who the hell else was looking for him?"

Fisher approached the body. "Hell if I know. We should've made finding him a priority after Guzman." With a pen from his pocket, Fisher pulled open the nightstand drawer. "Wallet's in here. ID says it's Ceballos. Son of a bitch. What the hell does this guy have to do with any of this?" He slammed the drawer closed again.

Duncan grabbed her cell phone. "Reid, Ceballos is dead. Michael Garza could be next."

18

T wo names were now at the top of everyone's mind. Xavier Medina and Michael Garza. One, of whom, could already be dead.

By late afternoon, the team had returned to the Somerset station with few answers. Kate eyed the photos of the deceased Ceballos on the conference table inside Brown's office. "It'll be days before the M.E. gets back these labs. And maybe that doesn't matter because I can't see how he's connected to our other victims. At this point, Medina remains our strongest lead. So, unless Ceballos and he are connected, I'm at a loss as to where this man fits."

Duncan set her gaze to the captain. "Still no luck finding Garza?"

"No, ma'am," Brown replied. "He's not home and he's not at his workplace."

She nodded. "Then it's time to issue a BOLO on his vehicle."

"I agree 100 percent," he replied.

Surrey moved in and peered at the photos on the table. "Like you said, Reid, the connection of this murder to our investigation is non-existent."

"If that holds true, then there seems to be a lot of killers living in this town," Kate added.

"Can I just jump in here?" Romero raised his hand. "Walsh and I spent the day talking to the local cops, friends of the victims. And let me tell you something, the unsubs we're looking for are only interested in women around the ages of our victims. Now, you two learned that our buddy, Medina, was in Laredo at the very location of Marissa Padilla."

"Right," Kate replied.

Romero pointed to the photos. "This man, Ceballos? His buddy, Garza? Hell, I don't know, but I gotta think they could be some sort of acquaintances to the unsubs. Because to think they don't have Jack Squat to do with our investigation isn't gonna fly with me. No offense to any of you folks, but Richard Ceballos knew something. Maybe Michael Garza does too. Point being, if we don't find out soon, we aren't gonna find him alive, I'll tell you that much. And Xavier Medina may be holding the answers."

Kate regarded him. "Last I checked, no one's been able to find Medina either. The fact that both these men are currently MIA suggests their involvement. So, if you know where to find either one, I'm all ears."

INSIDE THEIR 2-BEDROOM APARTMENT, Lupe curled up on her sofa after cleaning the dishes from lunch. She would have to go back to work tomorrow or risk losing her job. Having called in sick for a few days would only go so far.

She glanced at Vangie, who sat next to her. "What if there's more than what Ma said to those agents?"

"What do you mean?"

"I mean, what if she's keeping some things to herself?" Lupe pressed on.

"Why would you think that?"

Lupe sat up. "I need answers, Vangie. I want to know the truth. A crazy man took me. I thought I was going to die like the rest of those girls buried in the ground. Don't you understand that?"

"I do understand, but if you start asking around, you know what's going to happen," Vangie replied. "Whoever this person is who killed these girls, he could come after you for real this time." Tears streamed down her cheeks. "Please leave it alone, Lupe. I'm begging you. Let the police and the FBI handle this, okay?"

Lupe turned her gaze to the television and quickly realized Vangie wasn't going to back her on this. Fine. But she wasn't going to sit back and do nothing. Someone had to know more about her father's murder. The man who took her turned out to be a cop looking for revenge for his daughter's death. What made him think it was her father? He had to have been wrong about the shoe prints. Ma said Dad went back to Juarez to see his brother. If so, then maybe he has answers. If her mother wouldn't say more, then Lupe was left with no choice but to learn more on her own.

RED and blue lights flashed in the rearview mirror. "Son of a bitch. I'm only doing 5 miles over." He peered into the dimming sky ahead and noticed the approaching off-ramp. "God damn it." As the ramp neared, the police car's headlights flashed at him. "Yeah, I know, I know. I'm pulling over."

The tires on his red Hyundai Sonata rumbled as they hit the dirt shoulder and kicked up a light plume of dust. The particles floated in the early evening light. He rolled to a stop and kept his eyes trained on the rearview mirror. The patrol car stopped a few feet behind him, lights still spinning, and the officer stepped out. He walked around to the passenger side of the red Sonata and made a gesture to show that he wanted the window to be rolled down.

The man complied. "Hello, Officer. Can I ask why you pulled me over?"

The officer was tall, a solid 6 foot 1, maybe 6 foot 2, on the thinner side with a clean-shaven face and what looked like dark hair under his hat. "License and registration, please."

"Yes, sir." He dropped down the glovebox and retrieved the registration. "My license is in my wallet, sir. Can I reach for it in my back pocket?"

"Slowly," the officer replied.

With the license and papers ready, he handed them over. Several moments went by while the officer examined the information. "Is everything okay, Officer? Do I have something expired? I tend to let those things go now and again and it usually comes back to bite me in the butt."

"Step out of the car, sir, and walk over to me. Slowly." The officer stepped back and placed his hand on his weapon. He waited for the driver to step out and when he did, he continued. "Mr. Garza, do you know why I pulled you over?"

"No, sir. I'm completely stumped," he replied.

"Your license plate has a tinted cover on it. Those are illegal in the State of Texas."

"Oh, I see. You know, I only recently bought this car. I guess I didn't pay much attention to that. I'm real sorry and I'll remove it as soon as I get home."

"I'll let you off with a warning today, Mr. Garza. But you do need to get that off there." The officer handed back Garza's documents. "Get home safely, sir."

"Thank you, Officer."

THE SOMERSET POLICE STATION teemed with worried citizens. The local news had broken the story and now it seemed everyone had a tip to offer. Either that, or people were just plain scared and looking for answers.

The captain's cell phone rang in his pocket while he sat at his desk. "Captain Brown here."

"Captain, it's Kate Reid."

"Yes, ma'am. You folks make it back to the field office yet with Agent Romero?"

"Yes, sir. We just arrived. Listen, I know your officers have been looking out for Medina, so I wanted to let you know we reached out to the M.E.'s office to ask what they knew. Turns out, he showed up for work last night. We're hoping he'll show up tonight too, but his shift doesn't start until 11pm. They said to expect a call if he turns up and I have SAPD on standby if he does. They'll be the ones to bring him in."

"Sounds to me like we don't have much of a shot he'll show," Brown replied.

"It's the only shot we have right now. That said, where do we stand on the BOLO for Michael Garza's vehicle?"

"I sent a car out to his home, once again, with no luck. Oh, but I did get word back from his employer. They say he was taking vacation days, but didn't know where to. However, with all the hubbub here at the station with these reporters, I've had my hands full, and I haven't issued the BOLO yet. Let me get on that right now."

"Thank you, Captain. I'll touch base with you later this evening on our return."

"You got it. We'll speak again soon." Brown ended the call and pressed the intercom button on his landline.

"Yes, sir?"

"Hey, is Louisa still around?" Brown asked.

"I think she just got back. You want to see her?"

"Yes, please. Go ahead and send her to my office, would you?"

"Will do, Captain."

Brown put on his reading glasses and peered at his computer. A moment later, he heard steps approaching from the hall and glanced up. "Louisa, come on in."

"You wanted to see me, Captain?"

"It appears that our FBI friends are itching to find Michael Garza. He wasn't at home and his employer says he's out on vacation. They've asked us to issue a BOLO on his vehicle. Can you push that through for me?"

"Yes, sir. I'll do it right now. Regional, or statewide, sir?"

Brown appeared to consider the question. "Well, it's the FBI. They want to find him, so let's cast a wide net."

"I'll get on it now."

THE OFFICER's computer in his car alerted him to the incoming message from Dispatch. He pulled into a grocery store parking lot and peered at the screen. Computer aided dispatch sent out a wide variety of information to multiple law enforcement agencies all at once. This alert was for a Be on the Lookout, or BOLO.

He read on to see what the alert contained. "Red Hyundai Sonata." His face turned deadpan as he read the plate number.

"Damn it. You gotta be kidding me." He picked up the radio. "Dispatch, the BOLO just issued on the Hyundai?"

"Go ahead," the dispatcher replied.

"Damn it if I didn't pull over that car about an hour ago."

AGENT ROMERO HUSTLED down the hall, brushing by his colleagues without a word. Most of the agents in his office had gone home for the night, but when a case involved ten-plus victims, clocking out at the usual time wasn't going to happen. And now that he'd received the news, he had to get to the comms room where the BAU agents continued to work.

The door flew open, and Romero was slightly out of breath. "Someone saw his car."

Kate spun around. "What? Garza's car?"

"Yes, ma'am."

She stood from the table. "Who's got him in custody?"

Romero shook his head. "No one. An officer in Corpus Christi got the BOLO alert and called his dispatcher. Told them he'd pulled over that car an hour earlier."

"Jesus." Surrey pushed up from his chair. "What time would that have been?"

"Almost two hours ago now," Romero replied.

"And the officer was sure it was Garza?" Walsh asked.

"Damn sure. I have the coordinates. The officer said Garza was headed north." Romero looked at Kate. "What do you want to do?"

Kate walked to a map pinned on the wall that marked the locations of where the victims had lived. "He was spotted in Corpus Christi and was going north. Why would he have gone so far south? Had he planned on catching a boat?" She turned around.

"Have we checked the airports? Where's the nearest one to Corpus Christi?"

"There is a major airport there," Romero added. "You want me to flag his name?"

Kate looked at Fisher. "We don't have anything on this guy other than his association with Ceballos and Eduardo Cordova. And according to Brown, his employer said he was taking planned vacation days."

"He might be heading out of town, which, if he was in danger, could be the best thing for him," Fisher began. "Unless you subscribe to the theory that he's got a part in all this. Hell, for all we know, he decided to kill Ceballos and then head out for a vacation. Either way you slice it, he needs to be located."

Duncan stood from the table and approached Kate. "We don't know that he's heading for a flight. This is just a precaution."

"You're right." Kate turned to Fisher once again. "I think we should flag him."

He nodded. "Then let's do it. Romero, you want to make that happen?"

"I'm on it." Romero turned to leave once again.

Fisher checked the time. "I'd like to make one more run at the M.E to see if I can push him a little harder on Medina's swab as well as updating us on the remaining victims. I say let's get someone at DOT to search highway surveillance, and red-light cameras for the red Hyundai in that vicinity. Whoever we can still get hold of tonight, let's do that."

While Fisher stepped out to make the call, Kate turned back to the map.

"It hasn't changed since you put it up." Walsh moved in next to her and peered at it.

"I know. I keep thinking I'll see something. That's how this is supposed to work, right? I find the small stuff." She laughed. "That's what I do."

"Sure. Sure." Walsh folded his arms and nodded. "But I think we both know that it doesn't always work that way—for any of us."

"I'm not seeing something I should, Levi," Kate added. "Maybe Eduardo Cordova and his friends knew these unsubs we're after. Maybe they knew Medina. I mean, think about it. Guzman, came here in search of these friends, knowing Cordova was dead."

"He was convinced they had a hand in his daughter's murder," Walsh replied.

"Yeah, but maybe he wasn't seeing the whole picture and now that he's dead, we'll never know just how far down the rabbit hole he fell." She took in a deep breath. "I don't know why, but I just don't think Eduardo Cordova was the bad guy here."

"We'll know more when we find Garza and have a sit down with him. More importantly, it's Medina who we should be focused on. He needs to answer for his appearance at the last known spot our victim was seen. Son of a bitch better show up for work tonight. Both these men could be the ones we're after. Shit, right now, everyone's looking guilty as sin." Walsh studied her a moment. "You look worried about more than just the case. You talk to your husband yet today?"

"No. I doubt he's had a moment to think, let alone call anyone," she replied.

"I haven't even been watching the news to see if the trains are back up again. I'm sure he'll call when he can. He doesn't like it much when you're away. He worries."

Kate chuckled. "Which was part of the problem when he was our boss."

"I suppose so. Now you just got me." He patted her on the back. "But I don't worry about you, not one bit."

"You don't?" she asked.

"No, ma'am. I've seen you in action. You can take care of your-self just fine."

DARK SKIES RETURNED as Surrey sat behind the wheel while Kate was in the passenger seat. They were headed back to Somerset and back to the uncertainty and growing fear in the community.

Kate peered through the passenger window. "Brown said more reporters were there today."

"The storm's coming." Surrey glanced at her. "We did what we could today. We made some progress."

"Not enough." Her tone was hushed as she rested her arm on the door and lost herself in the darkness of the passing desert. She cracked the window to let in the cool breeze. "I think this evening was the first time that I've seen Fisher so decisive."

"I suppose you're right. It takes a while to get used to being a leader when you've never been one before. A little like you, I imagine."

She continued to peer through the window. "Sure. I'm the take-charge kind of gal. Everybody knows..." Her face turned blank, and she pulled back her shoulders.

"Reid? You okay?"

She shot him a look. "We have to go to the burial sites."

"What, now? Tonight?"

"Yes. I need to see something. I need to see if I'm right," she replied.

"Right about what? What's going on?"

"Surrey, please. Can we just go now?"

"Yeah, okay. We're almost back in town anyway. We'll hit the first site and go from there. Will you at least tell me what's happening here?"

"I don't know yet." She turned to him. "But I'll tell you when I do."

Minutes later, they arrived at the site found on Mr. Ortega's property. The excavation was complete. No more lights, but still police tape wrapped around sawhorses and Palo Verde trees surrounding the massive hole.

He stopped several feet away. "It's dark as hell out here. What do you think you're going to find?"

Kate pulled out her phone. "I'll just be a minute. You can stay here or come. I don't care." She opened the door and stepped out. The ground was hard from a lack of rain. Dust covered her shoes quickly as she aimed her phone at the ground.

"Reid, wait up." Surrey caught up to her. "Okay, are you gonna tell me what you're looking for or do I have to guess?"

When she reached the site, she stopped and turned around, aiming her phone's light back toward the road.

"What, do you see something?" Surrey narrowed his gaze and peered at the road alongside her.

"No. Just bear with me a second." She turned back and looked at the excavated grounds before deciding to walk around the area, slowly, with her phone light aimed down as though searching for something. A moment later, Kate jumped into the hole.

"What the hell are you doing?" Surrey stood at the top and peered down at her. "Get out of there. You don't know what got left behind. You could be contaminating the scene."

She ignored him and squatted low, using her phone to see. "Oh my God." Kate moved a few steps. "This is it. I thought I saw this before, at the other scene. At least the one."

"You mind telling me what that is?" he pressed on.

Kate looked up at him. "It's a pink rock. Painted pink. I saw this before. I know I did."

He shrugged. "Okay. It's a rock. What does it mean?"

Kate climbed back up, leaving the stone on the ground. "There may be others. I think they're leaving them around where the victims are buried. That one probably fell into the hole when they started excavating."

"Leaving what?" Surrey asked.

"A pink rock. It's a symbol. When I explored my theory about femicide, I did a lot of research. In many places, Juarez among them, pink crosses are left to memorialize the victims, but also to bring attention to femicide." She pointed to the rock again. "I need to see the other sites to be sure, but I think they're leaving a pink rock behind with the victims as a symbol, reminding us of what their goal is."

"Which is?" Surrey asked.

"That the only crime these women committed was that they were born women."

It was almost 11pm when Walsh spotted his colleagues walking into the lobby of the hotel. Sitting at the bar, he turned to Fisher and Duncan. "There they are."

Fisher peered over his shoulder. "Good. I was about to call the cops to go look for them."

"Something must've come up." Walsh raised his arm to garner their attention.

Kate started toward them with Surrey behind.

"Where the hell have you two been?" Fisher asked. "I thought you left shortly after we did."

Surrey thumbed in Kate's direction. "This one over here got a wild hair, so we had to make a few detours."

"A few?" Duncan asked. "Where did you go?"

Kate retrieved her phone and opened the pictures. She held it up. "We found these left in the burial sites."

"*She* found these." Surrey was quick to correct her.

Walsh leaned in for a better view and squinted at the image. "Is that a pink rock?"

"Yes. And we found multiple rocks left at all three sites," Kate added. "Some were partially buried. Some were in plain sight. All were missed or possibly dismissed by the San Antonio PD, and the field office."

"What does this mean, exactly?" Fisher asked.

"We are dealing with people who know about the epidemic of femicide. I think they're using it as cover. Depending on how we interpret this, they want to point us in opposite directions," Kate replied.

Duncan set down her glass of wine and turned around on her stool. "A diversion?"

"I think so," Kate continued. "Could be a way to get us to focus on the notion that this is nothing more than Mexican citizens coming here to do what they do in Juarez and many other places. Like you said, a diversion."

"An easy scapegoat," Fisher jumped in.

Kate pulled out a stool to sit down. "Scapegoats, or these people are followers of the belief that women are less than. A lot like what incels spout off online. Has anyone heard whether Garza's vehicle has been spotted?"

"Nothing yet," Duncan replied. "Now that you've discovered additional characteristics in the case, it could change the trajectory."

Surrey ordered a beer and took a sip before eyeing his colleagues. "I don't want to take our eyes off the ball, here. Reid makes a good point. Now is the time to reinforce our objectives. First thing we need to understand is how long this has been going on. We know it goes back at least five months. But the M.E. hasn't finished with all the autopsies yet. I heard he brought in a senior assistant with the Austin Medical Examiner's office to pitch in. Good news for us. And soon, we'll know whether Medina's going to turn up for work. We need something to break in our favor right now."

Fisher regarded Kate. "What do you think, Reid? These pink rocks have some significance, but how does this propel the investigation forward?"

It was an important find, but Kate didn't know how it would help. That part of the puzzle hadn't revealed itself to her yet. Sometimes, it was only pieces that showed up and then left it to her to fit together. However, in a moment of swift revelation, an idea sparked. "These pink rocks, they're painted florescent. We know for a fact that at least one of the victims had been in the ground for roughly five months. That's a long time for a typical household latex paint to last in that environment. Shifting temperatures. The clay in the soil shrinking and expanding with the weather. Most spray paints or acrylic hobby paints would've faded or chipped away."

"But these were a bright florescent pink," Surrey added. "Industrial?"

"Possibly. This is the kind of paint used to mark roadways, sidewalks. Infrastructure. Thermoplastic paints that last," Kate replied.

"A construction worker would have access to that kind of paint, right?" Surrey continued.

"Anyone who works in traffic, roads...construction, yes," she replied.

Fisher regarded her. "Can the general public buy this type of paint?"

"I can answer that," Walsh cut in. "It requires a special machine that mixes the ingredients. Heat is applied as well. I know because I've worked with it in the Army. Briefly, but yeah, it's pretty specialized. The average Joe wouldn't buy it. But someone who works for a city traffic department, or a road construction firm would conceivably have access to it and could tint the paint any color they wanted."

Kate cocked her head. "Or maybe someone who works on a construction site? Not unlike where one of the burial sites was located." Her phone rang and she retrieved it from her pocket. "It's the M.E." She answered the line. "Agent Reid here."

All eyes were on her as she listened to the caller. "Okay, thank you so much. I'll let them know. Good night."

Surrey appeared to note the look on her face. "He didn't show."

Kate cast down her gaze a moment and sighed. "He didn't show." She returned her sights to the team. "Well, if we weren't sure whether Xavier Medina played an important role, it's now safe to assume he does."

"Good night, Eva. I'll see you in the morning." Kate unlocked her hotel room door and checked the time on her phone. "Well, I'll see you in about 4 hours."

"Hey, we'll find him, Kate. Garza too," she replied.

"Yeah, I know. Eventually, we get our guys. How many they take down along the way is the only variable."

"Don't I know it." Duncan revealed a gentle grin and headed to her room next door.

Inside, Kate slipped off her shoes and set down her laptop bag. A part of her believed her assumptions about the mysterious pink rocks were too big a stretch. But it was something until they knew more about the victims or found the two people who seem to have simultaneously vanished.

D.C. was an hour behind, and she considered whether Nick might still be awake. It would be nice to talk to him after the day she'd had. When they'd worked together, they always discussed their cases and she'd taken it for granted. With her phone in hand, she made the call and smiled when he answered. "Hey."

"Hi." He unleashed a heavy sigh. "It's so good to hear your voice. You doing okay?"

"Fine. I just got back to my room. It's been a long day and we're slogging along, but I think we've found us a legitimate lead to follow."

"That's good news, babe."

"You sound tired. Did I wake you?" Kate slipped off her dress pants and pulled down the bed covers."

"No. I'm still at the office."

"What? It's 2 o'clock in the morning there," she replied.

"I know. I don't think anyone in Washington cares how late it is. They want this to end. The trains are still offline. Our team, Amtrak, DHS, NSA, CIA. Whatever acronym you can think of, we're all working this situation."

"And are you close?" she asked.

"Not close enough. We think we know where the group is located, and I can't say over the phone, but I'm sure you can guess."

"I'll bet I can." Kate turned on the television. "You don't sound good, hon."

"I'm okay. This has just been, well, it's not like anything I've experienced before. I have a lot of eyes on me. Important eyes. You know I don't do well with people looking over my shoulder."

"I know. I'm sorry about that. If it's any consolation, I miss you," she said.

"I miss you too. I did hear something about your case on the news tonight. Sounds like word is getting out. Is Fisher prepared for what's coming?"

"I think so," she began. "He's been different with this case. I think he finally gets that he's the one in charge and the buck stops with him."

"That's a good thing. I knew he had it in him. Maybe breaking it off with Duncan was the best thing for him."

Kate furrowed her brow. "Why would you say that?"

"Well, it was something hanging over his head. Something people could use against him, so he was cautious to a fault. That doesn't fly in that job. You know that. If you're afraid to take chances, you're not doing your job."

"I get it. Quinn used it against you and me, and it practically destroyed us," she replied.

"I think we both know it can change your perspective. But anyway, I'm glad to hear that he's adjusting and hopefully, there aren't a lot of hurt feelings going around," he said.

"Things do seem a little off, but they've both been professional about it. I just feel bad because I know Eva loves him."

"I'm sure he loves her too," Nick replied. "Listen, I want nothing more than to talk to you for the rest of the night, but I'd better go. I have a briefing in an hour, if you can believe that. We have to update the president every hour on the hour. Get some rest, Kate. I love you."

"I love you, too."

19

Louisa Espinoza was slumped low in the driver's seat of her personal car. She sat in the parking lot in front of Xavier Medina's apartment building and had been since Brown was informed the man hadn't shown up for work last night. Now, at almost 3 o'clock in the morning, he still hadn't returned home.

The FBI said he had been at the restaurant the day one of the victims disappeared. No one believed that was by accident. And especially not Louisa. The recent call she'd received also put Medina squarely in her sights. She was a good cop, and while her husband hadn't been happy about her staking out the apartment, he understood.

The sun would be up in a few hours, and she had no idea whether Medina would show. Going back empty-handed would make her feel like a failure, so Louisa had to press on.

A bag of chips lay open on the passenger seat, and she peered inside it. "A few left." She reached into the bag and retrieved a handful, plucking them into her mouth one at a time.

Landscape lights shone around the buildings and shrubbery in front of her. Her eyes were heavy, and she needed to pee like crazy. It was time to go back behind the bush she visited earlier.

Louisa stepped out of her 2018 white Honda CRV and walked toward the large pink oleander that would shield her from view. Unbuckling her uniform pants was a pain in the ass, but she pulled them down and squatted. "So much better." Finished with her business, she pulled up her pants again and started to button them when she heard a noise behind her.

A meaty hand slammed down over her mouth. Louisa's eyes widened as she quickly patted at her waist, but her gun was inside the car, still in its holster that she'd taken off because it was uncomfortable. She moaned and dug her nails in his hand, trying to pry it from her mouth.

He used his free hand to slap down her arm and yanked it behind her back. "You shouldn't be here."

Louisa tried to cry out again, but the sound was muffled. She twisted to free herself and felt the point of a knife dig into her ribcage.

"Don't move and keep your mouth shut."

The sting of the blade's tip piercing her skin came first. Her muscles clenched around it as he pushed it in and thick, warm blood trickled down, soaking her shirt. Louisa moaned again as the knife went in deeper. Her knees grew weak, and her vision blurred. She couldn't see her attacker, but it didn't matter. Staying alive was what mattered.

Her body spasmed as he withdrew the knife and plunged it in again. And again. And again. She finally fell limp.

∾

THE LIGHT from Kate's phone illuminated the darkened hotel room with an incoming call. She stirred a little and with blurry eyes, checked the time. "4:30." On answering the call, she began, "Yeah, this is Reid." Her brow knitted as she slowly sat up in bed. "Wait, hang on. You found what?" She turned on the bedside lamp and the bright light stung for a moment. "Are you at the office? Okay. And you haven't been able to confirm with the employer yet? No, I realize the time. So we need to get confirmation and you have the DOT video you can send me. Good. Hey, this is great work, Romero. I'll round up the crew and we'll head down there ASAP. See you soon."

With a deep yawn, she got to her feet and picked up her phone. "Hey, sorry to wake you."

Surrey cleared the frog from his throat. "I was getting up soon anyway. What's up?"

"I just got off the phone with Romero. He's in the office and did a follow up on Michael Garza. DOT cameras picked up his red Hyundai Sonata on Route 290, headed northwest. Local PD picked him up."

Surrey snapped to attention. "They have him in custody? Where?"

"In a town called Dripping Springs, about 100 miles north of San Antonio and close to Austin. Romero's in communications with Captain Brown as well as the local PD that has Garza."

"We need to get up there now," Surrey added.

"There's one more thing. After we went back to our rooms last night, I sent Romero an updated profile that reflected what we discussed."

"You mean about the unsub potentially working at the construction site?" he asked.

"Yes. He got back with me on that too. Guess where Michael

Garza works?" Kate didn't give him an opportunity to reply. "Signal Butte Paving."

"A place that would likely have an ample supply of thermoplastic paint."

Kate nodded. "You got it. So if we learn that his company has a contract with the housing developer, we might want to change our approach with him. I'll let the others know and let's plan on meeting in the lobby in say, 30 minutes?"

"I'll be there. Hey, what about Medina?" Surrey asked.

"No word on his whereabouts yet. I'll see you downstairs."

The housing development where one of the burial grounds was discovered had been shut down since that time. And to learn that Michael Garza worked for a paving contractor appeared to be a sizable piece of the puzzle. Whether he was the killer or whether he had acted alone was a bigger piece still missing.

Kate quickly readied herself and arrived at the lobby to find Walsh alone. "Levi, good morning. Where is everyone else?"

"I'm here." Surrey approached them wearing a fitted grey button-down and black tailored pants. He held a cup of coffee. "Decent continental spread back there if anyone's hungry."

"I might grab a cup." She glanced at Walsh. "Want one?"

"Yeah, thanks. Two sugars..."

"Extra cream. I remember." Kate walked toward the buffet restaurant and reached the elevators when the doors parted. "There you are."

Fisher appeared somewhat flustered and cleared his throat. "Good morning. Is everyone else down here?"

Duncan stepped out and avoided direct eye-contact with Kate, offering only a slight nod as she headed toward the lobby.

"They're over there. I'm just grabbing a coffee for Levi and me. I'll see you in a minute." Kate didn't want to make the awkward situation worse, so she continued, though it was clear what she'd just seen. "None of my business," she whispered.

After filling the paper cups with steaming coffee, Kate returned to the team and handed a cup to Walsh.

"Thank you. I needed this." He took a sip.

"Romero's waiting on us," Kate began. "We'll head to the field office. He's coordinating the effort to bring Garza back and talk to him. It'll be a little while for them to make the drive back here." Her phone rang in her pocket. "Hang on." Kate answered. "Captain Brown. I was going to wait a little bit to give you a call since it's still so early..." She drew in her brow. "What? When? Oh God. I'm so sorry. What can we do? Uh, we were just headed to the field office. I got a call from Agent Romero. They found Michael Garza, so we were going to talk to him." She glanced at the team. "Yes, of course. We can split up. I'll let them know. Thank you, Captain." Kate ended the call and lowered her head. "Louisa Espinoza was found murdered at Xavier Medina's apartment complex about half an hour ago." Her eyes reddened. "She was stabbed to death and left behind a row of bushes."

"What was she doing there?" Surrey asked.

"According to Brown, she had been staking out his apartment all night in her own car. She knew we were looking for him and wanted to bring him in." Kate's voice faltered. "He asked if we could come down and help investigate the scene."

"You and Surrey go talk to Garza," Fisher began. "The rest of us will figure out what the hell's going on with Medina and help the captain in any way we can. First Guzman was murdered, then Ceballos, and now Espinoza. I sure as shit don't like this trend."

"And that doesn't include the 10 buried bodies," Walsh added. "If we don't get a handle on what's happening around here, we're gonna find ourselves in a shitstorm."

THE SKIES WERE overcast as the morning wore on. Kate and Surrey arrived at the field office to meet with Romero and learn just how Michael Garza was tied to this case. The news of Espinoza's death rattled Kate. What was worse was that no one knew where Xavier Medina was, making him the obvious suspect. But the obvious wasn't always the right answer.

As they stepped out of the car, Surrey regarded her. "Are you okay?"

She kept her eyes ahead and reached the entrance. "Not really. A good cop is dead. She shouldn't have been there on her own but was too young and naïve to know any better."

"I don't know whether it was Medina, or the people out there killing these women, but it's starting to look like they could be working together." Surrey opened the door. "We should keep that in the back of our minds as we speak to Michael Garza."

They continued inside and Kate noticed Romero waiting in the lobby. "Do you ever sleep?"

"Only after I've caught the bad guys. No, I can't take all the credit. I had help." He shook her hand and regarded her with concern. "What's going on? Did I miss something?"

Surrey stepped up. "Somerset Police Officer Louisa Espinoza was murdered early this morning. She'd been staking out Xavier Medina's apartment."

"Ah, hell." Romero looked away for a moment. "Was it Medina?"

"We don't know. He hasn't been located," Kate replied. "In regard to Garza, we should consider the idea he could be involved in the deaths of Ceballos, and now Espinoza. The guy's been out of pocket long enough that it raises the hair on my neck. You learned he worked at the paving company. His connection to at least one of the burial sites is there. Not to mention the pink rocks. It's a good lead. The best we have right now."

"Garza's just been brought in. Let's see what he has to say for himself." Romero headed toward the holding room and opened the door.

Michael Garza, the 45-year-old native of Somerset, Texas, sat in the interview room and saw the agents enter. Thick-set with broad shoulders and a weathered face, he looked much older. "It sure would be nice to know why the hell I'm here and not on my vacation, like I had planned."

Romero walked inside and sat down. "Like my agents told you before, Mr. Garza, there was an alert out on you and your vehicle. You have not been charged with anything and you have the right to contact an attorney."

"What did I do? I was just on a trip to visit my mother near Austin. What the hell's going on here?" Garza asked. "Who are you people?"

"I'm FBI Agent Victor Romero. These good people here are Agents Kate Reid and Jonathan Surrey. They've come to the great state of Texas all the way from D.C. and we're all here to talk to you about what's been happening down in Somerset. Your hometown."

"About those bodies? Yeah, I heard about that. What's it got to do with me?" Garza asked.

Kate pulled out a chair to sit. "Mr. Garza, did you know a man named Eduardo Cordova?"

"Yes. He was a friend of mine, till he died a few years' back. Why?"

"And Richard Ceballos?" she continued.

Garza shrugged. "Yeah, I know him. I guess you could say we was friends." He regarded the agents. "I still don't know what this has to do with me."

"Were you aware that Mr. Ceballos was found murdered yesterday?" Surrey asked.

Garza turned stone-faced as he pushed back his shoulders. "What? He was murdered?"

"Yes, sir. Found face up on his bed, shot dead in his own home," Romero added. "You don't know anything about that?"

"No, sir. Why the hell would I? I knew Rich, but shit...I ain't seen him in maybe a year or more."

Kate peered at him. "What about a man named Xavier Medina? You know him?"

"Listen, no disrespect, lady, but should I just give you a list of people I do know? Because I sure as shit don't get why you're asking me all this. And no, I got no idea who Xavier Medina is." He leaned in. "Should I?"

"We're just asking questions, Mr. Garza," Surrey cut in. "I understand you work for a paving contractor that's doing a job over at the new housing development on the outskirts of Somerset."

"Yeah, so? It's a job, isn't it?" Garza replied.

"You heard that bodies were found in the community park being built, right?" Kate pressed on. "I mean, you worked on the site, and it's been shut down. You must've known why."

Garza grew frustrated. "Look here, I still don't know why you people are questioning me. Yeah, I know all about the murders. I got a television. But if you think I got something to do with them, you're mistaken. I didn't know Rich was dead, okay? And I'm damn sorry to hear it. And I don't know any Xavier Medina, all right? So what the hell you want from me?"

Kate got to her feet. "Would you excuse us for a moment, Mr. Garza?" She eyed Surrey and Romero and started back into the hall. When they followed and the door shut, she looked at them. "Either he's a damn good liar, or he really doesn't know about any of this."

"He's lying. Has to be," Surrey replied. "We know he and Cordova and Ceballos were friends."

"He did say he knew the men," Romero cut in. "And didn't you say, Reid, that Lupe Cordova had only seen those men at her dad's funeral and not since? Maybe he's telling the truth. Maybe we just hit another dead end. It happens."

Kate wore disbelief. "Then I was wrong about all of it. The rocks—everything. We're no closer now than we were before. If Garza had no recent association with Ceballos, then the man was killed either at random, or he had someone after him."

"But who would come after him if it wasn't the Juarez cop?" Surrey asked.

"I don't know, but we have nothing to hold Garza on. The fact he works for the paving contractor at that housing development isn't nearly enough." Kate considered a new plan. "Our next step should be to get a statement from him as to his whereabouts over the past 48 hours. See if he has a legitimate alibi. That could potentially rule out involvement in Espinoza's murder as well as Ceballos. Then, we go for broke and ask him for a DNA swab. We'll have two to compare to whatever's been found on the victims."

Romero scoffed. "After this, you think he'll volunteer for a swab? That's a stretch."

She peered at the door. "Let me go in by myself for a moment, would you?"

"Have at it," Romero replied.

"Might as well see if you can get anything from him," Surrey added.

Kate returned to the interview room. "Mr. Garza, do you want anything to drink?"

"I'm fine. I'd like to get the hell out of here and be on my way is what I'd like."

She sat down again. "You work for a paving company, is that right?"

"You know I do," he replied.

"Do you do the striping and things like that or work in the office?"

"I'm on the jobsites, mostly. Been with that outfit going on five years. What's my job got to do with anything, Agent Reid?"

"Mr. Garza, I understand your hesitancy to talk to us." She pulled out one of the rocks from the pocket of her sweater and set it on the table.

He glanced at it. "Am I supposed to say something about this?"

"You said you were friends with Eduardo Cordova. You went to his funeral?"

"Course I did. We was friends."

Kate nodded. "Did you know that Mr. Cordova had visited his brother in Juarez on occasion some years ago?"

"I knew that. Yes, I did."

She held his gaze. "What's happening in Somerset. It's happened before and continues to happen in other places, like Juarez. Do you know what I'm referring to?"

Garza swallowed hard. "The murders of all them women and girls. Yeah, I know. It's a tragedy is what it is."

"I agree with you," Kate began. "And it's come as an unwelcome surprise that it could be happening in Somerset—your community."

Garza scratched at his stubbled chin. "Yes, ma'am."

"Do you have a daughter, Mr. Garza?"

"No, I don't have any kids," he replied.

Kate needed to find a way to get through to him. She was no Sherlock Holmes, but her hunches were usually on target. "Eduardo made a good life for him and his family in Somerset before he was murdered. In fact, it's still an open investigation."

Garza placed his hand on his chest. "You think it was me? You think I killed my friend?"

"Honestly, I don't know what to think right now." Kate leaned back in the chair and pushed forward the stone. "Mr. Garza, that rock right there? I found pink rocks all over the mass graves we've uncovered so far. It's a lot like the pink crosses you see all over Juarez memorializing the deaths of a lot of women."

Garza remained stone-faced and locked eyes with Kate.

"That paint is pretty durable, wouldn't you say? Seems like the kind you'd find in a construction setting. I'm starting to think you know a lot more about what's been happening in Somerset, but maybe you're afraid you'll end up like your friends."

He looked away from her.

She noticed a tiny crack appear in his harsh mien. "I think you know at least part of what's going on. And I think it's time you tell us what that is."

20

Outside the Somerset Police Station, news vans, cameras, and reporters gathered. The national story had broken. Social media feeds were filled with photos of the burial sites, though the police had kept onlookers at a distance. Now, the head of the BAU team, Cameron Fisher, had no choice but to cap off the constant drip of information.

Inside the captain's office, Fisher pulled back from the window. "We're going to have to say something to them soon."

Brown was slumped in a side chair with his gaze turned away. The news of Espinoza's death left him numb. "Say whatever the hell you want to say to them, Agent Fisher. I just want to find Xavier Medina."

Duncan approached him and sat down. "I know how you're feeling right now, Captain. Our profilers are talking to Michael Garza now. Reid can get to him. I know she can."

"And what if he knows nothing?" Brown shot back. "What the hell was Louisa doing there alone?"

Walsh appeared in the doorway. "Excuse me?"

"Come in," Fisher replied. "Do we have anything new from the M.E.'s office?"

"He hasn't reached out yet. I came here to say that I just got off the phone with Reid. She thinks she's close to getting something from Garza."

"Something? Like what?" Fisher regarded him. "We need more than just something."

"She went in alone with Garza to press him about his connection to the construction site and his job. A moment ago, she stepped out to update Agents Romero and Surrey on her progress. It's looking like he knows something, but Reid says she needs a little more time with him."

"So, y'all have nothing, is that what I'm hearing?" Brown asked.

Walsh turned to him. "I'm saying Reid is on the verge of a breakthrough and we need to give her time to make it happen."

Brown pointed to the window. "And what about those vultures out there, huh? Should I tell them we almost have something that might be relevant to something else? How do you think that'll fly, Agent Walsh?"

"Captain, I know you're upset about..."

"Upset, Agent Duncan? You think I'm upset that one of my officers was murdered in the early hours of this morning? You think I'm upset that I have the San Antonio FBI, and the Quantico FBI assisting me and yet one of my own was still murdered and I'm no closer to finding whoever killed at least ten women in my city?" He pushed off the chair and marched toward the door. "God damn you."

When he left the room, Walsh stepped toward her. "Cut him some slack. He just lost one of his officers."

"Yeah, I know." Duncan held his gaze. "In order to tie Espinoza's murder to our investigation, we need to learn whether the same type of knife was used on her as with the other victims. And as it happened in front of Medina's apartment, it stands to reason he's our suspect. Let's not forget where he was when Marissa Padilla disappeared. All signs are pointing to Xavier Medina right now."

"Espinoza's body has been taken to San Antonio," Fisher began. "We'll inform Dr. Bauer of what we need ASAP. And I want everyone in the entire state out looking for Xavier Medina. Son of a bitch can't hide forever." He peered through the window again at the reporters. "Walsh, get on the phone with Reid again. Tell her to get something we can use from Garza and if not, cut the son of a bitch loose. I'm done wasting time."

KATE STOOD outside the interview room with Surrey and Romero. "I should go back in. He's been stewing long enough."

"You don't want help?" Surrey asked.

"Not yet. Just give me a little more time." Kate reached for the door and looked back at the agents. "Are we good?"

Romero raised his hands. "All good, Reid. I hope you're right about this."

"I'm right." Kate opened the door. "How are you holding up, Michael?" The door closed behind her and she returned to her seat at the table. "You have an opportunity to make this right."

"You have no idea, do you?" He scoffed.

Kate leaned back against the chair and folded her arms. "Then explain it to me. What do you know about what's been happening in Somerset? I should tell you that you are a suspect in this investigation. The only suspect. So if you have a chance to shed some light, I'd suggest you do that."

He swallowed hard and raised his gaze to her. "Okay, fine.

You're right about the pink rocks, but I didn't put them there. Trust me, if I'd known where the victims had been buried, I would've gone to the police. I'm not a monster, but there are monsters all around."

"Who?" Kate pressed on. "And why are they leaving the stones? What point are they trying to make?"

"Point? There is no point to any of this." Garza appeared to consider his words carefully. "What I can tell you is that whatever you think is happening has nothing to do with Juarez."

"What do you mean?" she asked.

"After Ed was murdered, me and Rich, well, we figured it was because we got nosy—Ed got nosy. I have no proof of this, but we were pretty sure he was killed as a means to stop him from getting too close to learning who these folks were. After that, we got scared. Me and Rich didn't talk much after Ed's funeral."

"Who are they, Michael?" Kate asked. "Who's leaving these rocks? Is there more than one person out there doing this? Is Xavier Medina involved?"

Garza pounded on the table in frustration. "I don't know! I don't know, okay? All's I can tell you is that there's a guy. A guy from back when me and Ed and Rich were hanging around. I thought he up and took off, but then about six months ago, he shows his face again."

Kate fixed her gaze on him, waiting for him to continue.

"We all worked in construction, me, Ed, and Rich. Knew a lot of the same folks. This guy worked in the business too."

"What guy? You've had suspicions about a man for what, two years and never said anything?" Kate asked.

"Look, you want answers or not? I don't care what you believe. All I can tell you is what I know. He worked for Signal Butte Paving up until a couple months ago," Garza said.

"Same place you work. Okay. What happened then?"

Garza folded his arms over his chest. "He got fired for coming in after hours and using equipment."

"Using equipment?" she asked.

"After hours, and shit. Yeah. He messed up one of the machines that heats up the paint we use for roads, that was why he was fired. So when you talk about the pink stones, I remembered seeing one or two of them in the shop where the paint was kept. Like he dropped them or something. I didn't think much of it then."

"Who is he, Michael? I need a name," Kate demanded.

Garza licked his lips and averted his gaze. "Guy Jacobs."

Kate did it. She got a name. "Okay. So, before we go any further, Michael, I'm going to need you to give me a timeline of where you've been over the past 48 hours. I said you were a suspect. That doesn't change until I can verify your whereabouts. And, I need to know where he is. Where can I find Guy Jacobs?"

WHY LUPE's family hadn't understood what she had gone through was perplexing. Even Vangie hadn't wanted anything but for Lupe to close the book and move on. That wasn't who she was. She was her father's daughter and she had been taken by a man for reasons she couldn't understand. But now was the time to find out.

Outside in the afternoon sun, she stepped into her car and pulled out of the parking spot in front of her apartment unit. As far as she'd known, the federal agents had visited her father's shut-tered workshop only once and hadn't found anything left behind by her now deceased abductor.

The building was owned by the bank and no one else had an interest in it, so it sat rotting and in various stages of disrepair. But her family had never gone to clear it out. Her mother hadn't wanted anything to do with it after the murder. Vangie had been too young.

The building sat at the end of the old airstrip where small warehouses and machine shops were housed. She parked in front of the building and stepped out. The sign on the door still read, "Cordova Custom Cabinets."

The windows were boarded, but Lupe came prepared. With the crowbar lodged between the sill and the board, she pried loose the nails and one of the boards fell inside. Lupe climbed in.

The Juarez cop who took her had done the same thing, but the bank had sent someone to repair it. They hadn't done a good job. She climbed over the sill and stumbled inside. The concrete floor was cold and as she pushed off the ground, her mind flashed back to that night. Lupe swallowed down the lingering fear and stood again to peer into the abandoned space. The former cop had insisted her father had been involved in something horrific. She had to know the truth.

Lupe wandered inside with a rising pulse. Anxiety filled her bones and for a moment, her stomach turned with nausea. "Calm down. You can do this. You have to do this." She pulled back her hair and wrapped an elastic band around the thick ponytail. "Just walk into his office."

If there was anything to be kept, it would've been found in the office. The loss of her father had been devastating and none of them handled his affairs, though in hindsight, Lupe knew that as the eldest daughter, the duty should have fallen on her.

Within the cold space, she walked to the rear of the building and to the office. Inside was an old desk, a printer covered in dust, and two filing cabinets on the front wall. Two years had gone by and who knew what she would find, if anything.

Lupe opened the top cabinet and sifted through the files. Mostly just customers or suppliers. A few utility bills. She opened the next drawer and found kitchen design prints. "Damn it. None of this means anything." She slammed it shut and turned around to survey the desk. Nothing lay on top of it except a thick layer of dust. "Who were you, Dad? What did you do?"

She walked around the desk and opened the pencil drawer. Two pens, a sticky note pad, and a black plastic organizer were inside. Angry, she yanked out the drawer and spilled its contents onto the top of the desk. "What did you do!" she yelled.

Her eyes were drawn to something taped to the bottom of the plastic organizer. Lupe gazed at it. "A key." She peeled off the painter's tape that secured the small key to the back of the organizer. It looked like a key to a file cabinet, maybe a post office box. She surveyed the office. The file cabinets didn't lock, so it wasn't that. Lupe stepped back into the main floor area where some equipment remained. Nothing appeared to require a key. "What is this for?" She examined it again, and as she gazed at it, the memory resurfaced. "Oh my God. I know what this is for."

Kate rushed out of the interview room and hustled to find her colleagues. They waited for her inside Romero's office and she soon arrived. "Guy Jacobs."

Surrey bolted upright in the chair. "That's our unsub?"

"At least one of them. That's what Garza claims. He says he worked with him at the paving company for a while until he got fired for damaging equipment used to paint the roads. Garza says after Jacobs was fired, he found pink rocks where the man had been and didn't think anything of it until..."

"Until you told him," Surrey cut in. "Where's Jacobs now and how do we find him?"

"Garza didn't know where he was, so we'll have to dig up

whatever we can to find him," Kate replied. "And we'll need to verify his alibis. He says he's been traveling to see his mother and when I asked him about Corpus Christi, he claimed he made a stop off to see an old friend."

"How wonderfully vague. Do we know where that friend is?" Surrey asked.

"Conveniently, the friend was moving out of state and that was the reason for his visit," Kate replied.

"Christ, you know how long it's going to take to verify his alibis?" Surrey asked.

"Days, I imagine," Kate replied.

Romero grabbed his laptop. "I'll run a background now on Jacobs and see what pops."

While Surrey peered over Romero's shoulder, he looked at Kate. "When was Jacobs let go from the paving company?"

"A couple of months ago. Garza hadn't seen or heard from him since." Kate glanced up a moment.

"What? What are you thinking?" Surrey pressed on.

"I'm just thinking about the stones found at all the burial sites. The multiple knives used."

"You're pretty certain we've got more than one unsub out there."

She nodded. "I still believe that. Now, more so than before. What Garza said about Cordova. He said he was killed because he was getting too close to the truth. And this was two years ago."

"We don't know how long some of those bodies have been in the ground, or whether there are more sites," Romero cut in. "Two years seems feasible."

"Right," Kate replied. "But I still don't see a connection to Juarez, which is throwing me off. I mean, the cop, sure, but what else?"

"Medina, who we still can't find," Surrey replied.

"Okay. So we have burial sites with multiple bodies being dumped in them. Multiple killers, who seem to know where to go with their victims." She hesitated a moment and considered an idea. "They're marked."

"What's marked?" Surrey pressed on.

"The burial sites. The rocks are being used to mark the locations. How did I not see that before? I thought they were being used to symbolize something, to make a point, but Garza said there was no point to any of this." She looked at Romero. "Anything show up for Jacobs yet?"

"I'm searching the state-wide database. It'll take a minute." He continued to key in commands.

Surrey turned back to Kate. "I hate to even mention this, but are we going to keep Garza in custody? That'd be a hard sell unless his alibis don't track, which, like I said, will take days."

She glanced at Romero. "This is still your case. What do you think?"

Romero sat back in the chair. "I think you did what you could, Reid. We got no legs to stand on with Garza for the moment. Let's put our focus on Guy Jacobs."

"Okay." Kate scrambled to think of a reason to keep Garza, but there was nothing they could do. Romero was right. "We'll do our best to keep tabs on him, but I guess we have to let him go."

21

The key Lupe recovered had been from a toolbox sold to her father's friend, Richard Ceballos, days before the funeral. She hadn't thought much of it at the time and made him aware she hadn't had the key. He wanted the toolbox anyway. Maybe this was why her suspicions were now raised. Who wanted a toolbox they couldn't get into? And a hidden key wasn't hidden without a reason.

She climbed through the same window of the cabinet shop and laid the plywood over top of it again. Upon returning to her car, she made the call to the one person who would know how to get in touch with Rich Ceballos as she'd long ago lost his contact details.

"Agent Reid here."

"Um, hello, Agent Reid, this is Lupe Cordova."

"Lupe, is everything okay?" Kate asked.

"Yes, everything's fine, but I have to ask you something. I was wondering if you found Rich Ceballos. I needed to ask him about something of my dad's that I sold to him years ago."

"Lupe, I'm so sorry. I haven't had a chance to tell you..."

"Tell me what?"

"Richard Ceballos is dead," Kate replied.

"What? I don't understand. I thought the man who took me was killed and that, well, he didn't have a chance to find the men I told him about."

"We're working to learn who killed him, Lupe. I wish I had more details for you, but I don't. A lot of things are happening right now. Has Captain Brown spoken to you at all?"

"No, ma'am." Lupe noticed the line was quiet for a moment. "Agent Reid?"

"Yes, you said you sold something to Mr. Ceballos?"

"Yeah, I found a key and I know it goes to a toolbox I sold to him after my dad died. The key was inside my dad's old office taped to the back of an organizer in his pencil drawer."

"You went back to your dad's workshop?" Kate asked. "Why?"

"I just—something isn't right, Agent Reid. What that man said about my dad and then he gets killed. And all these girls getting killed." Her voice fractured. "My dad wasn't a bad man. I swear it."

"I don't doubt you, Lupe. This toolbox, what do you think is inside?"

"I wish I knew. Maybe nothing, but then why hide the key?" Lupe sighed. "I feel like this means something. But with Rich dead too, I'm scared now, more than ever. What's happening, Agent Reid? So many people are dead."

"I know you're afraid and I would do anything to assuage those fears." Kate paused a moment. "Maybe there is something I can do. I can help you track down this toolbox, first and foremost. If Ceballos still owned it, it'll either be in his home or in his car. And if I'm not mistaken, his car is at the SAPD right now getting swept for evidence. Secondly, do you have family outside of town where the three of you can stay for a while?"

"I have a cousin in Austin," she replied.

"Good. Here's what I want you to do. Meet me at the SAPD in say, an hour. Get your family packed and drive to Austin after that."

"But my job..."

"I understand, but this is the way it has to be for a little while, Lupe. I'll do what I can to make sure you don't lose that job, but this is what needs to happen."

Lupe peered through her windshield at her father's shop. "Agent Reid, is there something you're not telling me?" The line went quiet again. "Something else happened, didn't it?"

"I shouldn't be the one to tell you this, but you deserve to know..."

"What?" Lupe's eyes filled with tears. "What's going on, Agent Reid?"

"It's Officer Espinoza. Oh, God, Lupe, I'm so sorry, but..."

"No." Lupe sobbed. "No, she's not dead. She's not! What happened to her? Was it the same people who killed the other women?"

"I don't know yet. She was doing her job. She was trying to protect the people in her community."

Lupe wailed as tears streamed down her cheeks. "What do I do? What am I supposed to do?"

"Take a breath. Just breathe, okay? I'm going to need you to be strong for me right now. You want to learn whether this toolbox means anything, then I need you to meet me at the SAPD station in an hour. Can you do that, Lupe?"

She choked back her tears. "Yes. Yes, I can."

"Okay. But I need you to calm yourself first. Don't drive like this. Please tell me you won't."

"I won't." She wiped away the tears. "I'll see you in an hour." Lupe ended the call.

Surrey was next to Kate and noticed her staring at her phone. "You want to tell me what that was all about?"

Kate released a deep sigh. "Lupe Cordova. Damn it. I shouldn't have told her something like that over the phone. Two people she knew, one she was friends with, and I told her they were dead."

"It didn't sound like you had much of a choice," Surrey replied. "You were talking about a key or something?"

"She'd gone back to her dad's workshop and found a key to a toolbox. Turned out, she'd sold that toolbox to Rich Ceballos and wanted to know how to get in touch with him to give him the key."

"Why the hell did she go back there?" Surrey pressed on.

Romero glanced up from his laptop. "We didn't find anything left behind. That Juarez cop knew what he was doing."

Kate turned to him. "I don't think she was looking for what he might've left. I think she was looking for answers about her dad. Lupe's sure there's something important inside this toolbox."

"And Ceballos is dead," Surrey replied.

"Just our luck. Look, this could be nothing, but while Romero's tracking down Guy Jacobs, I'd like to do more than sit on our thumbs. Garza's free to go, pending confirmation of his alibis."

"You tell Brown about that?" Romero asked.

"I'll do it now and send him Garza's statement. His guys can knock on doors and verify quicker than we can," Kate replied.

"The Somerset and San Antonio police forces are looking for Xavier Medina," Surrey began. "So, if there's a mysterious toolbox that Ceballos had and it came from Eduardo Cordova, what the hell can it hurt to check it out?"

"I'm glad you agree because I told Lupe we'd meet her at SAPD in an hour," Kate replied. "We should head there now."

∽

THE BAU AGENTS returned to the SAPD where they held Ceballos's vehicle. The CSI team was on loan to Somerset for the time being while the two police forces worked together to end this investigation.

"Afternoon. I'm Sergeant Grady." The CSI investigator offered his hand.

"Nice to meet you. Agent Reid. This is my partner, Agent Surrey. We're here at the request of the San Antonio FBI field office. Thank you for letting us come and take a look at what you've got. We're waiting on Lupe Cordova to meet us here. She has a key to something I'm hoping is inside Richard Ceballos's SUV. I understand it's here."

"Yes, ma'am. Come on back. I'll let you have a look."

Kate followed him and waved Surrey on. "Have you found anything interesting yet?"

"It only arrived late yesterday. We're in the process of checking for fibers, prints, blood. Anything that might point to his killer or if he'd been involved in another crime."

Kate nodded. "Any chance I could stick my head in the car a minute? I won't touch anything."

He peered at her with concern. "Are you looking for something specific?"

"Actually, yes. I'm looking for a toolbox. Have you come across one?"

He eyed her as though she'd made an odd request until he raised the corner of his mouth into a half-grin. "Funny you should ask. We did find one. It was taken out of the back behind the third-row seat and we put it over here." Grady walked toward it. "This what you're looking for?"

A toolbox that was slightly larger than a fisherman's tackle box rested along the back wall with a tag on it. "I hope so." Kate crouched low to examine it. "Have you opened it?"

"No, ma'am. It's locked and we haven't gotten around to trying to get into it. You have a key?" Grady asked.

"Not yet, but I might very soon." Kate stood again. "In fact, that's why we're waiting on Lupe Cordova. She should be out front by now. You mind if I run up there and collect her? Then if you're good with it, we'd like to see if the key she has will open it."

"I don't have a problem with that. Do what you gotta do, Agent Reid. If you don't mind, I'd better get back to the car."

"Of course. Thank you, Sergeant." She turned to Surrey. "You want to check out the SUV while I run out front?"

He nodded. "Can do."

Kate returned inside and noticed Walsh approach. "Hey. I wasn't expecting to see you here. I'm waiting on Lupe Cordova and was headed up front to get her."

"I came because the captain and I found some interesting information regarding Eduardo Cordova's brother. I figured you and Surrey needed to know about it ASAP."

Kate studied him a moment. "Let me guess, this isn't good news."

"That depends on how you want to look at it. We know Cordova used to visit his brother in Juarez and Brown learned from his friend over the border that this brother left there a few years ago," Walsh replied.

"Any idea where he went?" Kate asked as Surrey approached.

"Walsh, what are you doing here? What's going on? Is Lupe here yet?" Surrey asked.

"Still waiting. Walsh was about to tell us more about Cordova's brother." Kate turned back to him.

"As I was saying, he did leave Juarez, but he has been picked up on radar recently," Walsh added.

"Okay. Where is he?" she asked.

"He's here, Kate."

She leaned closer as if she'd misheard him. "Here?"

Walsh eyed his colleagues. "As in, here in Somerset. His prints turned up in the US and Mexican passport databases."

"Both of them? Is he a dual citizen?" she asked.

"Not exactly. His prints turned up in the Mexican crimes database because he'd served time in Juarez. Brown's contact over there cross-referenced those prints with the passport database and he got a match to a Mexican national named Alejandro Cordova. But that's not all. The official also got a hit on a visa that had been issued with prints matching Alejandro Cordova's, but they were listed under a different name."

"A different name?" Kate asked.

"That name was Xavier Medina. The official reached out to the captain to make us aware and that's when we found Medina's US passport that had been issued some years later." Walsh held Kate's gaze. "Alejandro Cordova changed his name and somehow got a very legitimate-looking US Passport. It would've cost him thousands. That passport is under the name Xavier Medina."

Kate's lips parted and her brows raised. "You're telling me Medina is the brother of Eduardo Cordova?"

"Yes, ma'am, and his real name is Alejandro Cordova. He was telling us the truth when he owned up to serving time in Juarez. But he failed to mention that he'd already changed his identity and had been traveling back and forth to Mexico under a falsified US passport. When he was sent to jail for assaulting that woman, he used his US identity, assuming it would likely help him get out of jail. It didn't," Walsh replied. "So when he was released, he came here to Somerset. It would've been around the time Eduardo Cordova was murdered."

"It was him," Kate began. "He killed his brother. It had to be him. Eduardo must've figured out what his brother had done to that woman in Juarez, and it got him killed."

"My guess is, Eduardo figured out more than just that. I'm thinking he learned that his brother was doing a whole lot of bad things in Somerset," Walsh continued. "And that was probably the reason the retired cop came here looking for Eduardo's friends. Something led him to believe that a Cordova had been responsible for his daughter's death, only..."

"It was the wrong Cordova," Kate cut in. "So, if Eduardo knew who his brother was, is it possible he kept that information inside this toolbox Lupe sold to Ceballos?"

"For what purpose? You're telling me Ceballos just held onto it for two years?" Surrey asked. "He had no key. No way to know what was inside."

Kate looked away a moment while her mind raced through the possible scenarios. "Unless Eduardo told Ceballos what he had and that he'd put it away for safe keeping for reasons I can't speculate on. After Eduardo was murdered, maybe it was Ceballos who went to Lupe asking for the toolbox. She hadn't known anything about it and figured if the guy wanted it, why not? I realize how this sounds, but for what other reason would Ceballos have been murdered, unless he knew what Eduardo knew."

Walsh pulled back his shoulders and cocked his head. "I suppose the only way we're going to get to the bottom of this is to see what's inside the toolbox. What we do know is that Medina is a liar and probably a killer. A cop killer. What I want to know now is where does Michael Garza fit into this picture?"

INSIDE THE SAN ANTONIO field office, Cameron Fisher reviewed the victims' background details they'd just received. He set his gaze on Duncan and Romero. "There it is, in black and white.

These women all worked in the same place, at one time or another, over the course of the past couple of years."

"Which leaves us looking for another employee who had known them, or crossed paths with them while they were employed," Duncan replied.

"Gotcha," Romero cut in. "And when the M.E. identifies the others, we'll know to check the employment histories to see if any of them also worked at this facility."

Fisher continued to eye the report. "But I don't want to wait. We need to question the management and, or owners as soon as possible to cross reference these names and the rest of the staff. That needs to happen now."

"Should we contact Reid and let her know what we found?" Duncan asked. "This is our best shot at confirming whether this ties Guy Jacobs to the victims. If he worked there too…"

"Yes, let's reach out now and give her a heads-up." Fisher retrieved his phone and made the call. "Reid, it's Fisher. I have you on speaker with Duncan and Romero."

"What's going on?" Kate asked.

"Hey, Duncan here. We found something interesting. It looks as though, at one time or another, the victims who we've ID'd, worked at the same warehouse in San Antonio."

"They knew each other?" Kate asked.

"We don't know that for sure," Fisher cut in. "But we'll be heading there soon to speak with management. What we do know is that they worked there over the past two to three years at various times. So we'll be looking for staff who had been there the entire time and knew these women. We're hoping the name, Guy Jacobs, pops up."

"Hey, Reid, it's Romero. Jacobs' employment history I managed to get my hands on doesn't show he worked at this facility, but we have to ask the question. Could be an oversight, I don't know, because otherwise, I haven't found squat on Jacobs. No arrests, no recent addresses, nothing for the past 24 months."

"How is that possible? Did he fall off the face of the Earth?" Kate asked.

"Maybe he did," Romero replied. "Best we can do is talk to these folks at the facility and see if we can figure out who else worked there at the time of our victims."

"I have another name you should be looking out for," Kate added. "Something Walsh and Captain Brown unearthed regarding Eduardo Cordova's brother."

Romero drew in his brow. "What did y'all find out?"

"He has a falsified US passport, and his name is Xavier Medina."

"Are you shitting me right now?" Romero asked. "No way. No God damn way."

"Brown's contact in Juarez uncovered this. It's true. We're at SAPD's office with Walsh and Lupe just arrived. She has a key to a toolbox found in Ceballos's SUV. We're about to find what's inside and whether it will help us. It may not, but who knows? At this point, nothing would surprise me. It's looking more and more like Medina killed Officer Espinoza. He must've figured we were getting close to learning his true identity. We're thinking that if he has disappeared and if he still has connections in Mexico..."

"Then that's where he probably fled to," Duncan replied.

"Yeah, okay." Romero nodded. "Let us get with the warehouse and find out who their employees are. That'll firm up what we suspect about Guy Jacobs and now, possibly Xavier Medina."

"I'll let you know what we find, if anything. We'll touch base soon." Kate ended the call and looked at Lupe. "How you holding up?"

Her eyes were red and swollen. "I just feel numb inside. I want to end this, Agent Reid."

"I know you do. We all do, so let's go see what's inside this toolbox, huh?" She started down the hall and pushed through the door to the warehouse. "Sergeant Grady. This is my colleague, Agent Walsh. You already met Surrey. This is Lupe Cordova. The toolbox originally belonged to her father."

"Nice to meet y'all. I'll take you back." Grady walked toward the back wall where the toolbox lay. "My team and I are still searching Ceballos's SUV, so I'll leave y'all to it. Let me know if you need anything."

"Appreciate it," Walsh replied and peered at Kate. "Shall we?"

Kate placed her hand on Lupe's shoulder. "Would you like me to open it? Might be better if it was law enforcement."

"Yes, please." Lupe handed her the key.

Kate pulled on latex gloves and squatted. She inserted the key and the lock popped open. "You were right. It fits."

Walsh knelt down next to her and peered inside. "Some old tools. Wrenches, screwdrivers. Pretty much what you'd expect to find."

Kate reached inside. "Let me move some of this around." She peered back at Lupe. "Do you have any idea what it could be that we're looking for?"

"No, ma'am," Lupe replied.

Kate removed all the items inside and lifted the top insert. "What is this?"

Surrey leaned in closer. "It's a picture of Xavier Medina, but who's he standing next to?"

"Damn. That's not all." Kate closed her eyes a moment. "A pink stone. He knew. Eduardo Cordova knew and didn't come forward."

"That means this has been going on for years," Surrey continued.

"And probably not just here in Somerset," Walsh added. "My God, how wide-spread is this thing?"

"What are you talking about?" Lupe glanced at the photo. "That's my father and that's his brother, but what did you just call him? His name is Alejandro."

"How much do you know about him, Lupe?" Kate pulled up again.

"Not much. My dad hardly ever talked about his brother except that sometimes my mom and dad would fight because he gave my uncle money when he went to visit him in Mexico. We didn't have much to give." Her eyes welled. "Agent Reid, was my dad killed by his own brother? And he's here under a different name?" She swallowed hard. "He's been here this whole time?"

Walsh placed his hand on Lupe's back. "Why don't we go up front where you can sit down a minute?"

Lupe followed him but stopped and turned back. "Agent Reid, please tell me my uncle didn't kill all these girls, too."

Kate felt the sting of tears but forced them back. "I don't know, Lupe. I just don't know yet." She waited for them to disappear beyond the corridor.

"What the hell, Reid?" Surrey placed his hands on his hips. "If Ceballos knew all this, then Garza sure as hell did too."

Kate eyed the photo and the pink rock. "Son of a bitch was lying to us. How much you want to bet his alibis aren't checking out?"

"We'd have to follow up with the captain to find out," Surrey replied.

"My gut told me Garza killed Ceballos. It told me he was a part of all of this." She eyed Surrey. "And I just let him walk."

22

The Millstone Warehouse had employed at least three of the victims discovered in Somerset. Now, the rest of the team had to find the connection to their killer.

The afternoon sun sparked a glare in the windshield while Fisher spied the road ahead. "That's the building there on the right, inside the commercial complex."

Agent Romero turned right onto the property and glanced at Duncan through the rearview mirror. "Did you get that list of missing persons from this area?"

"I have it. If any of the missing women on this list worked here too, I'll bet a few of them are laying on tables in the M.E.'s office waiting to be ID'd."

Romero parked near the entrance and stepped out of his car. They walked inside and the San Antonio agent glanced back at them as they entered. "If y'all don't mind, I'll tee them up first."

"The floor is yours," Fisher replied.

Inside, Romero approached the reception desk. "Afternoon."

He held out his credentials. "FBI Agent Romero. These two are with me. We're here to meet with Mr. Becknell."

The young man behind the desk, who wore a navy-blue polo shirt, smiled brightly at the agents. "One moment, please. I'll let him know you're here."

Romero nodded and turned to the others. "Here's to hoping we don't get pushback from these folks."

"I don't want to waste time getting a judge involved," Fisher replied.

"Excuse me, Agent Romero?" the young man called out. "Mr. Becknell is ready for you. He asked that you go ahead and go up." He pointed to the elevators. "Second floor. Third office on your left."

The agents rode the elevator up to the second floor, and when the doors parted and Romero started into the hall, he came up to Becknell's office. "This is it. You two ready?"

"Right behind you," Fisher replied.

Romero knocked and then opened the door. "Excuse me, Mr. Becknell?"

The older, heavy-set man looked up from his desk and spotted the agent in his doorway. "You must be Agent Romero. Come in, please." He stood from his desk and revealed an oversized paunch sheathed in a white button-down oxford. "I gotta say, this is one hell of an unexpected visit from you folks."

"We appreciate you taking the time." Romero extended a greeting. "I've brought in experts from Quantico to help out our field office." He turned to them. "This is Agent Fisher. He runs the department in charge of hunting down serial killers. And this is Agent Duncan."

"Serial killers? Well, I'll be. It's a pleasure to meet you both, although that seems a bit paradoxical." Becknell stepped out from behind his desk. "Why don't we all take a seat over here at my conference table and we can go over why y'all are here."

Romero pulled out a chair. "You know why I called, so I'll get to the point as to what we're looking for."

"By all means." Becknell sat down.

"As you know, we've identified some of the victims found in Somerset, and have come to learn that they had been under your employ at one time or another. We need the employment records of those victims," Romero continued. "In addition to that, Agent Duncan has a list of missing persons from the San Antonio area. We'd like your people to cross reference these names against all employees to see if any are a match."

"I just can't imagine those young women you found worked for us over here. How is that possible? Good Lord, we're a family here, I don't mind telling you. If what you say is true, it'll be devastating for every last one of my staff." Becknell removed his glasses and rubbed his eyes. "I can't hardly believe it myself. Not to question your expertise in any way, but are you folks sure about all this?"

"When we learned who the first few victims were, standard procedure dictated we run background on them," Romero began. "Talk to their families and friends. So, when we started doing our due diligence, Millstone Warehouse popped up in these victims' employment records. They all worked here over the course of the past few years, Mr. Becknell."

"Good Lord, I can't comprehend what it must be like for those families right now. Course, I been seeing the news stories and all that, but never in a million years..."

"Mr. Becknell, sir," Fisher cut in. "I don't mean to be disrespectful, and I do realize how hard this news is to hear, but we have no time to waste. There are more unnamed victims, and we know the killer or killers are still out there."

Becknell cleared his throat. "Yes, sir. Of course, I understand.

I'll send over the information to our HR department on the double."

"There's one more thing you should know, sir." Romero glanced a moment at his colleagues as if hesitant to speak. "If these women did in fact work here, there's a strong possibility their killer did too."

"What's that now?" Becknell asked. "You believe I have a murderer in my ranks?"

Duncan regarded him. "It's no coincidence that at least three of the victims worked here in the past few years, Mr. Becknell. As hard as this is for you to hear, chances are very good they came across their killer at your warehouse. Your company is the only connection these women have to each other. It stands to reason someone else who worked here might well have taken their lives."

Becknell pressed his lips together until they formed a thin white line and held out his hand. "May I see your list, Agent Duncan?"

She handed it over.

As Becknell read the list of names, his brow knitted, and then his gaze softened. The look on his face spoke volumes.

"Mr. Becknell, do you recognize any of those names?" Duncan asked.

He sniffed loudly and cleared his throat. "A couple, yes, ma'am."

CAPTAIN BROWN STOOD inside Xavier Medina's apartment. He was certain the man had murdered one of his officers and was now on the run. The apartment appeared untouched. Clothes remained in the closet. Toiletries lay next to the bathroom sink.

The investigation had been thrown into a tailspin after news of

Medina's true identity surfaced. It made sense now, the captain thought, why Medina ran from the FBI. "You knew they'd find out who you really were."

An officer tapped him on the shoulder. "Excuse me, Captain?"

Brown was drawn back to the moment. "Yes?"

"We've cleared the place, sir. No murder weapon was found."

"Thank you, John. What about the manager? Have you spoken to him yet?" Brown asked.

"Lichtner's with him now, actually," the officer replied. "And Espinoza's car was towed back to the station. Her husband is at the morgue, last I checked."

"Okay. I'll head over to the manager's office and see how far we are on obtaining security footage. You and the rest of the team can head back to the station and write up your reports. Any evidence will need to be logged in. I'll have the FBI handle it since they can push it through the system fast."

"Got it, Captain."

Brown walked outside and made his way to the manager's office. Police tape was strung across the hedgerow where Espinoza was found. He stopped and set his gaze to the spot. When they'd arrived earlier this morning, he examined the scene where his officer took her last breath. Now that her body was gone, he walked toward it again.

The beige landscape rock was stained blood-red. One of the otherwise perfectly shaped shrubs now had a large dent where it had been crushed when she fell. Brown had never lost an officer under his watch. Sure, he'd been to plenty of cop funerals during his career, but never one of his own. Louisa Espinoza had only been there less than two years, but he'd taken a liking to her. Well, he had taken a liking to all of his officers. It was just who he was— for better or for worse. But she was different. Kind, yet strong. She believed in the gray. That not everything was black and white where people were concerned.

As he continued toward the spot, he wondered why she went on a stakeout alone and in her own car, no less. It wasn't procedure and not in her character to do so. Had she suspected more than she let on?

This was it. Brown stood just feet away from the bloody rocks that had already dried in the winter sun. He raised his gaze out toward the parking lot where her car had been parked. The line of sight was clear. If it was Medina, and there was little doubt in his mind that was the case, he would have been able to see her well from anywhere around this immediate area.

Espinoza was properly trained, so why would she risk exposure behind her? Brown spun around and gazed down the walkway leading up to this spot. "Wide open." And in the early hours of the morning, darkness would've been the killer's friend.

"Captain? Captain?" Lichtner ran toward him from the manager's office.

Brown stepped away from the tape and back onto the sidewalk. "Yes?"

"Sir, I went through the security tape. They only have cameras on the edge of the buildings." He turned and pointed. "So there's a camera right there."

"Did you see Medina?" Brown pressed on.

"No, sir. There's a blind spot where she was..." he trailed off. "But I did see her inside her car on her phone. It didn't appear that the conversation lasted long because she stepped out of her car and came over here where I lost visual."

"Who was she talking to?" Brown asked. "Do we have her phone records?"

"I made a call to her husband while I was back there. I asked him if he could check their cell phone usage online. He did."

"And?" Brown appeared impatient.

Lichtner handed him a sticky note. "This was the number. Her husband didn't recognize it."

"Then we'd better find out who she talked to only minutes before she was murdered."

THE PICTURE WAS proof of Xavier Medina's identity and Kate held it in her hand. The question was now, how would this help find the man suspected of murdering Officer Espinoza and possibly being involved in the death of Eduardo Cordova and countless women? Kate walked ahead toward the CSI officer. "Excuse me, Sergeant?"

He stepped away from Ceballos's SUV. "Yes, ma'am? You find what you needed in that toolbox?"

"We found something. Not sure it's exactly what we needed," she began. "How much longer until you're finished with the car?"

"We're pretty well wrapped up. I think we've found everything we're going to find. Now, it's time to run the prints to see if they match Ceballos, or if any other prints turn up. Same with the hair and fibers." He turned back to the car a moment. "I can keep you posted if something new hits, but like I said on the outset, Richard Ceballos was murdered in his home. We're not likely to find much inside his car, then again, stranger things have happened."

"Yes, they have," Kate replied. "Thank you for your help. I'd like to take a copy of the photo and I've taken pictures of what we found inside the toolbox. We'll leave it in your possession to log in as evidence."

"Yeah, of course. No problem." As Kate started to walk away, he called out again. "Agent Reid?"

"Yes?" She turned back.

"What's so important about that picture, if I might ask?"

"This?" Kate held it up a moment. "Oh, it's just a couple of brothers smiling for the camera."

"That's it? It doesn't help you?" Grady pressed on.

"It does. I just haven't worked out how yet." Kate returned to Walsh and Surrey. "I want to make sure Lupe gets her family out of town as soon as possible."

Surrey appeared concerned as they started into the hallway. "That's the best course of action. God knows what Medina might do once he realizes we know who he is."

"I'm not sure we'll see that man back in Somerset again," Walsh replied. "I have no idea if we'll ever track him down."

"We have to start thinking about Michael Garza, too. He was connected to Eduardo and Rich Ceballos. No way he's not part of this," Kate cut in. "The captain is at Medina's apartment now. I'm going to call the M.E. and ask if he's been able to identify the murder weapon used on Espinoza. Our best option at connecting Medina to her murder and the others is if he's gotten back the DNA sample."

Kate stepped away while the line rang through. "Yes, this is FBI Agent Kate Reid. I'd like to speak with Dr. Bauer if he's available. It's urgent. Thank you. I'll hold." She glanced back at Walsh. "Yes, Dr. Bauer, it's Agent Reid. I know you have your hands full, but is there an update on Officer Louisa Espinoza?" She nodded. "Okay. Okay. Yes, I know you've pinpointed other possibilities. Just this one, though, Doctor. Uh-huh. It is. Okay, thank you. You'll keep me posted? Thank you and yes, we are on the hunt for Xavier Medina. Thank you, Dr. Bauer." She ended the call. "No DNA back yet, however, the knife used to stab Espinoza appears to be the same style as the one used on the victims found on Ortega's property."

Walsh eyed her. "Making Medina the likely suspect. Then let's make damn sure the Cordova family gets the hell out of Dodge right now."

23

A knock on Becknell's office door drew the attention of the agents who were inside. The door opened and a middle-aged woman in black dress pants and a long-sleeved blouse appeared. "Mr. Becknell, I have the employment records you requested."

"Come in, Beth. This is what these fine FBI agents have been waiting for."

She handed him the folder. "I hope this helps." A polite nod to the agents and she took her leave.

Becknell pushed up his glasses and reviewed the contents of the folder.

Duncan studied his mien and returned a knowing gaze to Romero and Fisher. "How many?" she asked Becknell.

Becknell appeared stunned. "Excuse me? Oh, uh, yes ma'am. It appears five more. Eight, in total."

Duncan appeared relieved. "Now we can finally ID some of these women."

"Let's put the pieces together first, so we understand where we're at here," Fisher added.

Romero drew back in consternation. "With respect, Agent Fisher, no way this is a coincidence eight times over." He looked again at Becknell. "Do you have data on those who worked here at the same time as each of these women?"

Becknell pulled off his glasses. "HR is also working on that. It'll take some time. It's a lot of records to sort through. I just can't believe it."

"Now that we're certain we're on the right track," Duncan added. "We have two names we need to examine immediately. Xavier Medina and Guy Jacobs."

"That's right," Romero said. "Mr. Becknell, can you ask your HR team to run those names?"

He picked up the phone and made the request. "Done."

It wasn't hard to see that the otherwise jovial middle-aged man was shaken to his core by the news. Anyone would be, and so while they waited, it was Duncan who attempted to console him.

"Mr. Becknell, I wish this wasn't true, for the sake of you and your company. But I hope you understand that you've helped us to identify multiple women whose families had no idea what had happened to them. And this could very well lead us to the person or people who are responsible for their deaths."

His eyes welled and tears threatened to spill over. "That's kind of you to say, Agent Duncan, but we're a family here. At least, I thought as much. I simply can't wrap my head around the notion that I had a murderer here and I let that person prey on my own people."

Becknell's door opened again, and Beth walked inside. "Here you go, Mr. Becknell. I had everyone working on this so we could get it to you quickly. This includes the names you just asked us to run."

"Thank you," He opened the file and examined it a moment before sliding it across the table to Fisher.

Fisher pulled it closer and read the report inside. "Son of a bitch." His eyes darkened with anger as he darted a glance at the agents. "It's goddam Michael Garza."

Romero cocked his head. "What the hell's going on? Mr. Becknell, are you damn sure about this?"

Fisher shook his head in disbelief. "Guy Jacobs was a goddam ploy. Garza wanted to throw us off his scent."

Becknell appeared confused. "Agent Romero, that's the name on the report. I'm sorry, but this is the man who worked here during the time these eight young women did as well. Am I missing something here? Isn't this what you wanted?"

"If it was Garza, and we had him..." Duncan picked up her phone and waited for the line to answer. "Where are you?"

"Still at the SAPD," Kate replied. "What's going on?"

"It's Garza, Kate. It's Garza and we let him go." Duncan's face masked in anger.

"I knew it. God damn it. What did you find?"

"HR checked for names of those employed during the time our victims were employed. His was the only one on our radar. Not Medina, not Ceballos, and it sure as hell wasn't Guy Jacobs."

"That makes a little more sense with what we just found then," Kate replied.

"What do you mean?" Duncan shot a look at Fisher.

"A pink stone. We found one inside a toolbox that belonged to Eduardo Cordova. That, and a picture of Alejandro Cordova, or as we know him, Xavier Medina. Look, it's a long story how this all came about, but it did, and now with what you've discovered." She scoffed. "I let him walk. I let Garza walk."

"I'm going to step out on a limb, here, and suggest it was Garza who killed Ceballos," Duncan said. "Let's comb over his statement and put together a timeline to see if it was feasible. Medina appears to be a part of this and he likely murdered Officer Espinoza. And at this point, we should consider Garza did not work alone. Like we assumed Medina was a spotter in Laredo, it's possible Garza was a spotter too. These men may not be the only killers out there."

"I gave Garza time to create an exit strategy," Kate added. "Maybe all of them."

"We'll come back so we can put our heads together. Be there in 30." Duncan ended the call, and looked at Becknell. "Can you give us everything you have on Michael Garza? Last known address, phone numbers, family. Anything you have."

"Yes, ma'am. Whatever you need."

KATE DROPPED down onto a chair inside the SAPD lobby and held her phone in her lap.

Walsh sat down next to her. "This isn't your fault, Kate. We had no way of keeping Garza in custody."

"He fit the profile, Levi. He fit it and I ignored it. Of course he knew Xavier Medina because he was his friend's brother. Maybe not much of a friend. And whoever the hell Guy Jacobs is. Probably someone Garza worked with and didn't like. A big red flag should've sprung up in my mind the moment Romero said he couldn't find anything on Jacobs in the past two years."

Surrey stepped in. "What's done is done, Reid. We all made the wrong call on Garza. We have to live with that. It's now time to find him and bring him into custody. We can armchair quarterback this another time."

Walsh nodded. "I gotta go with Surrey on this one. When are the others coming back?"

"They're leaving now. We'll all have to head back to the Somerset station," Kate replied. "At least the Cordovas will be out of harm's way."

"Exactly. Staying with extended family is the best thing for them until this shit is over," Walsh replied.

Kate turned her gaze to him. "Eva thinks Garza likely killed Richard Ceballos. I think she's right. He would've been the only one left who could've known who Xavier Medina really was."

"Only way to know for sure is a ballistics report, and whether the timeline works," Walsh replied.

"Garza was headed south when that cop pulled him over in Corpus Christi," Kate continued. "Then he turns around and heads north toward Austin. He would've had enough time and been in the right place to kill Ceballos."

"Medina was still talking to us at that point," Walsh replied. "But that's not to say he didn't have time to head back to his place in the middle of the night when he didn't turn up for work to find Officer Espinoza waiting for him."

Surrey tossed his laptop bag over his shoulder. "The only way we'll get answers is to pull phone records on both of them. Check for credit card usage. Tracking down these men is how we finish this."

WALSH DROVE Kate back to the Somerset station while Surrey followed in another vehicle. The other agents were headed there too. Nothing in this investigation had gone the way Kate thought it would and her entire way of thinking had been thrown into disarray. Every time she thought she had a grip on this job, it slipped through her fingers like melted butter.

"Look at that," Walsh began. "Even more news vans than yesterday."

"No doubt it's because of Espinoza's death." Kate peered through the windshield. "Fisher's going to have to get out in front of this pretty damn quick."

"With what? We don't have anything to offer them." Walsh drove around to the back of the station. "We can't let the media distract us. We're about to lose the only lead we have, and it wasn't much of one to begin with."

Kate opened the car door. "Tell me something I don't know."

As they walked in through the rear entrance, Duncan marched toward them in the distance. "Tell me you know where to find Michael Garza."

"His phone records should be with Brown. His people were verifying Garza's statement," Kate said. "Now we just have to figure out who he was really going to see when he got pulled over by highway patrol. Like hell he was going to visit his mom."

"Let's find out." Duncan headed back to Brown's office with Kate beside her.

The captain stood from his desk chair. "I have the records, Agent Reid. What can I do to help?"

It was then that the rest of the team arrived. Fisher pushed ahead to see Kate. "Garza and Xavier Medina. That's who we're after for now. But it's looking like they might be the tip of the iceberg."

"Yes. We're awaiting ballistics on the gun that was used to kill Ceballos. I'd like to say that it'll tie to Garza, but we'll just have to wait and see," she replied. "And you already know the deal with Medina, Eduardo's brother."

"I'm tired of getting sucker-punched, Reid, so tell me how we plan on finding these men before they decide to head straight to Mexico," Fisher said.

The pressure was on and it was up to Kate to find a way through the mess she made. "Captain Brown has Garza's cell phone records and tower data. We need to look for calls placed in a radius of where he was pulled over in Corpus Christi. We believe —I believe—he could've been headed there for help. It's possible Xavier Medina was headed in that direction too," Kate continued. "The M.E. informed me that the knife used to kill Officer Espinoza matched the same type of knife used on Lisa Gutierrez and others. That leads me to believe it was Medina who murdered her." Kate stepped back and raised her chin. "Believe me, I don't want either one of us to get punched in the gut again."

Fisher softened his gaze. "No sightings on the vehicle BOLOs?"

"None yet," Brown interjected. "Agent Reid's got a good plan, so I say let's see where these calls were placed. We know the date and approximate time thanks to the officer in Corpus Christi who pulled him over." He distributed copies of the report. "I haven't looked at this yet. I only just received it. I'm also running on a call that Louisa made minutes before she was murdered. After I returned from Medina's apartment, I asked my team to reverse ID it."

"Where are they in that process?" Duncan asked.

"I'll run that down now while you folks take a look at these records." Brown headed out.

Fisher peered through the captain's office window. "Look at those guys out there. All waiting on a soundbite they can cue up for the 6 o'clock news."

Surrey sat down and examined the report. "Who has a laptop here we can use to access the tower locations?"

"I do." Duncan pulled it out of her bag and set it on Brown's desk."

While she logged into the servers, Walsh approached Fisher,

who was still at the window. "You're going to have to give them something, man. They're going to overrun this place and soon."

Kate headed over to Surrey. "What did the paving contractor say about Guy Jacobs? Was Garza spinning a tale on us?"

Surrey turned his sights on her. "They're looking into it. Said they'd get back to me as soon as possible."

Kate scoffed and dropped onto the chair next to him. "Geez, can't we catch a break?"

"No one could've predicted this would turn into the shitshow that it has, Reid. Not even you," Surrey replied. "These people, Medina, Garza, whoever else, they've been doing this a long time. They've gamed a system that doesn't care much about seemingly random women being sliced and diced. I mean, are you kidding me with the SAPD not connecting those dots of the missing women? How the hell does that happen? Months, maybe years this shit's been going on and they didn't look to see that several of these missing persons, at one time or another, worked at the same location?"

"I appreciate you trying to deflect, but I should've found a way to keep Garza in custody," Kate replied.

"I'm in," Duncan interjected. "I'm pulling up the cell tower locations now to see which ones pinged Garza's phone."

Fisher walked toward her and peered over her shoulder. "Who the hell did he call? We need an address."

Walsh's phone rang and he peered at the caller ID. "Excuse me, folks. I gotta take this." He stepped into the hall. "Walsh here. What do you have for me?"

"Agent Walsh, ballistics came back on the bullet found in Richard Ceballos. The striations of the bullet match that of a Ruger EC9S 9-millimeter," the caller replied.

"Okay. Can you run registration on a Michael Garza and

Xavier Medina, Somerset, Texas? See if either of them owns this type of gun."

"I'm on it. I'll call you right back."

Walsh returned inside. "Well, ballistics came back."

"And?" Fisher pressed on.

"Ruger 9-mil. They're running a reg check on both our suspects now. I should know soon," Walsh replied.

"Uh, how about a town called Kingsville?" Duncan cut in. "It's near Corpus Christi, where Garza was pulled over. And not that far from Laredo."

"Where Marissa Padilla was taken," Kate began. "And where Medina was seen the day she was taken. Garza's phone pinged a tower there?"

"Twice that morning, actually," Duncan replied. "What do you guys think?"

Walsh's phone buzzed in his pocket and he turned away to answer. "Yeah, Walsh here. Yeah, okay, send it my way, would you? Appreciate it." He ended the call. "Sorry for the interruption. Garza is a registered owner of a Ruger 9-mil."

"So he did kill his friend, Ceballos," Surrey replied.

"Not just Ceballos. I reviewed the cold case on Eduardo Cordova when Brown first mentioned it. I know the bullets lodged in him also came from a Ruger 9-mil. So, I think we have Garza on the Ceballos murder as well as the Cordova murder," Walsh replied.

"What about his brother then? The man we now know as Xavier Medina?" Kate asked. "I thought he was the one who killed Eduardo Cordova."

"Sounds to me like these two men have been working together for a while," Fisher cut in. "And maybe Eduardo Cordova knew that. Eventually, Ceballos learned of it too. Now they're both dead." He looked at Duncan. "Track down the call to that tower.

Find out who owns that phone number. It's looking like these two could be in Kingsville."

Captain Brown returned and appeared to note Duncan's expression. "What's going on?"

Kate walked toward him. "We're close, Captain. We think we know where these men are located."

"Good Lord, I hope so." Brown returned his gaze to the agents. "I know who Louisa talked to in the minutes before she was murdered. Apparently, she'd been in communication with a woman in town, undocumented, by the sounds of it. I just got off the phone with her. After some reluctance, she admitted to making the call. Only days earlier, this young woman managed to escape from a man who'd attacked her. A man who had been at the Dorado bar."

"Lupe had seen someone hanging around there too," Kate added. "Did this woman know him?"

"No. But she'd approached Louisa because she trusted her. Gave a description." He paused a moment. "I think I know why Louisa was there at the apartment. She wanted to confirm her suspicions. The woman described someone who looked an awful lot like Xavier Medina as her attacker. She knew we already suspected him, so she wanted to be the one to catch him." He swallowed hard. "Except that it cost her life."

"We will find him, Captain," Kate began. "Louisa's death won't have been for nothing."

Duncan unfolded a street map on the captain's conference table. "I've marked the cell tower location here. It connects to calls made from these few blocks that I've circled. So when Garza used his phone, the number pinged to this tower and was shown to connect to a number somewhere in the vicinity of these two blocks. We know where Garza was last seen when he was pulled over right here." With her index finger, Duncan pointed to the highway. "That was two days ago. There's no way to be certain he's returned to this area or whether Medina is with him."

"Then we head there and find out," Fisher replied. "We can coordinate with the local authorities and have them help us canvas the area."

"What happens, assuming these men are there, when they see cops all over the place?" Surrey asked. "My guess is, they won't stick around. Isn't there a way we can narrow this down so our team, and maybe one local team, can knock on doors?"

"Garza would've taken off shortly after he was cut loose, meaning he might not have had a chance to go home, or didn't want to risk it," Kate said.

Fisher returned a curious gaze. "What are you getting at?"

"We have enough for a warrant to search his property. If he left behind a computer, that would go a long way to helping us find his associates. One of them is helping him or Medina, maybe both."

Captain Brown nodded. "We do have probable cause to retrieve it. No need for a warrant in this instance. Evidence points to him being the one who pulled the trigger on two murders and he hasn't been seen since. I'll send one of my guys out now to have a look around." He stepped out again.

"We don't have time to search for a laptop or whatever we think we'll find on it," Fisher began. "What specifically are you looking for, Reid?"

Kate hesitated, but for only a moment. "We are all but certain these men are part of something larger. The pink stones marking the burial sites. The Juarez officer who shot at one of the killers we know wasn't either of our current suspects." She looked at Surrey, who appeared to offer his support. "I don't think this is about the mass murders in places like Juarez and other countries. That doesn't mean I would rule out that any one of this larger group wasn't inspired by those crimes. However, I do think this is about a group of disenfranchised men taking out their hatred and self-loathing on unsuspecting women."

"The incels," Duncan replied.

"Yes. And I think Garza and Medina are getting help from a member of that group who lives in Kingsville."

"Okay, I'll bite. What do you hope to find on Garza's laptop, assuming he left it behind?" Fisher pressed on.

"Contacts. I know how this sounds, but I need you to back me up on this. If we don't get something specific, something concrete, like a name, we'll be hunting around for these men in Kingsville for too long and they'll vanish."

THE FRONT DOOR WAS AHEAD, and Officer Lichtner peered at the side window. No lights were on inside the home. He had no key, but how to get inside without alarming the neighbors was his main concern. He walked down the porch steps and toward a front room window.

"Excuse me?"

Lichtner twitched and went for his gun before he spun around and saw a teenaged girl a few feet away. "Oh, good Lord. Don't ever sneak up on a cop."

"I'm sorry." The girl held up her hands. "Please don't shoot me."

He returned his gun to its holster. "I'm not going to shoot you. You just caught me by surprise. Do you know the man who lives here?"

The girl, not more than 13, nodded and gazed at him with doe eyes.

"He doesn't seem to be home. Do you know where he is?" Lichtner asked.

The girl shook her head. "I haven't seen him in days."

"I'm Officer Lichtner. What's your name?"

"Gabrielle. I live next door."

"What do you know about Mr. Garza, the man who lives here?" He pressed on.

"I know he has people over at his house a lot, other men. They stay over for a long time and sometimes I can hear them from my bedroom when they leave late at night," she replied.

So far, Lichtner hadn't heard anything illegal. But maybe this girl knew more. "Do you know what they were saying? Did you happen to overhear their conversations?"

She nodded. "Sometimes. Sometimes I would hear them talking about where they would meet. Like, it wasn't always here. Like, they would meet at other people's houses, I think."

Okay, now they were getting somewhere. He continued on. "Do you remember anyone's name in particular? Someone else's house where they would go?"

Gabrielle shot a glance back and forth as though someone might hear her. "Um, I remember hearing the names Xavier and Clay. That's all. I don't know where they lived, though. They would all just stand around outside on the driveway and talk real loud."

"Xavier," Lichtner nodded. "Do you recall a last name?"

"No, sir, but I don't think Mr. Garza, or his friends were good people," she replied.

"What makes you say that?"

She looked away as if embarrassed. "I think they wanted to hurt people. That's all. What are you doing here, anyway?"

"You're right, Gabrielle. Mr. Garza wasn't a very good person. I'm here to go inside and collect some of his things."

The girl nodded. "Oh, okay. I won't tell anyone." She turned away but stopped short. "I don't think I like him, so I hope he won't come back here anymore."

"He won't if I can help it, Gabrielle."

24

The evening rolled in when Lichtner returned with Michael Garza's laptop. He hurried inside Brown's office. "Captain, I got it."

"Thank God," Brown replied. "Did you have any trouble?"

"No, sir. Well, I almost shot a child..."

Brown jumped up from his chair. "What?"

"Nothing, Captain. I didn't, obviously. It was just a neighbor girl who snuck up on me. Anyway, it doesn't matter. What matters is that she said Garza usually had men over at his place and when they'd leave late at night, she heard them talking on the driveway sometimes. I prodded her a little and she recalled a couple of names for us. Xavier and someone named Clay."

"Any last names?" Brown asked.

"No, sir. I got inside the house shortly after that and found the laptop straight away. You'd think he would've taken it with him if he took off."

"I have a feeling he didn't get a chance to go back home once he learned what Medina did to Espinoza," Kate interrupted. "May I hand this to Agent Duncan?"

"Yes, of course," Brown replied. "The sooner we find these men, the better for everyone in this community."

Kate set down the laptop in front of Duncan. "You're up."

She opened the lid and smiled. "You gotta be kidding me?"

"What?" Kate asked.

Duncan viewed the Home Screen. "No password."

Walsh leaned into Kate's ear. "What were you saying about not catching a break?"

"We got lucky this time. Now, we need to find out who he's been talking to online. If we can get names, I know one of them will be the person they'll turn to in Kingsville," Kate replied.

Fisher appeared impatient as he folded his arms and stood over Duncan's shoulder. "I hope to hell you're right about this, Reid. We're wasting time not heading down to Kingsville right now. These guys won't stay put for long."

"How about I make a call to the locals? I'll give them a heads-up that they could have killers in their city and that we'll be heading their way soon," Surrey replied. "That way, they can keep eyes out for us in the meantime with the BOLOs and we won't be blindsiding them."

"Appreciate that, Surrey. That'll help," Fisher replied.

The gesture hadn't gone unnoticed as far as Kate was concerned. Surrey bought her some time and every little bit helped. She turned to Duncan. "The information you got for me about the incel groups?"

"Yeah?" Duncan replied.

"Let's start with that."

"Got it." Duncan keyed in the commands. "When I first investigated this, I found a couple of groups whose members referenced San Antonio. I don't recall much more than that since we came here a couple of days later. Let me pull that up again and see if Garza had an account."

Walsh approached her. "How would you be able to tell if he did?"

"It's an easy assumption that Garza lived alone and didn't use a password to protect his laptop because of that. If he had, I wouldn't get very far without sending this to a lab first. Given that, I can pull up his browser history to see if he was part of the group. If he was, he probably had the 'remember me' function selected so that the username and password would populate automatically." She continued to type. "Let's see how far I get with that."

Walsh nudged Kate. "You have a minute?"

"Yeah." She followed him into the hall. "What is it?"

"Listen, uh, I know we have our hands full right now, but I wanted you to see this." He held up his phone.

Kate's brow creased as she took hold of it. "He sent this to you?"

"Have you checked your phone lately?" Walsh asked.

She retrieved her phone and noticed a missed call. "Looks like Nick tried to call me."

"Which is probably why he texted me. I had also asked him about a case he worked back at the WFO. He emailed me the files, but I didn't see anything useful. Anyway, I know it's a text and all, and things get lost in translation, but he sounds worried. You should talk to him. Duncan's going to be a while."

"Yeah. Okay. Thanks." She stepped away and made the call. "Hey, it's me. I'm sorry I missed your call. Is everything okay?"

"I know you're right in the middle of things. I texted Walsh to give him a heads up," Nick replied.

"What's this about?" Kate asked. "Did something else happen?"

"I was asked to make a statement to the media about an hour ago," Nick began.

"Which was when you called," she replied.

He was quiet for a moment. "I was asked about you and I didn't handle it all that well."

"What do you mean? Who asked you about me and what was the question? Who the hell even knows in the media that we're married?"

"It's public record," he replied. "But what I want to say is that you'll probably start getting calls asking about all that shit that went down back in Rio Dell."

Kate closed her eyes and sighed. "Well, it wouldn't be the first time. I just thought we'd experienced the last of it long ago."

"So did I, and that's why I had to talk to you. And why I gave Walsh a heads-up. I don't want it to distract from what you're doing, so I figured if you were prepared..."

"Yeah, of course. I get it. But what about you? You said you didn't handle it well. Nick, you're not in a position to start pissing off people. What did you say?"

"Nothing important. It may have involved a four-letter word, but he caught me at a bad time."

Kate chuckled. "That's it? You cursed at him?"

"Well, it was a little more than that and apparently, the Administration is planning on making sure I know that's not how things are done in situations like this. So, I've already gotten on their bad side."

"Oh, Nick, I'm sorry. You know this will all blow over. Once you all figure out who took out the trains, everyone will forget what was said."

"Maybe. But listen, I just thought you should know in case your phone blows up. I've briefly seen on the news all that's happening over there. You doing good with it?"

"Yeah. We're close. Really close. And I'm fine. I'm doing what I should be doing. I'd better get back inside. You'll be okay?"

"I'll be fine. You?"

"You know I will. We'll talk later." Kate ended the call and noticed Walsh had already returned inside. She walked back in and Duncan caught her gaze. "What? Did you find something?"

Duncan grinned. "Clay Melgren. I think he's letting Garza and Medina hole up for a while. He lives in Kingsville."

Kate turned to Fisher. "So are we leaving now?"

"You bet your ass we are."

THE LARGE MAN wearing a bomber jacket with jeans and work boots stepped out of his car and started toward his front door. The sky had darkened but a hint of grey remained, and the dusky light made it tough to see.

"Hey."

The whisper that came from his front bush forced him to spin around in surprise. "What the?"

"Clay, it's me, Michael." Garza emerged from the shrubbery and surveyed the area. With his hands in his pockets, he stepped toward him. "Hey, man, you gotta help me."

"The fuck are you doing here, man?" Melgren quickly appeared worried. "You were supposed to be long gone by now. That was what we agreed."

"Can we go inside?" Garza looked around. "I don't want people seeing us."

Melgren shook his head and unlocked his front door. "Get inside, dumbass." He waited for Garza to step in and followed him, closing the door behind them. "You mind telling me why the hell you're still here?"

"Xavier and me need a place to lay low for a while," Garza replied. "Frickin FBI, man. They're all over our shit."

"How do you know?" Melgren dropped his keys on the living room side table.

"Have you seen the news, brother?" Garza held up his phone. "Shit's everywhere."

"Melgren yanked off his baseball hat and tossed it onto the couch. "I hope to hell you turned off your GPS on that phone of yours."

"Uh," Garza glanced at it. "Yeah, I did. What the hell are we going to do, man? I know we should've left town after Xavier took off like a bat outta hell and those agents found him at his apartment. He just runs off like a little bitch and he wonders why they caught up to him again."

Melgren sat down on his couch and rested his elbows on his knees. "Fine. You two can keep your sorry asses here until shit blows over. Stay off the computer. Stay off your phones. We'll ride this out."

WHIRLING atop the San Antonio field office was a helicopter prepared to take the BAU team to Kingsville. All signs pointed to the home of Clay Melgren. Duncan, once again, exhibited her expertise when she had traced back an avatar in an online group focused on the life of incels. Melgren's name came up as the one who lived near the cell tower that pinged on Garza's phone days earlier.

Agent Romero checked his weapon's holster as he and the other agents readied for departure. "It's time, folks. We have to move now. The bird's waiting."

"I've informed the local police we're headed their way. The plan is to briefly meet with them to rundown the situation. From there, they'll offer us backup as we serve the warrant to Clay Melgren." Fisher eyed his team. "We arrest our two fugitives, ideally, without incident. Melgren will be brought in on charges of aiding and abetting unless we uncover more details of his potential involvement. I asked Captain Brown to hold off on any press statements until we have these men in custody."

"Our department is preparing to issue an update to placate the media, which I'm hopeful will alleviate some of the pressure on the Somerset police," Romero added. "So, if there's nothing else?"

"We're ready," Walsh replied.

"Then let's move." Romero led the way to the elevators and held the door as the team stepped inside. When the doors parted on the rooftop, he stepped out to a gust of wind generated by the whirling helicopter blades. "Keep low," he shouted.

As the team reached the chopper, Walsh waited for Kate and Duncan to step inside. He turned to Surrey. "Bet you didn't think this case could get any more interesting, huh?"

"Where our team is concerned, nothing surprises me anymore." Surrey slapped him on the back and stepped inside. "You need a hand?"

Walsh took his hand and Surrey pulled him in. He glanced to Romero. "That's it. Everyone's accounted for."

Romero nodded and turned his attention to the pilots. "We're in. Let's move."

A moment later, the chopper floated into the evening sky. A ring of dust on the rooftop below scattered as they ascended.

Kate pulled on her seatbelt and Walsh glanced at her. "You doing all right?"

"Yeah, fine. I'm still trying to get my head around the planting of the pink rocks. At this point, it had to have been Garza since he had access to the equipment. But why? It only implicates him further."

"It's possible he was looking to point the finger at Medina, knowing he's a Mexican national. Maybe he thought, if he was going to be questioned, he could squirm his way out by turning our aim toward his partner," Walsh replied. "The evidence has to speak for itself. Can't do a damn thing about that. All we can do is leave it up to the attorneys."

They had exhausted all theories during the course of this investigation and what Kate initially believed turned out to have been right. She felt good about finding the men they were after. The problem was, she had no idea the extent of the crimes committed. That was what would keep her on her toes.

"Agent Romero." One of the pilots turned to him. "We land in five."

Romero returned a thumbs-up and looked to the team. "Five minutes. We brief Kingsville PD and then we drive out to Melgren's home."

Within minutes, the police station appeared below. The helicopter began its descent and prepared to land on the parking lot. No rooftop helipad at the local stationhouse. These guys were about to be overrun with federal agents.

The helicopter landed and Romero jumped out. "Let's go folks. Time's a wasting." He lent a hand and the team stepped out.

Two men approached, both wore badges on their belts and were dressed in off-the-rack suits.

"You must be Agent Romero. I'm Lieutenant Brock. This is Detective Cruz. We understand you're on the hunt for a serial killer."

"Yes, sir. Two actually," Romero replied. "These folks heading up are from Quantico. They're the experts in finding people like the men we're after."

Cruz glanced toward them. "Yeah, I heard all that's gone down over there near San Antonio. Crazy shit. What can we do to help?"

"Let me introduce you to the senior agent," Romero cut in. "This, here, is Cameron Fisher. He's in charge of the team."

"Good to meet you." Fisher tendered a greeting. "We could use your help. A couple of units for backup." He waved over Kate. "This is Supervisory Special Agent Kate Reid." He turned to her. "You want to show them who we're after."

Kate opened her tablet and pulled up the photos. "These men here, we believe, are responsible for the murders of several women in Somerset. Most of the women are from San Antonio. One of them lived in Laredo. There could also be more suspects, but these two are our current targets."

"Not far from here," the lieutenant replied.

"No, sir. We believe they're holed up with a man named Clay Melgren. That's where we're headed tonight," Fisher added.

"Melgren?" the detective asked.

Kate spotted a hint of recognition in the detective's eyes. "Yes, sir. You know him?"

"We just had a tip called in earlier today. A young woman said she'd been approached by a man in a silver sedan. When she wouldn't stop for him, he gave chase. She got away and called it in. She got a plate number, and the car was registered to one Clay Melgren."

"Then he's part of it," Kate replied.

"Part of what, ma'am?" Lieutenant Brock asked.

"We thought he was sheltering the men we're after, but it sounds like he's an active participant." She peered at Surrey. "It's starting to make sense now knowing Marissa Padilla was taken from Laredo. Garza spotted her, made sure Melgren could take her."

"And she did work at the warehouse for a short while in San Antonio, too," Surrey replied. "The parents mentioned that to us."

"Yeah, I remember." Kate turned back to the lieutenant. "I don't know how big this operation is, Lieutenant. I don't know how many people we'll find in Melgren's home. But we need to make this happen now."

The lieutenant nodded. "We're ready when you are, Agent Reid."

～

"HEADS UP, FOLKS," Walsh began. "We're about to turn down Melgren's street." He made the turn and slowed down as he drove on.

Kate peered at the homes as they drove by. "This is a nice neighborhood. If people are home, they'll be curious. Last thing we need is bystanders."

"I'll give PD a heads up to keep folks at bay," Romero replied.

Walsh slowed to a stop in front of the next house down. "That's Melgren's silver sedan in the driveway. Things are looking up for us." He turned to Kate. "Are we doing this now or what?"

"No time like the present." Kate stepped out of the backseat and checked her weapon. "Romero, you may want to let those local guys know to hang back."

"Gotcha. I don't want this to be a free-for-all. I want these men alive and taken without incident." Romero walked back to the waiting patrol cars.

She waited for the others to join her. "Fisher, you want us to split up?"

He turned to the team. "We'll cover all exits. We believe we'll encounter three men inside, but let's be prepared for more. Don't hesitate to do what you have to do to protect yourself. Kingsville PD will be there if we need them." He checked the radio. "We've all got one of these. Use it if necessary." Fisher looked ahead at the house. "Let's bring these guys in."

Surrey raised his hand. "I'll take the lead at the front door."

"I'm right behind you," Kate replied.

"Then I'll head around the left side," Fisher said. "Duncan, don't let them get to the car. Walsh, mind the right side. If Surrey and Reid push in, we go in after them."

Romero caught up to Surrey and Kate and waited on the bottom step of the porch while Surrey prepared to knock.

The screen door rattled as he rapped his knuckles atop it. "Clay Melgren, FBI."

Kate observed the home. It had been well cared for. Recently painted. The lawn in good condition with green winter ryegrass planted in the front. Not exactly what she would expect from a man who was a member of a subculture appeared intent on blaming women for their own shortcomings. And now, it seemed that he may be a willing participant in Garza and Medina's sick game, according to Detective Cruz.

Surrey pounded again. "Melgren, open up. FBI. We have a warrant."

The door opened and Melgren stood on the other side. The tall, full-waisted man looked down at Surrey from behind the screen door. "Yes, sir? Can I help you?"

"Are you Clay Melgren?" Surrey asked.

"Yes, sir. What's this about?"

"FBI." Surrey held out his badge. "We'd like to ask you a few questions about what's been happening in Somerset, near San Antonio."

"I'm sorry? I don't think I'm aware of what you're talking about," Melgren replied.

"Then we'll be happy to fill you in if you just sit down and talk with us for a minute. I have a warrant, so we can be civil about this, or me and the ten people I have behind me will come inside and find what we're looking for."

"Well, I don't think I can do that with you right now. But I'd be happy to make a trip to—Somerset, you say? And have a sit-down with you tomorrow," Melgren replied.

Kate noticed he'd kept the door close to him, but she spotted someone out of the corner of her eye through a side window. "Excuse me, Mr. Melgren, I'm FBI Agent Reid. We're looking for Michael Garza and Xavier Medina. Do you know those men?"

"Gosh, ma'am, I sure don't."

"There he is!" Duncan spotted a figure running past what looked like the dining room window. "That's Garza. I saw him." She rushed over from her position on the garage side of the house.

Surrey stepped back and trained his weapon on Melgren. "Step aside, sir."

"You're making a mistake...."

Fisher and Walsh heard the commotion and hurried to their colleagues. Walsh looked on. "Shit." He cocked his gun.

Surrey kept his weapon on Melgren. "You need to step aside, Mr. Melgren. Now."

A crash of glass sounded in the back of the house.

"He's running!" Surrey dashed around to the side of the house and Kate followed.

Fisher knocked open the side gate and hustled to the backyard. Walsh was right behind him.

In the uproar, Duncan took her eyes off Melgren. On returning her sights to the home, she trained her weapon straight ahead and walked inside.

In the distance, and in the dimming light, a shadowy figure clung to the rear yard fence.

Fisher pumped his legs hard. "We have to get him before he jumps!"

"Stop! FBI!" Walsh cried out.

"I got him!" Fisher darted ahead and reached out to clutch the man's leg. With a final lunge, he grabbed hold of Garza's pant leg at his ankle and pulled hard.

The two stumbled and fell to the ground.

Kate looked on. "Where's Eva? I'm going back inside." She hurried to the back of the house where a glass door lay in shards on the ground. Kate ran inside with her gun ready. She carefully walked through the kitchen and toward the living room. The overhead lights in the ceiling were on and illuminated her way inside. She listened for noise, but the house was quiet. A quick glance outside and the car was still there. Melgren was still in the house.

The living room was clear and as she started toward the hall-way, footsteps reached her ears. A quick pivot and her gun was aimed at Duncan. "Jesus." Kate immediately lowered it.

Duncan lowered her hands. "This way," she whispered. The two continued into the hall.

"Show yourself, Melgren. We have Garza. We just need you to talk to us. We need to know where Xavier Medina is." Kate stopped and glanced at Duncan. It seemed they'd both heard the sound. Kate pointed to the room ahead on the right. "There are too many of us, Melgren. You won't find a way out."

A sound from the room forced Kate and Duncan to take shelter in the adjacent doorways and prepare to fire on Melgren.

Duncan nodded at Kate and continued, "Come out slowly with your hands up."

A hand appeared from the doorway. Kate tightened her grip

on the gun and steadied her aim. "Slowly. Keep your hands where we can see them."

The large man continued to emerge as instructed. When he appeared at the end of the hall, hands in the air, relief washed over Kate. "You're under arrest, Mr. Melgren. Turn around, place your hands behind your back and walk backward toward us."

"I got him." Duncan kept her gun trained on the man.

Kate retrieved the zip ties from her holster. "That's far enough." She took a few steps forward and grabbed his wrists.

Melgren flung out his arms and swung around, pushing Kate to the ground. She lay on the floor when Duncan fired her weapon. One, two, three shots and he was down.

"Oh my God. Kate!" Duncan hurried to her side and helped her up. "Are you okay?"

"I'm fine. I'm fine."

Walsh ran inside with his gun aimed.

Duncan spun around and saw him. "We're okay! The suspect's down."

"Jesus." Walsh put away his gun and peered at the bleeding body of a dead man. "What the hell happened?"

Kate steadied herself. "He was cooperating and then he wasn't. Eva took him down. What's happening with Garza?"

"Garza's in custody."

"Then where the hell is Medina?" Kate eyed Duncan. "Did you see the shed out back? Maybe he made it over the fence before we saw Garza." She started back through the home and into the kitchen.

"Reid, wait." Walsh caught up to her. "If he's here, we'll find him."

She nodded and continued through the back. "Hang on." Kate stopped on a dime and looked back toward the living room."

"What is it?" Walsh whispered.

"We didn't clear that room. Melgren stepped out of there to surrender." Before she could finish her explanation, Kate quickly started back toward the hall.

"What are you doing?" Duncan had reached the front door. "Reid?"

Kate continued on with her gun at the ready. She walked into the hall.

Duncan caught up to Walsh. "What the hell's she doing?"

"I don't know, but we'd better be ready," he replied.

"Xavier, it's Agent Reid," Kate called out from the hallway as she stepped over Melgren's lifeless body. "You can't run from me this time. Melgren's gone. Garza's sitting in the back of a patrol car right now. It's over." She slowed her steps. "We know your Eduardo's brother. We know everything." Kate reached the back bedroom. She glanced over her shoulder to see Walsh and Duncan backing her up. A moment's pause and she walked inside. "Xavier, come on out." She peered at the bottom of the bed, then toward the closet. And then she spotted the bathroom. A flicker of light peeked through the closed door. When her team reached the door, she looked back at them and pointed to the bathroom.

Kate stood to the side of the door and turned the handle, pushing it open. A gunshot rang out.

Walsh yanked on Duncan's sleeve. "Get down!"

Kate spun in front of the open bathroom door and fired on Medina, striking him in the leg.

Medina collapsed to the floor and clutched at his calf, writhing in pain.

"Drop your gun. Now!" Kate stood in front of him. "Drop it, or I swear I'll kill you." Her eyes burrowed into his as he held his weapon. "Do it, Xavier. I'm not asking again."

The two locked eyes for several more seconds before he finally released his gun.

Relief swelled in Kate's chest. "Push it toward me."

He pushed it a few feet away, close enough that Kate could pick it up. "Xavier Medina, you're under arrest for the murder of Louisa Espinoza, Lisa Gutierrez, and probably a whole lot more."

He still clutched his grazed calf and raised his eyes to her. "Good luck with that, Agent Reid."

25

S omerset Police Officer Lichtner spotted the agents arrive at the rear entrance of the stationhouse. News of the operation in Kingsville had reached social media when shots were fired at the home of Clay Melgren. Plenty of neighbors held out their phones and recorded the man's body being removed by the coroner.

Lichtner opened the back door while the agents approached with the remaining suspects in their custody. When Kate reached him, he regarded her. "Which one of these men murdered Espinoza?"

The look in his eyes was unmistakable. It was a look Kate had seen before. "We still have to prove it, and I understand how you feel. Trust me on that. But let us do our jobs now."

The officer's eyes reddened. "Maybe you leave the son of a bitch out back for a minute, huh? He won't be a problem for anyone after that."

She patted him on the shoulder and continued inside.

Fisher soon joined her. "You see the mob out front?"

"I did. Are you offering yourself up for sacrifice?" Kate replied.

"Hey, I offered, but Brown insisted on handling it himself." Fisher stopped and turned to her. "After those two are officially booked into custody, let's put them in separate rooms and see what we can get. If there are more bodies out there, or if we can get them to turn on each other, the better the D.A.'s case will be. And for the officers here? We have to drop the hammer on Medina for the loss of one of their own."

Fisher headed toward Brown's office, leaving Kate to find a way to make that happen. She spotted Romero approach.

He raised an index finger. "Hang on. My phone's ringing." With his phone to his ear, he answered. "Romero here."

"Agent Romero, it's Dr. Bauer. Do you have a minute?"

"Course I do, Doc. It's getting late in the day for you to still be working. I hope that's good news for us."

"I understand you have my janitor in your custody," the doctor said.

"Word travels fast. In fact, we do, sir. He's not who any of us thought he was, I'll tell you that much."

"So I hear," Bauer replied. "And I'm sorry we didn't figure that out before he did what he did. That said, since he submitted a swab early on, I have that sample back and plan to run it against Louisa Espinoza's profile and the other victims as well. It could go a long way to proving your case."

"Yes, it would. How long you think that'll take? I know the good folks here in Somerset want to know who killed their colleague. And then of course, the rest of the victims."

"I plan on staying for as long as it takes, Agent Romero. Now that you have these men in custody, I want to do what I can to identify the remaining victims to give you all the ammunition you'll need."

"You sound like you're holding a grudge, there, Doc," Romero added.

"I had a murderer working for me. Considering what I do for a living, that's not sitting well. I'll keep you posted, Agent Romero."

"Appreciate that, Doc." He ended the call and looked at Kate. "Bauer got the DNA profile back from when we swabbed Medina. He'll work his magic and see what turns up against the victims and Officer Espinoza."

Walsh made his way toward them. "We have them booked. It's time for them to give us names, and whether there are more bodies yet to be found. Fisher said he wants to separate them and get them to turn on one another. I agree. It's the only way to get to the truth."

"I want to talk to Garza," Kate jumped in. "I want to scare him. Tell him that his friend, Medina, will end up being sent back to Mexico and the entire thing will fall on his shoulders. And that will include the murder of Armando Guzman. I'll make clear that the sheer number of victims we currently know about will see him on Death Row, especially here in Texas."

Fisher returned from the captain's office, appearing to have overheard the conversation. "And your point in scaring him?"

She whipped around toward him. "To get to the truth. To get Garza to name and shame everyone in this incel group, Medina, included. We bring them all down. Even if they had no hand in the murders themselves, we'll get them for being co-conspirators. And do you know how easy it'll be to get public opinion on our side? Garza was using these pink rocks, a symbol for the femicide in Juarez, to shift blame. When what he was really doing, in my opinion, was marking the graves. He was telling others in his group, Melgren among them, that the bodies could be dumped there."

Walsh regarded her. "It's a dangerous game, Kate. Getting the media to side on a case before it's tried. We can't be the ones to do it, that's for damn sure. You, of all people, should know that."

The rest of the team had joined them, and Surrey narrowed his gaze at Kate. She picked up on the look. "What my good friend, Levi, is referring to is a time when I was the target of the press because of resurfaced memories of my abductor as a child." She considered the call earlier from Nick and how the press still hounded her. "They, in particular one, who I now consider a friend, tried to claim that I couldn't possibly finger a suspect based on resurfaced memories."

"Kate, I don't mean to bring that up," Walsh cut in, "It's just that shit like that happens. When the media turns against you or works with you; neither results in justice."

Fisher reached into his shirt pocket and retrieved a pack of toothpicks. He placed one between his lips. "Fine. I'll agree to your participating in the interviews, Reid, but you don't go it alone. This is Romero's investigation. I won't put everything on the line to bring forward a case only to have it dismissed for a technicality. Romero, this is your call. How do you want to run this?"

Romero eyed Kate. "Turning these men against one another is the best way we get to the truth. I'll go in with Medina. Reid, I'd like you and Surrey there. We have the DNA profile on Medina. We'll be sure to mention that the doctor is running it against the victims. I think Walsh and Duncan should hit up Michael Garza and find out just how deep he was into this group and who else was involved."

"Okay." Fisher nodded. "I'll work with the captain to piece this thing together and get a joint statement ready for the vultures outside."

"I got no problem with that," Romero replied.

It wasn't what Kate wanted, but it was the best she was going to get. "Fine. We'll talk to Medina."

On their return to one of the interview rooms, Medina sat up at attention.

"Sorry to have kept you waiting, Xavier, or should I call you Alejandro? You must be thirsty. You want a soda or water?" Kate asked.

"No. I just want to know if I'm gonna be charged with something. Cause you can't keep me here otherwise," he replied.

She pulled out a chair to sit. "Oh, there are several charges we can levy against you. I think you know that by now." Kate noticed his eyes flicker. "So it seems you have a pretty interesting history. Terrible thing, what happened to your brother."

Surrey joined her. "What we want to know, Mr. Medina, or Cordova, or whoever the hell you are, is where the rest of the victims are buried and who else is involved in your group."

"With Clay Melgren dead, you and your friend, Garza, are facing multiple murder charges," Romero added. "And that's just the beginning. You're here under a false identity, so if there's any more information you have to share, we're all ears."

Surrey leaned over the table and held Medina's gaze. "How about we talk about your brother, Eduardo. The timing of his murder is awfully suspect. You turned up with a new name, a US passport, and social security number. And you got a job inside the medical examiner's office fairly recently. Unfortunately, they didn't verify your social because if they had, they would've seen that it was under Eduardo Cordova's name. So, how did you get involved with this group of men who seem hell-bent on blaming women for their problems?"

Medina's face screwed up. "What the hell are you talking about? I still got a right to a lawyer."

Kate pulled back. "Oh, I'm sorry, did you think you had any rights here? I'll tell you what, how about we skip all this, and I'll get the Mexican authorities to meet you at the border now. We'll hand you over and let them figure out what to do with you. I'm sure they'll be thrilled to know you killed a retired Juarez cop."

"I didn't kill a cop," Medina shot back. "I didn't kill anyone." He looked at her and scoffed. "Lady, you don't know how wrong you are."

Kate shrugged. "Then why don't you clear things up for us?"

EVA DUNCAN's role in this investigation had fallen outside her wheelhouse. Interviewing suspects was better left to the profilers. But Fisher had thrown her in with the wolf. Whether it was out of necessity or just plain curiosity hadn't mattered at this point. She was here and while Levi Walsh stood behind her, Duncan wouldn't let this wolf find a way out of the trap.

"Why had you gone to see Clay Melgren? Was he going to help you get out of the country?" she asked.

"I didn't kill Rich. He was my friend. I don't know who killed him," Garza replied.

"The bullet lodged in Ceballos's body came from the same type of gun that is registered to you. All we need to do is check it against your gun to confirm the match. But that's the least of your problems, Michael. Why did you leave the rocks at the burial sites?" Duncan pressed on.

"I told you people; it was Guy Jacobs. He got fired for screwing around with the painting machines. I got nothing to do with any of this," Garza replied.

Walsh pulled out a chair to sit down. The former Army Intelligence Officer had plenty of experience with these situations both from the military and his time with the BAU. He was no stranger to the killers' tactics, their narcissism, and their penchant for bragging about their crimes. And while Garza still feigned innocence, the time had come to get him to show his true colors. "Your options here are few, Mr. Garza," Walsh began. "There is no Guy Jacobs. Well, he exists, just not how you suggested. You had to realize we'd figure that out. But then again, you probably thought you'd be long gone before that happened. So, you should answer Agent Duncan's question. Because I'll tell you what, we have your buddy, Medina, over in the next room. He'll be looking for a way to save himself and it won't be good news for you."

"I didn't kill Rich. You have to believe me. I didn't do any of these horrible things to these women. I didn't know Clay Melgren was part of any of this. I went to him to ask for money."

"Why were you asking him for money?" Duncan said.

"'Cause I knew he had it," Garza replied.

"So you were trying to leave the state? Why would you do that if you were innocent of Ceballos's murder and claim to have had nothing to do with what Melgren and Medina were into? We know you worked at the warehouse where several of the victims had been employed over the past few years." Duncan regarded him. "Michael, you've lost this battle."

Garza lowered his gaze. "Someone told me y'all were still after me. I figured after I offered to talk to Agent Reid, this was all over. So, I thought I'd better lay low until this shit died down." He leaned over with his hands still cuffed. "Look, I went to a couple of Melgren's meetings, okay? I'll admit to that. But after hearing the shit they came up with, I was like, no way, man. That's messed up."

"And what about Eduardo Cordova? He was your friend too, right?"

Garza nodded. "We were friends. He was killed. Nothing more to say about that."

Duncan eyed Walsh and tossed a glance to the door. She turned back to Garza. "Excuse us for a minute." She stepped out and Walsh followed. When the door closed, she looked at him. "What the hell is going on?"

Walsh sighed. "He's acting like he's got nothing to do with any of this. We know he worked at the warehouse. We know he owns the same kind of gun used to kill Ceballos. He's grasping at straws because he's up shit creek right now."

"It's only a matter of time before he cries out for a lawyer," Duncan replied. "Without his DNA on any of the victims, what do we have?"

"We can hold him on suspicion of murdering Richard Ceballos long enough for us to confirm it was his gun used to kill Ceballos and Cordova. But the fact remains, we have a pile of bodies. The media is pounding down the door of this stationhouse. And a Mexican national, who could very easily get handed over to Mexican authorities, is in the next room saying God knows what."

Duncan eyed the door to the interview room. "Okay. We find something that really scares Garza." She started back toward the room and walked inside. "As we speak, your phone is being searched for texts, emails, calls, GPS. All of it. We will piece together a timeline of events that proves it was you who killed Richard Ceballos and I'll bet we'll find texts between you and Clay Melgren." She eyed Walsh as he sat down. He nodded for her to continue. "Are you afraid of Xavier Medina? Is he part of something bigger?"

A tear streamed down Garza's cheek as he shrugged. "I wasn't lying when I said I went to some of these gatherings. By then, I was in too deep. Melgren promised he'd get me out."

"Give us their names," Walsh cut in. "I don't give a shit how you were conned or whatever bullshit you want to pass off as the truth. I care about who else is out there killing women."

Garza eyed him. "Xavier Medina is a dangerous man. I left the rocks, yes. It was my job to make it look like the murders were part of what's been going on in Juarez and other places. It was my job to help them find...." He trailed off. "Melgren knew the FBI would think it was connected. That was kind of the whole point. And the rocks were used for others to know where they were."

"Others?" Duncan pressed on.

"Others in the group. Clay Melgren led the group. He had the money and the means to get me and Medina out of the country. That was why we went to him." Garza peered at the agents. "I'm not saying anything else without a lawyer."

MEDINA WORE A COCKY GRIN. "You people even bother looking into the man you shot a few hours ago?"

"Melgren?" Romero answered. "We know that Michael Garza contacted him via cell phone and that was how we figured out where you two were holed up."

"But you don't know nothing about him, do you?" Medina pressed on.

"We're not here to justify our actions," Kate jumped in. "We tracked you down. We killed Melgren because he resisted arrest. And we do know that he was a major player in this group of incels you and Garza are part of."

Medina was a stocky man, square-shaped, and short-legged. He looked about as intimidating as the ice cream man. But he'd murdered a police officer and God knew who else. However, where he fit in this group remained unclear to Kate.

"You're right about me using my brother's social security number to get a job. But there's something else you should know. When I used to travel back and forth from El Paso to Juarez for work, I saw a lot of things."

"Like the attack on the woman who was later murdered," Surrey replied.

"Yes. I was sent to prison for that, but I didn't attack or kill that woman. I did see the man who did. After I was sent to jail, I learned that the woman who was murdered was the daughter of a police officer."

Kate traded glances with Romero and Surrey before turning back. "Who told you?"

"A man associated with the person who did kill her. I saw that man. And I later learned that his name was Clay Melgren. Because I knew what he did, the only way I would survive my prison stint was if I agreed to keep my mouth shut about what I knew."

"You're telling me that Clay Melgren murdered the cop's daughter in Juarez? An American citizen?" Kate asked. "And then, what, you got in good with him?"

"I did what I had to do to survive there. So, yeah, I got in with Melgren's people. His connections and money got me a new identity. I was living in El Paso, but I wasn't there legally. After prison, I needed clean documents. I needed to make a fresh start with my brother, who was here in Somerset."

Romero eyed Medina. "A fresh start with your brother? You said you used his social security number to get work after he was killed."

"I did, but it wasn't my choice. Melgren's reach was far. He has a network of people in Juarez, and several places in the south part of Texas, including San Antonio. When I crossed over the border again with a new identity, I went to see my brother. I told him what had happened in Juarez and that I wasn't a killer. That I didn't harm that woman in any way. And that I knew she was the daughter of a cop. Ed went back a few times to get to the truth. It wasn't long before Melgren figured that out. It was his people that came after Ed. They killed him and I couldn't do a damn thing about it."

"You couldn't go to the police?" Surrey asked.

"And tell them what? That I arrived on forged documents with a new identity? That I made a deal with a man I knew was a killer?" Medina continued. "If I didn't go along with him, my nieces and sister-in-law would've been next."

Kate stood up and headed toward the door. "Surrey, Romero." She motioned for them to join her. They walked into the hall and Kate continued. "Do either of you believe him?"

Romero folded his arms and widened his stance. "I'm not sure. The gun used to kill Cordova appears to match Garza's gun. And what about Espinoza? Did he kill her? All we have is that the same type of knife used on Lisa Gutierrez was also used on Espinoza. We don't know if it was Medina. Not yet. Jesus, Reid, what if it was Melgren all along?"

"Then how does Michael Garza fit into this?" Surrey asked. "And that doesn't explain why Medina took off and went to Melgren for protection. Who would do that when he knew the man had his brother murdered?"

Kate turned back to see the room where Duncan and Walsh were questioning Michael Garza. "Let's pull them out for a minute and see where they're at."

Surrey walked toward the room and opened the door. Kate listened while he asked them to step out. A moment later, the agents joined her.

"What's going on?" Duncan asked.

Kate regarded her colleagues. "What's Garza saying?"

"Some bullshit that he's been a reluctant participant. That Melgren was the leader, and he was forced to put the pink stones around the sites as a message to others in the group that the bodies were there. Claims he didn't kill anyone," Walsh replied.

"He says he didn't kill Ceballos either," Duncan added. "Until we can prove otherwise, and unless the M.E. finds his DNA on the victims, all we have on him is his association to the victims."

Kate nodded. "Medina is laying blame for all this at Melgren's feet too. And he says Melgren's people murdered his brother. He also claims to be a reluctant participant in the situation."

"Who the hell was Clay Melgren?" Duncan began. "His online presence suggested he led a group of incels, but what are we talking about here? How many people does he have under his thumb?"

26

The name, Clay Melgren, appeared to have a far greater influence than the team suspected. Yet had Kate followed through on her initial theory of this subculture known as involuntary celibates, she might've taken a deeper dive when Duncan first found the man's online identity. It was the second, and nearly fatal, mistake she'd made on this investigation. Letting Garza off the hook had been the first.

Now, Kate began to question the legitimacy of Captain Brown's so-called friend in Juarez who readily handed over damning details on Xavier Medina. That act drew the team in another direction. It seemed an intentional action, one that Clay Melgren may have perpetrated with this power he wielded, along with plenty of money. "If we don't understand how this man was involved, we could be leaving open an opportunity for someone else to fill his shoes. This has to end with Medina and Garza."

"Then we need some goddam answers." Romero reached for his phone. "Let me put in a call to the M.E. before we bring this up to Fisher. I want to go into him with answers, not more questions."

With the phone at his ear, the line rang through. "Yeah, hey, Doc, it's Agent Romero. Listen, I know you and your team are hard at work, but we're at a tipping point right now. If we don't have solid evidence against the men we have in custody, our case falls apart. We can't let that happen. Our time's up, Doc. Please tell me you have answers."

"Agent Romero, as a matter of fact, I've been trying to reach you for about an hour, but I kept getting your voicemail."

"Damn. I've been questioning the suspect. My phone didn't ring inside the room. What did you find?"

"We confirmed the presence of foreign DNA found on Louisa Espinoza," Bauer replied. "It matches the DNA found in Richard Ceballos's home, Louisa Espinoza, and two of the victims found on the Ortega property. We haven't finished comparing the profiles of the remaining victims yet, though considering the autopsy information, I can't be certain it's the same killer."

"Who is it, Doc?" Romero pressed on.

"The swab you got from Michael Garza when you booked him earlier? His profile was already in the system. Interpol's system. Came back almost instantly. It was Michael Garza. I hope this helps you."

"Dr. Bauer, you have no idea. Thank you. I'll pass along the message to the team." Romero ended the call. "Michael Garza killed Louisa Espinoza, Richard Ceballos, and two victims on the old man's property." He peered at them. "It's a DNA match. We got him."

"Why would Garza have murdered Officer Espinoza while she waited at Medina's apartment?" Kate asked.

Surrey turned to her. "Could be for the same reason Ceballos was killed. Garza was cleaning up either for Medina or for Melgren. Either way, we have Garza dead to rights. It's possible he'll cooperate with us now if he sees it could benefit him. We still got ourselves a lot of moving targets, but now we have leverage."

Walsh eyed the agents. "Let's give the news to Fisher and the captain. It's time we start shaping this narrative."

Captain Brown hung up his phone and eyed the agents as they appeared in his doorway.

Fisher turned in his chair at their arrival. "The gang's all here. This must mean something popped. Tell me what you have."

Kate relayed the details regarding the men in custody as well as the call Romero made to the M.E.'s office. "How do we want this to play out?"

Brown grew emotional after hearing who had been responsible for taking Louisa's life. He turned away toward the window.

Fisher eyed Romero. "You'll be the one building the case. What do you think? Is Garza our primary target? We have enough evidence to put him on Death Row."

Romero appeared to consider the question. "Reid, do you think he can lead us to a bigger target?"

"Bigger than Melgren? Hard to say. It's possible Duncan took out the head of the snake. I do think we need to find out who this man really was. There's still the question of Medina. He claims Melgren kept him close because of what he knew but stopped short of admitting he'd participated in any of the crimes," Kate replied.

Romero glanced through the captain's window. "I want to be able to go out there with the captain and tell those folks outside that we have the killers in custody. If there's a chance more could be out there, then I want to be damn sure we know about it. Medina's going to cooperate because he'll want to cut a deal. He's still guilty of co-conspiracy in my humble opinion, unless and until we get additional evidence. Garza might not be so willing and especially when he learns we have his DNA on more than one victim and a cop. Not much upside for him at this point."

"Then we'll throw out a possible deal if he tells us whether there are any more bodies. Don't know if he'll bite." Kate paused a moment. "Actually, there could be a way to get more out of him."

Fisher eyed her. "Go on."

"What if we get him to go into Melgren's group chat and draw out others? Others he knows are involved. Call it a sting operation. Rather than us dragging names out of him. Let's let him bring them to us. They reveal themselves to us, we pluck them from their homes."

"You're assuming there are others," Surrey added.

"I know there are just based on what Duncan unearthed. I just didn't understand if or how we tied it back to this group," Kate replied.

They'd already retrieved Garza's laptop. Now, Kate had to convince him this was the only way he stood a chance at helping his case. While Medina was in a holding pattern, it was time to get Garza to open up.

Kate entered the interview room with Garza's laptop where he waited. "We just received confirmation from the medical examiner that they have your DNA on several victims, including your supposed friend, Ceballos." She sat down and placed his laptop on the table. "I don't know how you thought you were going to get out of this, Michael, but lying to us wasn't the way to go about it. So, you have a couple of choices to make right now." Kate pushed the laptop toward him. "You log into Melgren's group and give us the names of the other people involved, or you take your chances with a judge who will have no reason to give you even the slightest bit of mercy for your crimes. You help us take down this group, a judge might be willing to let you see daylight before they put the needle in your arm."

Garza stared at his laptop for a moment. "I'm already a dead man. Besides, I told the other agents I wanted a lawyer. I'm not saying shit to you until I get one."

Kate leaned over the table and held his gaze. "Michael, you can wait for a lawyer if you want. It'll just mean we'll have to put you in a cell until we can get one for you. Do you know what happens to people like you in jail? People who've done what you've done to women, girls?"

He appeared to consider Kate's proposal and extended his hand. "Give it to me." A few keystrokes and he continued, "I'm in. You want to see what this is all about?"

Kate pulled the laptop closer. "And this is the group that Clay Melgren operated?"

Garza nodded.

"Where are these people located?" she asked.

"Everywhere, but there is a subgroup." He retrieved his laptop again and keyed in more commands. "This is a regional group. This is what Melgren ran from his house. And I don't mean the one you found us at. He has a place where we were supposed to take them. I know where it is."

"Tell me," Kate demanded. "Tell me where this place is now."

Garza looked away a moment and returned a smug gaze. "If I tell you where it is, and tell you who else is involved, then I need something from you."

Kate leaned back in the chair and smirked. "You're not in a position to demand anything. I suggest you don't overplay your hand."

Garza appeared to consider the alternative. "It's where they did the dirty work. Out of the way, quiet. Everyone called it the butcher shop."

"Jesus." Kate turned away for a moment in disgust. "Where, Michael? Tell me where this place is now, or I swear to God I'll make sure when they throw you into a cell tonight that everyone knows what you've done. I wouldn't count on you making it through the night."

THE DOOR of the interview room flew open, and Kate hurried out into the corridor. She reached the captain's office. "Excuse the interruption, but you all should hear this."

Fisher bolted up from his chair. "What did he say?"

She slapped down a piece of paper on Brown's desk with an address written on it. "We have to get to this house now."

Romero picked up the paper. "This is about thirty minutes south of here. What is this place?"

"It's where Melgren and others took the victims before burying them in Somerset. They called it the butcher shop. The evidence we'll find in that house will likely be enough to convict every single one of the people involved in the group." Kate peered at Surrey. "Garza showed me what we needed to see. No more circumstantial evidence. This is it. This is how we end this."

"Then what the hell are we waiting for?" Fisher shot a look at Brown. "Don't talk to the press until we get back."

"I'll try to hold them off a while longer," Brown replied.

Romero checked his gun. "I'm coming with you. This is still my case."

"Then let's go." Fisher eyed the other agents and they started out of the office. He turned to Kate. "Is there reason to believe we'll come across hostiles?"

"He didn't say whether anyone was there. I wouldn't take his word for anything. We should be prepared for a confrontation."

"The more, the merrier, as far as I'm concerned," Romero cut in. "Let's load 'em up and move 'em out."

LARGE DROPS of rain splashed against the windshield of Romero's SUV while he drove along the darkened highway. He turned on the wiper blades and smeared the water across his field of vision. "Hasn't rained in almost two weeks. Figures it'd rain tonight."

Kate was in the passenger seat. "Isn't that always the way?" She peered back at her team. "Map says we'll be there in five minutes."

"We're out in the middle of nowhere," Fisher said. "I doubt this place will have electricity."

"Could run on a generator," Surrey added. "Depends on whether anyone is out there and how fast word spread online about Melgren's death."

"Well, folks, we're about to find out." Romero nodded ahead. "That shithole-looking shack down the dirt road. That's gotta be it." He turned onto the road as the rain picked up. "It's gonna get real boggy real quick out here. Good news is we might be alone. I don't see any vehicles."

When he rolled to a stop, Kate opened the passenger door. "We'll need a forensics team out here if we find what we think we'll find." She looked back at Romero. "It's late, but do you have a team on standby?"

"I'll get them here, don't you worry about that. This needs to be put to bed tonight."

The agents stepped out of the SUV and onto the damp, softened earth. Duncan caught up to Kate and pulled her aside. "Hey, just so you know, you did this, Kate. I know you were feeling the pressure after we learned what Garza had done."

"Fisher felt it too."

"Yeah, there was tension," Duncan continued. "But just so you know, that wasn't all on you. Regardless, you got Garza to tell us about this place. You're one of the best agents I've ever worked with."

Kate's eyes softened and a gentle grin appeared. "I appreciate that, and back at you, Eva. But we don't know what we'll find in there. We'll either close this investigation, like Romero thinks, or we'll see that Xavier Medina was right. That this group has a far greater reach than we realized."

"I'm opting for the former." Duncan patted Kate on the shoulder and started ahead. "Okay, who's going in first?"

Fisher stepped up toward the front door. "I'll get the party started. The rest of you, be ready for whatever we find on the other side of this door." He tried the handle. "Locked. Not much of a surprise." A moment later, he turned to his side and with his shoulder, slammed into the door. "God damn it! That's gonna leave a mark."

"I have a few pounds on you." Walsh stepped up. "Let me give it a try."

Fisher moved aside. "Do your worst."

Walsh withdrew his weapon and steadied his stance. He rammed into the door and it flung open, splintering the frame. He stumbled inside and quickly regained his balance, aiming his gun into the darkness.

The rest of the team drew in close with weapons ready. Flashlights shone inside the darkened room. Fisher searched the wall for a switch and flipped it on. The room lit up. "What do you know? Power's on."

Kate set her eyes on the room. "What the hell is this?"

Surrey stepped toward her and placed his hands on his hips. "Some kind of—Christ, I don't know, an homage?"

"To what?" she looked on in horror.

Polaroids of dead women were pinned to the walls of what

appeared to be a living room. Their bodies still intact, face up and naked, eyes filled with terror.

Bile rose in Kate's throat. "My God. How many are here?"

Duncan approached them. "Far more than what we've found to date."

"Hey?" Walsh called out from down the hall. "We've got something here."

Romero started ahead. "I'm not sure I want to know." With his gaze down, he made his way into the narrow hall and toward Walsh, who stood in the doorway of a room. "This the only room in here?"

"I think so." Walsh stopped him. "Hang on. They all need to see this." He peered back. "Y'all need to come take a look here."

"What did you find?" Kate asked.

Walsh stepped aside. "A goddam nightmare."

She stepped in and gasped as though the wind had been knocked from her lungs. Her stomach turned. Kate closed her eyes while the others peered in.

Surrey placed his arm over her shoulder. "You want some fresh air?"

"I'm fine. I wasn't expecting this. I've never seen anything like this."

"I think I can safely say that none of us have." Surrey turned to Romero. "Call your forensics team. I don't want to risk contaminating anything. Get them out here to document this."

Kate took in the gruesome scene. Peg board was mounted on the walls. Knives dangled from metal hooks. Rope, tape, zip ties, all of it hung from hooks. "This is where they did it." A table lay in the middle of the room covered in plastic. Sealed buckets with dried red drippings were stacked against one of the walls. "Blood?"

Surrey nodded. "Probably. It explains why we didn't find much around the bodies."

Walsh sighed in exasperation. "We should step out of here. Let Romero's forensics team deal with this. There's nothing more for us to do now."

The team retreated to the small, covered porch out front while they waited. The rain fell hard now, and thunder rumbled in the night sky.

Kate set her gaze to the storm overhead. "There must be fifty, sixty photos inside."

"We know these killings have been going on for months, based on what the M.E. had found. Maybe longer," Romero added.

Eva paced the small wood porch. "This was all the work of a group of angry men led by an even angrier man, Clay Melgren. Those women did nothing to deserve what happened to them."

"They never do, Eva," Fisher replied. "Reid was right. These people felt emboldened the likes I've never seen before. And the leader incited all of it."

Kate turned to her. "Both Medina and Garza claimed Melgren's reach was extensive, but I never thought..."

"None of us did, Kate," Walsh replied. "What's important now is that you got Garza to call out these sons of bitches. They'll all be in custody in a day's time."

Senior Unit Agent Cameron Fisher stood inside the lobby of the Somerset Police Station alongside Captain Eli Brown. The statement was drafted, and they were ready to talk to the press.

Kate sat on a chair inside the lobby when Lupe Cordova approached her.

"Excuse me, Agent Reid?"

"Lupe, what are you doing here? You're supposed to be in Austin."

She sat down next to her. "I heard on the news that they'd been brought in. I drove back. The rest of my family is still there. I wanted to thank you for helping my family. And that you believed me when I said my dad wasn't a bad man."

"I believe that he tried to stop what was happening here," Kate replied. "Unfortunately, he was killed for it. And I'm sorry to say that your uncle might've been able to prevent it. Just so you know, your father's case will now be re-examined. Captain Brown said they have enough that it should be easier to identify who shot your father that night. Although, I suspect the white devil your mother spoke of was probably Clay Melgren. Someone in his organization, possibly Michael Garza, was the one who killed Eduardo. But rest assured that justice will be done for your father."

"Yes, ma'am. You helped a lot of people tonight. A lot of families who didn't know where their daughters or sisters or friends had disappeared to." She glanced away a moment. "I just wish I knew why they were taken. Why Louisa was taken."

"I wish I had an answer for you, Lupe. As much as I've seen, and do my best to comprehend, I'll never fully understand why," Kate replied.

Lupe stood again. "Anyway, thank you for believing me."

Kate smiled at her while she walked away.

But when Lupe turned back, Kate regarded her again. "Is there something else?"

Lupe's eyes reddened. "Girls, women. They get killed a lot in this country, in Mexico, in countries around the world."

"Yes, they do. They all deserve justice for what was done to them."

Lupe cleared her throat. "I was thinking that the world needs to hear that."

"Hear what?" Kate asked.

"What you just said. They all deserve justice, including

Louisa. Maybe other people will hear it and maybe some will finally start to listen."

When Lupe walked away, Kate pushed up from the chair and headed toward Surrey, Walsh, and Duncan as they huddled with Fisher, who prepared to speak. "Excuse me."

Fisher peered at her. "Hey. I was just about to head outside with Brown to tell everyone what happened tonight. Did you want to add something?"

"I was wondering if, after you and the captain are finished, if I could say a few words."

"You want to address the mob? Are you feeling okay?" Fisher joked.

She chuckled. "I'm fine, yes. But it was something Lupe said to me just now. I think I'd like to make a brief statement, if you're okay with it. A minute, tops. And I won't take questions. I know the drill."

Fisher regarded the team who appeared in agreement. "You're the lead profiler of the BAU team at Quantico. You and Surrey were the first ones here. If you want to address the media, I don't see a problem with that." He turned around and spotted Agent Romero. "You mind if Reid has a word with the press when we're finished with our statement?"

Romero eyed her a moment. "No, sir. Fine by me."

Kate nodded and stepped away while Fisher and Brown prepared to exit to the podium that awaited.

From inside, the team watched as camera lights illuminated in the darkness and the crowd closed in on the duo.

Walsh shoved his hands in his pockets and meandered over to Kate. "You sure you want to do this? Putting your face out there, people are going to look into you. They'll dig up your past and they'll throw it right back at you."

She turned to him. "Let them. It's already started, well, according to Nick, it has. This needs to be said."

"My friend, you're the best one to say it if I may say so myself." He nodded with a tight-lipped grin and stepped away.

While the rest of the team listened in on the statement, Surrey waited with Kate inside. She eyed him. "Do you want to try to talk me out of this too?"

"Me? Hell, no. When people see you and they hear you speak, they'll see the face of a fighter. I think I have an inkling of what you're planning to say and I think it's a hell of a good idea." He looked down a moment. "I don't know all that went down in your past. I'm not one to pry and I think you know that about me by now. But clearly, it's had an impact on your life and where you are right now. So I say, do your best, Agent Reid. This world needs more women; more *people* like you."

Fisher and Brown returned inside among shouts from reporters and flashes of light. Fisher looked at Kate. "You're up, Reid. I'll walk you out and make the introduction. The rest is up to you."

Kate followed him outside. He introduced her and she stepped to the podium. "Thank you, sir." She turned to the bright lights. "It's very late, so I won't waste your time. My job doesn't generally involve speaking to the press, though I have had my share of encounters, which I'm sure you'll all Google when I'm finished here tonight. But tonight isn't about me. It's about the victims of this horrific event that has occurred in this otherwise peaceful city of Somerset and community of San Antonio. It's also about the larger picture of violence against women. I've seen far too much and have, myself, been a victim of such violence. I was lucky enough to have survived and it compelled me into this life that I live now. I'm here speaking to you now on behalf of all the women who no longer have a voice. Those who were murdered for the simple fact that they were born female and reviled for it. The time has come for the world to stop burying its collective head in the sand, ignoring this tragedy. Pretending it doesn't exist. Statistics prove otherwise. I have seen otherwise. So let it be known that governments around the world must do more to shed light on an otherwise dark and troubling subject. These mass murders that have occurred in this small community should never be forgotten. The names of these women and girls should never be forgotten. Thank you."

27

His was the only face Kate wanted to see when she stepped off the plane at Reagan National Airport. She'd insisted he hadn't needed to pick her up, especially when the weight of the world had only just lifted from his shoulders. But Nick Scarborough had seen Kate's statement to the press, and he was concerned.

The smile on her face couldn't be contained as she hurried into his arms. "It's so late. I could've taken a cab home. Levi or Eva would've given me a lift too."

He gently pushed her back to look at her. "I haven't seen you in 10 days. I couldn't let Walsh or Duncan bring you home. I wanted to see your face."

When the other agents caught up, Nick smiled and offered his hand to Fisher. "Good to see you, man. Congrats on the investigation."

Fisher accepted the greeting. "Hey, this one here was running the show. I was only along for the ride." He thumbed to Kate.

"They all did a hell of a job, as usual. Good to see you, brother. We'll catch up soon, yeah?"

"You got it," Nick replied.

Fisher looked at Kate. "And I'll see you in the morning."

She nodded and watched as Duncan offered a hug to Nick and turned to her.

"Get some rest. I'll see you tomorrow."

"You too, Eva."

"Levi Walsh." Nick threw his arms around Walsh's broad shoulders. "Glad to see you're back and you brought everyone home safely."

"Wouldn't have it any other way, my friend," Walsh replied. "Hey, I saw you on the TV. Hell of a job your team did getting the trains back online."

"It wasn't just me, but thanks. We still have a lot of work ahead of us, but we have a direction."

"Good to hear. I hate taking the bus." Walsh smiled and looked at Kate. "See you tomorrow, Kate."

"See you tomorrow," she replied.

Nick turned back to her. "You ready to get out of here?"

"More than you know." She followed him to the parking garage and stepped inside his SUV. When he stepped behind the wheel, she looked at him. "Thanks for coming to get me. I can't imagine how crazy things have been for you since this started."

"And for you." He turned the engine and drove out. "What you said on TV, it was important. I'm glad it was you who said it."

"Thanks." She peered through the passenger window. "So what happens now? I mean, for you and your team."

"I think we'll be putting in place better protocols for the agencies working together. This kind of thing can't keep happening." Nick glanced at her. "I also think the president is going to sanction Russia. I heard it from a little birdie, so mum's the word."

"I won't say a thing." She turned back to him. "You stepped up to exactly where you were supposed to be, you know. The move to Unit 2 wasn't one you were sure about, but Nick, you got to meet the president and the upper echelons of his administration. I mean, that's incredible. That's the kind of thing that gets you promoted to cabinet positions."

He chuckled and raised his hand. "Let's not get ahead of ourselves. Besides, that's not what I want. I like our life the way it is. I'm happy. And I hope you are, too."

"You know I am." Her phone buzzed in her purse. She picked it up and smiled at the caller ID. "Tell me this isn't who I think it is." Kate's head reared back in laughter. "Oh, you think I don't sleep, is that it?" She glanced at Nick and returned her attention to the conversation. "Marc, it's been too long. It's great to hear from you, even if it is late." She nodded while he spoke. "You saw that, did you? It wasn't really planned, no. Uh-huh." She turned away a moment. "No, actually, I hadn't thought about that in years. You think I should?" She cocked her head. "I don't know. I mean, you know how crazy this job gets. I know you're some big-time national news anchor now, but I just can't." She sighed. "Fine. I'll think about it. I hadn't planned on coming to New York, but as I'm between cases at the moment, I might be able to squeeze it in. You'll have to buy me lunch, though." She laughed again. "Dinner? Well, that's even better. Okay. Yeah, I promise I'll think about it. It was good to hear from you too, my friend. Good night."

Nick glanced at her. "Marc? As in Marc Aguilar? What did he want?"

Kate returned her phone to her purse. "He watched my statement to the press. Said it reminded him of the old days."

"That was nice. You said you would think about something," Nick added. "What do you have to think about?"

"He asked if I thought it might finally be time to write that book. He said he could put together interviews, arrange for a ghost-writer."

"A book? About what?" Nick continued.

"About what happened—before Marshall died. Before you and I were a thing," Kate replied.

"He wants you to write your story about Joseph Hendrickson," Nick said.

"He does. He thinks it could help others. And given what I do for a living, that it would be inspirational." She regarded him. "What do you think?"

Nick was quiet for a moment and the only sound in the car was the muffled hum of the tires on the highway. "I think you should sleep on it."

She pursed her lips and turned away from him to watch the streetlamps pass by in a blur of white LED glow. "It's probably a bad idea. No point in rehashing the past, right?"

"That's not what I said," Nick cut in. "I said you should sleep on it. That's all. I mean, it's Marc Aguilar, for Pete's sake."

"He's my friend, Nick. You know that."

"You're right. I'm just looking out for your best interests."

Maybe he was right. Sleeping on it was probably the best idea. The time it would take away from her job; a new job at that. Not to mention reliving all that had happened. It wouldn't be easy. She'd just spent six months in therapy going over a lot of that crap and had only just gotten to a better place. Was it worth risking a setback?

Nick pulled into their building and parked up. He grabbed Kate's bag for her from the back seat. "Your bed awaits you, my love." He kissed her cheek and ushered her to the elevators where they rode in silence to their floor.

As they walked to the door, Nick opened it and set down her bag. "Can I get you anything to eat? You want some water?"

"No, I'm okay, but thank you." Kate walked inside and slipped off her sensibly heeled shoes. "I'm glad to be home."

"I'm glad to have you home." Nick wrapped his arms around her. "There was something I wanted to mention, but if you're too tired..."

"No, what is it?" She walked to the side chair and sat down.

Nick made his way to the sofa sectional and took a seat. "Well, I did get to see the president during all this."

"I know. That's huge," she replied.

"It was just for briefings, but he did actually mention something interesting."

Kate narrowed her gaze. "What are you trying to say, Nick? Did he ask you to join his cabinet?" She chuckled.

"No. No, it was nothing like that." He held her gaze. "I love you so much, Kate. I'm so proud of the work you did on this case. Seeing you up there talking to the media." He looked down a moment. "Kind of reminds me of me back in the day."

The smile on Kate's face faded as she continued to gaze at him. "What is it? What's going on?"

"So, the president, along with others from NSA, DHS, CIA."

"Yeah, I'm familiar with the letter agencies. What did they ask you, babe?" she pressed on.

Nick inhaled deeply. "I mentioned earlier about how they want to have a joint task force, so to speak, to tackle the growing cyber threats from both China and Russia."

"Uh-huh." She waited with anticipation.

"The president asked if I wanted to head that up."

A smile rose on her lips. "Really? Well, that's great, right? I mean, wow. But I thought you said you weren't interested in a change. You've only been with Unit 2 for, what a year?"

"A little less than that, but yes. I said I wasn't interested in being a member of his cabinet, which I would definitely not be. I don't have the stomach for political bullshit. I've suffered enough of that with the Bureau. But what this would mean, if I accept, which I haven't. I knew I needed to talk to you. But it would mean a move from Quantico."

"Okay. Where would you go?" Kate asked.

"HQ," he replied.

"In D.C.? Okay. That's not a big deal, is it?"

"No, it's not a big deal. I mention it because, well, it's still a big change. You know, we wouldn't be in the next building over anymore."

Kate smiled. "I think I'll survive. What's this really about, Nick? Why do you look like you have more to say?"

Nick licked his lips and folded his hands until finally, he peered at Kate and held her gaze. "Georgia works at HQ now."

She nodded slowly. "So your ex-girlfriend works there. It's a big place."

"She doesn't work in Violent Crimes anymore." He lowered his gaze for a split second before returning it to Kate. "Her expertise in profiling has been put to use with hackers. They're a narcissistic bunch and her insight helps with that. Kate, she would be working on my team."

Kate had always admired Georgia Myers and had learned a great deal from her. But it was Georgia who cheated on Nick insisting it was because Nick had loved Kate. It set in motion their current relationship. She also remembered how hurt he'd been at the time when he learned about her infidelity. "Okay. I get why you were hesitant to mention this to me, but you shouldn't have been. We're married now. Years have gone by and I'm sure she's married or in a relationship. I mean, Nick, this is a tremendous opportunity for you. You've said your light at the Bureau had dimmed while mine shone brightly, but that's not true. Look, I'm fine with you and Georgia working together."

"Are you sure? I can turn it down," Nick replied.

"Don't be ridiculous. I would never ask you to do that. Look, it's still in the D.C. metro area. We don't have to move. I don't have to choose another field office. This is a good deal all the way around." She reached for his hand. "If this is what you want to do, Nick, you should do it. You have my full support."

Nick stood and took her hand to help her up. "And if you decide to write the book, I'll support you one hundred percent."

"Thank you." Kate pulled him into an embrace and peered over his shoulder through their balcony door. The moonlight glistened off the bay while the boats swayed in their slips. Her smile faded. "Everything will work out just as it's supposed to. I know it will."

THE END

ABOUT THE AUTHOR

Robin Mahle has published more than 30 novels in the mystery/thriller genre. She also writes historical fiction as <u>Christine Chase.</u>

It is Robin's fast-paced style of storytelling combined with tense action and thrilling twists that bring her readers back for more. So be sure sure to subscribe to her newsletter to keep up on all the latest releases, sales, and giveaways. Go to robinmahle.com and sign up today!

Robin lives in Coastal Virginia with her husband and two children.

If you enjoyed Ms. Mahle's work, please share your experience by leaving a review on <u>Amazon.</u>

ALSO BY ROBIN MAHLE

**Visit robinmahle.com and sign up to receive Robin's Newsletter so you can stay up to date on her new releases, events, contests and even exclusive new material!

www.ingramcontent.com/pod-product-compliance
Lightning Source LLC
Chambersburg PA
CBHW060535180626
46817CB00002B/577